ALL MY LIFE

by

PRESCOTT LANE

Print Edition

Cover design © Michele Catalano Creative
Cover image from deposit photos by EpicStockMedia
Editing by Nikki Rushbrook

TABLE OF CONTENTS

PROLOGUE

MIA HOLLIS
Graduation Speech

I'M NOT GOING to do the usual graduation speech. No Dr. Seuss book or quote from Robert Frost about the road less traveled. I'm going to quote someone greater—my dad. He likes to say that we don't always want what we need in this life. He loved to throw that one at me when I wanted chocolate cake but needed vegetables. Think about it—we don't often want what we truly need. We want the big house, but all we need is a simple shelter. We want designer clothes, but off-brands work just as well. The examples are endless.

Everyone here knows my dad, Garrett Hollis. He never got this moment. His GED arrived in the mail, and he opened it with me in his arms. He calls me his unexpected blessing.

This is yours, too, Daddy. For teaching me how to read, taking that road trip to the museum when I was obsessed with dinosaurs, all the nights you stayed up late with me studying, the teacher conferences, the trips to the bookstore, the college tours. This piece of paper, who I am, doesn't happen without you. So while I really wanted a car when I was sixteen, I already had what I needed—you.

Not sure what he's going to do without me. Thirty-four years old and an empty nester. Anyone know a nice, single woman who can date my dad? You know where to find him. Hardware store in the town square. Just tell him Mia sent you.

CHAPTER ONE

GARRETT

THERE'S A WOMAN in that bed. How did that happen? Most thirty-four-year-old guys probably have that thought for entirely different reasons than me. Because somehow that young woman is my daughter, my baby girl has grown up. How did that happen? Where did the time go?

She's traded braids for a straightening iron. Teddy bears for earbuds. Sippy cups for coffee mugs. Graduated from high school and off to college in a couple months, soon I'll have an empty house. An empty nester at thirty-four, as Mia so eloquently put it in her valedictorian speech yesterday.

She looked so damn beautiful on that stage. It seemed like the whole town was there. They should be. Me and Eden Valley raised her. While I was a single teenage dad, I was never really alone.

Leaning my head on the doorframe to her bedroom, I listen to my daughter's soft breathing, knowing there won't be many more mornings like this, and remember her words.

"Unexpected blessing," I whisper.

Yes, she was the result of a teenage pregnancy, but she wasn't a mistake, an accident. She was what I needed. I didn't know it at the time. I'm not sure she always believes it. There were no tears on her face yesterday, only a big-ass smile, but I had to wipe my eyes listening to her.

I couldn't even be mad about her plea for my dating life. The crowd loved it, and I just rolled my eyes. Mia's always had this fear about me, this urge to take care of me. Maybe because it was just the two of us. She used to have these god-awful nightmares about me dying, wake up in fits of terror, or I'd be startled awake by her checking my pulse in the night. She hounds me constantly about eating my vegetables. Guess she's afraid now that she's going off to college, I won't have anyone to look after me. There are several things I can think of that I need a woman for, and making me eat salad isn't one of them.

Mia rolls over, and I see her shiny car keys gripped in her fingers, her graduation present. I finally got her a car—a used, little white sedan. It might as well have been a brand-new luxury car for the scream that came out of her tiny frame.

Glancing around her room, I remember when it used to be filled with princesses, castles, pink frilly things, and fairytales. She's always loved reading, and her room now looks more like a library than a bedroom, everything from her childhood favorites to classic British literature covering her floors and shelves.

At seventeen, she looks exactly like her mother did at her age—petite and blonde with deep brown eyes. Not at all like me, tall with blue eyes and brown hair. While I hate her mother, Sheena, I only have love for Mia. Life's been hard, but Mia is soft, tender. Not at all like that . . .

"Daddy," Mia says softly, giving me a sleepy smile.

"Got in pretty late last night," I say, raising an eyebrow. "Or should I say, early this morning?"

She yawns and rolls her brown eyes at me. "I was just at the Falls with everyone else."

I know exactly where she was, but it's my job to give her a little bit of a rough time. Our town, Eden Valley, sits right outside the Blue Ridge Mountains in Georgia, and is bordered on one side by a waterfall and natural springs. They throw a big party out there every year at graduation. Our town probably wouldn't be on the map except for that spot. It has more recorded rainbows each year than any other spot in the continental United States. People travel from all over to be married there. Folk legend has it that if you kiss someone while a rainbow cascades over the Falls, they will always be yours.

Personally, I think that's a crock of shit. Rainbows, waterfalls, and forevers sound like something in those Hallmark movies Mia makes me watch with her at Christmastime.

She sits up slightly in bed, and I take a seat next to her. "Did you have fun last night?"

She nods and tells me about her night. Who kissed who. Who broke up because they don't want to be tied down going off to college. Who got drunk and threw up. Mia tells me everything. I'm not sure if it's because I'm a young dad, but she always has. It's not always easy to hear. When she had her first kiss a little over a year ago, I wanted to threaten the boy's life. When he broke up with her, I wanted to ram my fist threw a wall. Still, she's seventeen, eighteen in a couple weeks, and I guess I'm lucky kissing is the extent of it. I was a dad at her age.

"I'm starving," she says, stretching her arms high over her head then hopping up out of bed. "Dad, did you wash my . . ."

I simply point to her dresser, where I left her clothes, folded and waiting for her to put away. She pulls out her favorite t-shirt from the pile then motions for me to leave. Thank God, Mia is modest. I see some of the girls from her school with their asses hanging out, stomachs showing. No fucking way would Mia walk out of the house like that. She hates it when her bra strap shows. Made it interesting the first few times I had to take her shopping for bras or products for that time of the month. By the time Mia started with all that, my mom had passed away. So poor girl was left with me to try to explain the ins and outs of the female menstrual cycle. There was no one else to do the job. No aunts, no sisters, no grandmother. Not that it would've mattered, Mia would have died of embarrassment if she knew I told a soul when she first started. Even her pediatrician was a dude. We tried signing up for one of those classes you take at the hospital explaining puberty, but no men were allowed.

By that point, I was used to it. I wasn't allowed backstage at her dance recitals with the moms because I've got a dick. When she was little, I had to cover her face with my hand any time she had to use the restroom in public, so she didn't see anything in the men's restroom. It's par for the course. So a few library books and a video or two, and we got through the female reproductive system.

We even had a system for when she needed tampons or pads. She'd leave the empty box by my keys. No discussion. Then I'd buy the stuff and leave it in her bathroom. Of course, now when she needs new bras or something, I just give her the money and she handles it herself.

"Out the door in five, kiddo," I say, heading out of her room and closing the door behind me. Whoever the lucky man is that marries her, a long, long time from now, will have me to thank for my daughter's ability to be dressed and out the door in record time. No hours of primping and makeup with Mia.

Before I have my keys in my hand, she's meeting me in our kitchen, pulling her hair through the back of a baseball cap. "Wanna drive?" I ask.

She looks at me like I'm crazy. I get that look a lot from her. "We always walk."

She's right. We've made this walk almost every day of her life. Our house is just a few streets over from the town square. It's one of the reasons she didn't get a car until now. She simply didn't need one. Most mornings, we'd walk the few blocks, grab breakfast at the local diner, then she'd head to school, and I'd head to the hardware store.

I open the backdoor for her, locking it behind us, seeing her staring up at our house. Mia's sentimental, and I know she's thinking about the day she won't live here anymore.

"I still think yellow would've been better," Mia says, ragging me over painting the house white with dark green shutters like my grandparents always had it. This time, it's me that rolls my eyes at her. "At least paint the door red," she says.

"Not gonna happen."

I brought her home from the hospital to this house. It was my grandparents' old place. They were both gone and the place was empty, so my parents let Mia and I move in here. They lived next door, so they thought it was the perfect arrangement. It forced me to grow up and be a dad, but they were close enough to help.

Those first few years, there's no way I would've made it without them. I continued my part-time job at the hardware store, same place as today. Only now, I own it. It's been a far cry from my dream of playing college football and becoming an architect, but I can't complain—the store lets me do projects for people around town. I'm not designing skyscrapers, but the church now has the best damn outdoor worship center, and the new mayor's sons' tree house is a fucking work of art.

"Morning," my dad calls out across our yards. "Off to Biscuit Girl?"

"Yep, you're at it early this morning," I say, seeing his hands stuck in the dirt. Not sure why the man retired from his law practice, he's always tinkering around with something, gardening, building stuff. I get that from him. I love building stuff. Got an old motorcycle in the shop behind our houses that I'll finish one of these days. He seems busier now than he did when he was working, even during his stint as mayor of our small town. With my mom gone, I worry about him getting lonely. He and Mia are really close. He's taught her to love sports, poker, car racing. Some guy is going to thank him one day. With Mia leaving for college in the fall, I'm going to have to make sure dad hangs out with me more.

"Granddad, want to come to breakfast?" Mia asks, running over and throwing her arms around his neck.

He holds his hands up. "Thanks, but not today, buttercup."

Edward Hollis is the epitome of a good dad. Strong when he needs to be and understanding as all hell. He and Mom had to be disappointed as shit when Mia's mother showed up pregnant on our doorstep, but not once did it show on his face. Anger—yes. But he never let his feelings overshadow mine. I was scared shitless. He knew it, and he was there. His hand on my shoulder, looking down and telling me that he wouldn't leave my side. He and Mom never did.

"Bring you back something?" I call out.

"Nah," he says, waving his hand. "Going to visit your mother."

I knew that. He goes to my mother's grave every day, rain or shine.

"I've got to tell her all about Mia's speech!" he says, picking at me. The man does love to goad me. "Maybe she's got some pull with the Big Guy and can send some ladies your way."

Mia flashes me a smile over her shoulder, still basking in her public plea for my non-existent dating life. Women have never been my strong suit. After the teenage pregnancy, dating just wasn't easy. You have to remember for most of Mia's childhood, I was in my twenties. Not many single women in their twenties looking to date a guy with a young kid. Rightly so, they want romance, nights out, to be the center of some guy's life. I couldn't offer that. I tried here and there, but it just wasn't in the cards. I can count on one hand how many women there have been over the years. None of them wanted to be a stepmother so young in life. From my perspective, none of them were really worthy of being a stepmother to my daughter, either.

WALKING THROUGH EDEN Valley is like walking through a gingerbread village. The buildings all have detailed latticework, porches. Verandahs are a staple in our town. If I didn't know better, I'd think the sidewalk was made from candy. The carpenter in me appreciates the craftsmanship, but growing up, this town bored the shit out of me. Raising my daughter here gave me new appreciation. Everyone knows everyone, but better yet, everyone watches out for everyone. That's the part Mia hates. She can't get away with anything. That's just the way I like it. Unlike me, she grew up slow.

I open the door to our daily breakfast hangout, Biscuit Girl, holding it open for Mia. We've been coming here since before Mia could sit in a high chair. In fact, she said her first word right at our usual table by the window. It was Dada, of course.

Like a lot of businesses in town, this one is family-owned and passed down from generation to generation. This one is named after the current owner. Her parents opened it when she was just a toddler, and named it after their own little biscuit girl. Devlyn Drake,

DD when we were kids, grew up in this diner, just like Mia did.

We take our seat at our regular spot, the usual smell of bacon, biscuits, and fresh baked breads surrounding us. This place is the epitome of Eden Valley, family-friendly, comfortable, and charming as hell. Decorated in vintage, distressed white furniture and bright flowers, it's as quirky as the owner.

Devlyn gives us a wave, indicating she'll be right over. She no longer brings us menus, knowing how we both take our coffee. Mine, black as night. Mia's, with so much cream and frilly shit it's not really coffee anymore.

Mia's phone dings, and she reaches for it. I beat her to it, flipping it screen down on the table. She knows the rules. No phone during meals. "But it could be Penny . . ." Before I can stop her, it dings again and again. "Seriously, Dad, it could be an emergency."

"Boys are not considered an emergency," I say, grinning at her.

"Boys are always an emergency," Devlyn says, placing our mugs down in front of us. "Emergencies are unexpected and dangerous. I'd say that's the definition of most boys."

Mia wraps her arm around Devlyn's waist. A year younger than me, Devlyn has watched Mia grow up in this diner. From my lap, to the highchair, to the booster seat. From braces to a beautiful young lady. Devlyn, like the rest of Eden Valley, has witnessed it all. Honestly, she's done more than that. Devlyn and Mia are close. Devlyn's the one Mia turns to when she needs advice on boys, clothes, hair. All the stuff that Mia thinks I'm an imbecile about.

"You have to take me shopping," Mia says, flicking up Devlyn's tutu.

"This is the uniform, honey," she says, giving us a twirl. She always did have a quirky fashion sense. When she took over the diner, she took to wearing different color tutus each day with a simple t-shirt that reads *Butter my biscuits*.

"So what are we having this morning?" Devlyn asks, playing with Mia's hair a little bit.

While our coffee orders are a constant, our food choices are anything but. "Yogurt and granola," Mia says.

"I'll have the bacon . . ."

"Fruit cup," Mia says, interrupting my need for grease. "Cholesterol, Daddy." Told you, she's got some weird fears about losing me. I'm hardly the picture of bad health. "Devlyn, help me out," Mia begs. "Tell him."

She squeezes my bicep and gives me a little wink. "He looks in good shape to me."

Mia groans, throwing her head down on the table. Devlyn begins to giggle at the dramatic nature gifted to all teenage girls. Devlyn's eyes catch mine. She immediately shakes her head, and I can tell she's giving herself an internal tongue lashing for saying that. No harm, no foul. I know she didn't mean anything by it. Devlyn and I are friends. The best of friends. Another day, another life, maybe.

Don't get me wrong, Devlyn's playful and fun, and she has killer curves. Her blue eyes and strawberry blonde hair don't hurt either, but there's never been anything between us. I've made it a point not to date anyone from Eden Valley. It would just be too hard when it ended. The whole damn town would be taking sides. It's a nosy bunch here. Besides, she's got a long-distance boyfriend.

"Mia," a loud screech calls out, coupled with an earth-shattering bang on the window, lifting my daughter from her teenage-induced drama.

We all look through the window, finding Mia's best friend Penny holding her phone out and jumping up and down. Mia waves her in. Now that my daughter is distracted, I seize the opportunity to order a bacon lover's omelet.

Devlyn smiles and greets Penny as she rushes though the door. "Why didn't you pick up your phone? I knew you'd be here." Mia points to me as the warden behind her cellular service. "Oh, hi, Mr. Garrett," Penny says, calming her voice just a little before starting back up again. "Mia, your video. Look, it's gone viral!"

"What?" Mia screams out.

"What video?" I ask, reaching for Penny's phone.

Penny holds it out for us to see. "The video of her graduation speech. It's got over a million views in just twelve hours."

"Fuck!" I blurt out. Mia and Penny's wide eyes both hit me. I try to make it a point not to curse in front of my daughter, but sometimes things just slip. My internal monologue tends to be much more R-rated than what I actually say out loud. "Can you take it down?"

"It's too late," Penny says, putting her arm around Mia. "It's already been shared and . . ."

"Garrett," Devlyn says, pointing to the television in the corner, the video suddenly playing on a morning news show.

"You're famous," Penny giggles out, shaking Mia, and the two start screaming and dancing around. They immediately start texting, their fingers moving at the speed of light. "Let's go find everyone."

Mia grabs her phone and rushes towards the door. "Mia," I call out. "Breakfast."

"Later. I'll meet you at the store in a little bit," she says, coming back to kiss me on the cheek before rushing out.

I look up at the television, and Devlyn's hand lands on my shoulder. "Looks like you're trending."

Letters to Mia

Fifth birthday

The quiet is my enemy. It's when the memories take over. They're like shadows, always lurking, and when I'm still, quiet, they roll in like the morning fog. This time of year doesn't help. The little girl I left behind is having a birthday. Every year, in the weeks leading up to this day, I feel like a prisoner on death row, hoping for a stay of execution, but knowing I deserve all the pain that's coming.

A pain that started with a boy.

Spending a couple months in some small, Podunk town is not what I had in mind the summer I met your father, but I was sixteen and didn't get a say in the matter. My dad had fallen on some ice the winter before and broken both his legs. It had been months of physical therapy, casts, pins and screws, and I don't know what else. My parents decided he needed a long break, and somehow had heard about this place Eden Valley.

It was just what they wanted—quiet, solitude. I wanted to be in New York with my friends. I lost that fight. They rented a cottage through just after Labor Day, when I'd have to go back to school. My whole summer.

They talked about the mountains, but I missed the skyscrapers. They commented on the air quality. I grew up on pollution. They loved the quiet. I missed the taxis honking at each other.

My dad slowed the car down as we pulled into town. I wondered if even the speed limit was slower here. They marveled at the quaint shops. I missed my chain stores, my big coffee shops. I had no idea how I was going to get through that summer.

Then I saw exactly how.

Tall, tanned by the southern sun, dark hair, and eyes so blue I could see them from the car. Yep, he was how I planned on passing the time. He smiled as we passed, tugging on the pigtail of a strawberry blonde girl tagging behind him. Poor girl, I could tell he only saw her as a little sister type, but that she had a huge crush on him. I could also tell she was the type of girl that hadn't discovered the power in being female. I learned that lesson young, having watched my mother flirt her way to getting anything she wanted. This girl had curves she didn't know how to use. She was no threat, dressed in some crazy red pants and yellow shirt. In fact, I doubted any girl in town could give me a run for my money.

What I didn't expect to happen was that I'd fall madly in love with that boy. Garrett Hollis.

Even his name does things to me, things it shouldn't after all these years.

He thought we met by chance. A small town, we would've run into each other at some point, but that wasn't good enough for me. So when I saw the strawberry blonde girl coming out of the town's diner, I followed her, knowing she'd lead me to him. I didn't have to wait long. He was right across the town square in the hardware store, working. I remember that first meeting like it was yesterday.

Perfect.

I walked right in, pushed my sunglasses on top of my head, holding back my blonde hair. He looked over at me, surprise in his blue eyes. "I'm new in town, and I'm a little turned around," I said. "I'm looking for the library."

That wasn't a total lie. I loved to read and would need to find it eventually.

"It's on the other side of the square," the strawberry blonde girl said, pointing toward the door. "I'll show you."

"That's okay," I said, not taking my eyes off his blue ones. "I'm sure I can find it."

"They show movies in the town square once a week in the summer," he said. "There's one tonight."

"Will you be there?" I asked.

"Garrett and I always go," the girl said, like she was stating some sort of claim.

"DD," he said warningly, taking a step towards me. "I'll be there."

"Save me a seat," I said, flipping my hair over my shoulder.

"I'll need your name," he said, grinning.

"Sheena."

Even now, I smile at the memory of meeting your father. I wonder if he's ever told you that story. I wonder what you know about me other than I left. I wonder what kind of cake you're having for your birthday. I'm eating a piece of chocolate cake. I even put five candles on it for you. Happy Birthday!

Until next year,
Your mom

CHAPTER TWO

GARRETT

NORMALLY, I'M NOT one for doing inventory. I farm that part of the job to my employees. Yes, I have to do paperwork, payroll, and ordering, but the part of owning the store I really love is getting my hands dirty outside of the store, doing building projects for people around town. Although today, doing inventory in the back is just what the doctor ordered. It seems like the entire population of Eden Valley has stopped by, some thrilled with the attention our town is getting via Mia's video, others offering up their nieces, aunts, cousins and friends to date me. The one thing they all have in common is finding the humor in my situation. So I escape to the storage room, having instructed Mia not to bother me for the remainder of the day, having had my fill of well-wishers.

My store is in the center of town square, and even though our town is small, I pride myself on having everything anyone might need, and if I don't have it, I'll get it. Like the rest of town, the store could be on a postcard for small town living. Just because we sell shovels and nails doesn't mean it can't be welcoming. I've reprimanded more than one employee for not greeting a customer when they walk in. A "hello" and "how can I help you" comes with the territory around here.

"Dad, we need to order . . ." Mia's voice trails off. She's spending part of her summer vacation helping me at the store, but I think she spends more time on her phone. I call out to her from the storage room, but she doesn't answer. After a few more tries, I make my way to the front of the store and immediately know why.

Mia turns to me, her eyes wide, her mouth dropped open. Standing in front of her is a woman, her eyes cast right on me. I know everyone who lives in this town. Yes, we get tourists, the occasional person just passing through, but I immediately know this is something else. I can sense it.

This woman is clearly on a mission, dressed in a short, tight black dress with black high heels and a bright red purse. She looks like she belongs in a nightclub in a big city, not small-town USA.

"You must be Mia's dad," she says, smiling at me.

"Can I help you with something?" I ask.

"She saw the video," Mia says, shrugging.

On instinct, I reach out to Mia. "Look, if you're a reporter or something . . ."

"I'm not a reporter," she says, taking a step closer. "I saw the video . . . and I . . . Um . . . I . . ."

"You came to date my dad!" Mia says, her voice a mix of joy and shock.

Holy shit! That can't be right, but one look at her nodding head and blushing skin lets me know my daughter hit the nail on the head.

"I don't do stuff like this. It's just, I saw it and felt something."

Mia elbows me in the side and whispers, "She felt something."

"It was a speech," I say. "I'm sorry you came all this way."

"Drove up from Florida," she says. "Through the night."

Frankly, I'm not sure what to think about this woman. Did she just escape from an asylum? Is this a joke? Am I on one of those practical joke shows? Not to mention, I certainly don't want my daughter thinking this is the way to meet someone.

Mia wiggles next to me. "Daddy, she drove here to meet you. You should at least buy her a coffee or something. That's the polite thing to do. I can watch the store for a few minutes. Besides, Biscuit Girl is right across the square." Mia turns to the stranger. "They have the best coffee in town."

The woman raises her eyebrows to me as if to say, "shall we?" I hold my finger up, indicating I need a minute with my overly excited daughter. Pulling Mia out of earshot but where I can still keep an eye on my new admirer, I say, "I know you think this is fun."

"She's pretty," Mia says simply.

I glance her way. "She is, but that doesn't change the fact that this is my life, our life and . . ."

"It's just coffee," she pleads.

"I had coffee already," I say. Not that I care what people think, but the locals would have a field day with this.

"You never get enough of Devlyn's coffee," she says, nudging me.

"Mia, this isn't how this works."

"Why not?" she asks, and I half-expect a stomp of her foot. "She's here. What can it hurt to just go have coffee with her?"

My pride? My ego? My man card will be revoked for allowing my daughter to set me up. Feeling me softening, Mia goes in for the kill, kissing me on the cheek. I hate to disappoint a woman much less two, so walking back over, I motion with my arm towards the door. I know I'm going to regret this. Mia squeals a little, and I mouth to her that's she's in so much trouble. She just smiles at my veiled threat.

The door is barely closed when she starts talking. "My name is . . ." Basically, she proceeds to give me her resume. What she does for a living. Her education. Relationship status. I get the whole lowdown on the short walk over to Biscuit Girl.

So here's the thing. I know within thirty seconds that I'm not interested in this woman. Yep, it happens that quick. We don't even make it to the gazebo that centers the town square. How do I know? Well, let's just say my dick isn't interested. Sad but true. A man's dick doesn't lie (unless we're drunk). It might be the most honest part of our bodies. Our heads can muck things up. Our hearts are even worse, but the cock always tells the straight-up truth. A man's dick is a good judge of character.

I open the door to the diner, and my coffee date places her hand on my chest. "Aren't you sweet? This place is so cute."

I motion towards a two-top table in the corner, not my usual table with Mia. We sit down, and I realize the drumbeat of her voice has stopped. Shit, must be my turn to say something. "So Florida?"

"I've lived there my whole life," she says. "I think a change would be good. I'd be open to moving."

See, the dick is right. This woman has driven the crazy train straight into town. She's met me for five minutes and seen one video, and she's ready to pack up and move.

"I think it's important you know that I want kids. I'm thirty-five."

Those words hanging in the air make me choke, and I start coughing. Do all women look at a guy and try to picture him as their husband and father of their children? Or do only the crazy ones do that? I feel someone pat my back, and a mug slips under my nose. I look up into Devlyn's sassy smirk. "Who's your friend?"

I look over at the woman, drawing a blank. She just giggles, introducing herself to Devlyn. "I saw the video of sweet Mia's speech, and just had to come meet the man that raised such a wonderful girl."

"Oh," Devlyn says, throwing me a look. She's going to have a field day with this. "Well, he is Eden Valley's very own bachelor." Devlyn reaches into a vase on a nearby table, pulling out a flower and placing it in front of me. "For the rose ceremony."

"I applied to be on that show!" the woman giggles.

Why am I not surprised? Is it too soon to bolt? Damn it, I should've had an exit strategy. Everyone of dating age should have one. I'm in so much trouble here. Devlyn takes her order then saunters off, throwing me a look over her shoulder. Damn woman!

My tablemate keeps talking about her favorite television shows, movies, anything and everything. Then she asks, "What would you like to know about me?"

It occurs to me that this lady hasn't asked me a single thing about myself. It's almost like she just wants a man and as long as we've got a dick, we'll do. I'm not rude, but it's been a long damn time since I've done this. I think of Mia and the things she likes to talk about. "What's your favorite book?" She gets this crease between her eyes like she's never heard the word before. "Or the last book you read?"

"I don't really have time to read a whole book," she says. "I like quick articles better."

Maybe I should buy her an audio book to listen to on her way out of town. "Uh huh."

The dreaded awkward silence follows. I can see her searching for something else to say. God knows, I've got nothing, and she's already told me her whole life story. What's left to ask? She starts fidgeting with her hair, looking around, giving me an uncomfortable smile. I'm sure she'll blame me for how terrible this is going, but she's the one who just showed up in town after seeing a YouTube video.

Suddenly, Devlyn appears, placing my mystery woman's coffee down in front of her in a to-go cup. Subtle!

Devlyn takes one look into my help-me eyes and says to me, "You know, you're really bad at this."

"Oh no," the woman says, waving her hand. "This is just an unusual situation."

"No, trust me. He's single for a reason." Devlyn leans in like she's about to spill my secrets. "Once, he missed a woman's birthday because of a baseball game."

The woman's eyes dart to me. I just shrug, not letting on that the girl was Devlyn, I was ten, and I only missed it because my team was in the Little League World Series.

"His priorities are all messed up," Devlyn piles on. "Anyone will tell you. Another of his relationships ended because of the woman's appearance."

"That's terrible," the woman says, grabbing her purse.

I bite the corner of my mouth not to laugh or spit out the truth, which is that the girl dumped *me* at the sixth-grade dance because she was taller than me and didn't want to dance with a short guy. At six-two, I got the last word on that one. Eventually.

"Maybe I should go," the woman says.

Devlyn places her hand on the woman's shoulder. "Some men just don't know a great woman when they see her." The woman straightens her posture. "It's really his loss, don't you think?"

"Absolutely," she says.

"You drove all this way just to meet him. You tried, you have to feel good about that," Devlyn piles on.

"I had to try," the woman says with a hopeless tone. "The heart wants what the heart wants."

Who came up with that stupid saying? Don't you have a brain? Who decided the heart is the body part to represent love, anyway? Why is that? Because it beats faster when you're with someone special? Well, my dick thumps, so maybe the penis should be on all the Valentine's Day cards. We could serve chocolates in a penis shaped container!

Is it because the heart is the center of your body? So is the cock. Is it because you can't live without your heart? I guess a man can live without his penis, but why would he want to?

The woman gives me the once-over then stands, telling me, "You really should learn how to behave on a date." Then she walks out.

I look up at Devlyn biting her bottom lip, trying to contain her laughter, but it comes out anyway. "Maybe there's an app for that."

I crack up laughing. "You totally saved my ass."

"You're welcome," she says. "I can spot crazy from a mile away, and that right there was crazy with a capital C."

She starts back towards the counter. "I owe you one, DD," I tease, knowing she always hated when I called her that in high school.

She turns back, cocks a smile, and says, "No double D's here. I'm a full C all the way, baby."

Chuckling, I see Mia rushing through the front door of the diner. "Daddy!"

I guess she saw her wannabe stepmother leaving and is trying to run interference. "Mia, she left because . . ."

"Forget her," Mia says. "I just took two phone calls from other women who want to meet you."

WHAT STARTED INNOCENTLY enough—a graduation speech—has quickly turned into a full-on festival of women. No joke. Eden Valley has become home to a parade of women all vying for my affection. Are women in this country so starved for single men that they have started responding to YouTube videos?

First, it was just the one woman, then a few phone calls. Eventually, the emails started. Then it was two women and a dozen letters. One week later, it's a full-on festival. Women from all over the country, even a few international, writing me, calling me. If I was on social media, I'm sure they would've found me there, too. Some sent pictures. Some sent resumes. Others sent flowers. One woman sent a pie, which went in the trash, like I'm going to trust that. I've avoided it all, choosing to ignore it, believing it will go away. Yet another, a personal shopper, offered to help me with my clothes. What's wrong with jeans and t-shirts? This is who I am. I'm not about to change what I wear to impress the mob of women who've invaded my town.

It's turned into a fucking free-for-all for my attention. The local bed and breakfasts are booked solid. I can't even get into my store. I've had offers from news outlets wanting to interview me and Mia. I've declined.

Our life works. Why complicate things? I open the door to the garage behind my house, flicking on the light, where the last piece of my teenage years is covered by a sheet. Before Mia's mom, before teenage pregnancy, there was that motorcycle—a 1972 Moto Guzzi Ambassador. Perhaps the greatest piece of metal ever saved from a junkyard. My dad and I worked on that bike almost every night. My mother hated it. Don't know why she worried so much, we never actually got it road ready.

After I found out I was going to be a dad, I covered it with a sheet. Over the years, I've fiddled with it from time to time. Kind of like me and dating. Every now and again, I mess around under the sheets, but ultimately, I leave and shut that door behind me.

"Dad, we need to get going," Mia says from behind me, but I don't turn toward her.

She's taken it upon herself to organize this chaos into some sort of mission of love for her dad, and there's no talking to her when she gets like this.

I've tried telling her that when I want to date someone I will. I've tried telling her that I don't need or want her involved in my love life.

Her response: It will be fun. Just humor me.

That I could fend off.

It's when her eyes grew weepy, and she said how much she worries about me that I caved. That's the ace in the hole every time. There's no saying no to her when she plays that card.

"Were you working on the bike?" she asks.

"Thinking about it," I say.

"You should," she says, like she knows we are talking about dating more than the motorcycle.

I open my arm for her to come over, and wrap it around her shoulder. This garage holds more than my lost youth, it holds what I gained, too. Over in the corner sits Mia's first tricycle. Up on a shelf sits the dollhouse she never played with. Running my hand over the wood of her rocking horse, I say, "I couldn't get you off this when you were little."

"Didn't you make it for me?" she asks.

I nod. It was the first thing I ever made for her. "Hours and hours, you were on that thing. You'd sing this little song. *Horsey, horsey, my horsey* over and over again."

"If only riding a real horse went as well," she says, laughing.

She'd begged me for riding lessons, so when she was eight I signed her up. Riding horses is an expensive hobby. I calculated it one time. It was a buck a minute. So the ten minutes she spent crying cost me a ten-spot. It only took her falling off the horse one time, and her equestrian career was over.

"We should go. Penny's meeting me," Mia says." She's going to help me make a spreadsheet of the . . ."

I turn her to me, my hands on her tiny shoulders. "Promise me this won't interfere with me and you. Our time together. I don't want your last couple months at home to be . . ."

"I promise," she says, wrapping her arms around my waist, her head resting on my chest.

"I love you," I say.

LOOKING OVER MY shoulder for women who want to be my wife, I walk towards the diner. I just left Mia at my shop. It's quiet around town, the haze from the morning still rolling off the streets, the morning dew making everything look fresh.

"Garrett?" I hear my name being called.

"Quiet," I bark, turning around to see Eden Valley's new mayor power walking through the town square.

"Eden Valley's very own economic boost in the flesh," the mayor boasts. He's a nice man. I wouldn't describe him as wise like my dad, but he loves this town, and what more can you really ask for in a mayor? His heart is in the right place, even if his nose is stuck in my business.

"Can I help you with something?"

"Just getting my morning cardio," he says, shuffling past me. If that constitutes cardio these days, we are in serious trouble.

Giving him a wave, I stop at Biscuit Girl and lightly knock on the front door of the diner. It's early, the place isn't even open yet, but if I want to avoid a mob of women and have my coffee in peace, I've got no choice.

Most men would love to have this problem, but I find it all ridiculous. How can anyone decide they want to meet me from one video? A video that, by the way, only showed me for about five seconds.

Smiling, Devlyn unlocks the door, letting me in. She's been opening early for me the past few mornings. "Coffee's not quite ready," she says. I shrug and collapse into my usual chair. "Where's Mia this morning?"

I point across the square at my daughter and her friend, Penny, setting up a table in front of my store. "She's decided she's going to vet these women for me. Interviews, resumes, or some shit."

Devlyn laughs. "That bad?"

"That bad," I say. "Yesterday, I stumbled upon a woman sunbathing topless in my backyard."

"I think most men would be all over that."

"Most men don't have a teenage daughter."

"Well, don't send them all away too quickly. Business is so good I may be able to retire early. I'm even thinking of naming a menu item in your honor. That way your suitors can learn your dietary habits. You know, Hamburger Hollis or Garrett's Garlic Fries."

Devlyn is always good for a laugh. "Don't worry," I say. "Mia hates the idea of me being alone. She is hell-bent on having me nice and settled before she goes off to college. I think she thinks she can get me married in the next three months."

"So what are you going to do?" Devlyn asks.

"What do you do with any woman who gets her head wrapped around something? Compromise!" I say. "I told her three dates with three women, and that's it. So she's sorting through and selecting her top picks for me. Then I'll pick three and be done with this whole mess."

"You don't sound optimistic," Devlyn says.

"Would you be?"

Her eyes lower a little. "Probably not." She's had her share of bad relationships. I know how that feels. "Did you ever think it would be this hard?" she asks. "Love, I mean."

"This isn't about love," I say.

"That's where you're wrong," Devlyn says. "It's about the hope of love."

Do I want that? I certainly haven't been hoping for it, but I guess Devlyn's right. That's why all these women are here. They are hoping to find love. I'm sorry to disappoint them, but I think they are in the wrong place.

I'd like to meet the asshole who said love was easy because they're fucking liars. Besides, it's the hard things that mean the most, not the easy things. "You're asking the wrong guy," I say. "Seems to me that hard love is the only kind there is."

CHAPTER THREE

DEVLYN

"I HATE HIM," I screamed into my pillow. Only I didn't hate him. I could never hate him. Most fifteen-year-old girls hang posters of their favorite boy band. If Garrett Hollis was in a boy band, he'd grace my walls.

Sobbing into my pillow, snot ran down my face. It couldn't be true. Sheena couldn't be pregnant. It couldn't be Garrett's. My mom had been on the phone non-stop as news spread through Eden Valley like wildfire, and I hadn't stopped crying since.

There hadn't been a teenage pregnancy in this town for as far back as anyone could remember. Out-of-wedlock was one thing, but teenage pregnancy didn't happen here. Or so everyone thought. According to my momma, Eden Valley had become the devil's playground.

I opened the door to my bedroom, hearing my parents in the kitchen. "I can't believe they are sending Garrett back to school," I heard my mom say to my dad. "And they enrolled that girl." She said "that girl" like it was a cuss word. "Can you imagine a pregnant teenager roaming the halls?"

When something like this happens, there's a ripple effect. It changes the lives of a lot of people, not just the main parties involved. Parents, grandparents, siblings all are affected. Neighbors and friends are on that list, too. Take me, for example. I'm no one. News of Sheena's pregnancy was my first heartbreak. Not that this was about me, I knew it wasn't. But it also rippled through the rest of the town, making parents of teenagers scared, cautious, and overly protective. Suddenly, the town's golden boy was a poster child for what not to do, and no one wanted their child associated with that.

My dad's eyes caught mine, and he nodded to my mother. She faked a smile for me, running her fingers through my hair. "I want you to stay away from Garrett Hollis. I know he's your friend, but that boy . . ."

"That boy" was now a cuss word, too. "Don't worry, Momma. I don't ever want to see him again."

I WANTED TO hate him. I did, but I loved him too much. Garrett was every girl's dream. He had these blue eyes and when he smiled, you'd swear they sparkled just for you. At sixteen, he was already six feet. His dark hair was always a little messy, and I wish I knew what it felt like. He played football for our school, and it showed in the way his shirt sleeves tightly hugged his biceps. Popular, gorgeous, on honor roll, and worked a part-time job at the hardware store in town—there wasn't much not to love.

Unfortunately, I wasn't the only one who loved him.

He had sex. He'd gotten her pregnant, and still I loved him. Any adult would say it wasn't real. They'd say it was just teenage puppy love. Someone needed to explain that to my heart.

Sheena wasn't from Eden Valley. She'd spent last summer here with her parents. They were from New York. They rented a place and were here until Labor Day. The day she walked into town and laid eyes on Garrett, I knew I'd never have a chance. When she left at the end of the summer, I was so happy. I didn't want Garrett to be heartbroken, but I hoped he'd finally notice me as more than a friend.

Then several weeks later, she shows up at his front door, having run away from home, pregnant with his baby. Rumor has it that her parents have disowned her. Not sure if that's true or not. Either way, Mr. and Mrs. Hollis took her in, got her enrolled in school, and are going to help them raise the baby.

The hallways of the high school were eerily quiet. You could've heard a pin drop when Sheena and Garrett turned the corner that first day they walked in together.

Her eyes were down, and he was gently rubbing her back, carrying both their school bags. Everyone, including me, stood frozen by their lockers. The boy who once walked down the hall to high fives and cheers was now the outcast.

I couldn't imagine what it was like for him to walk into school after news of the pregnancy broke. I'd never seen Garrett cry. Never seen him scared, but when his blue eyes found mine in the hallway, the sadness and fear shot right through me. I'd been his friend his whole life. Our parents were friends, we'd grown up together. We'd ridden bikes through town, skipped rocks at the springs, played touch football at Thanksgiving with other kids from town.

Now was not the time to stop being his friend. Not when it appeared he didn't have any left. He needed me. Adjusting my backpack on my shoulder, I walked toward him and Sheena as whispers filled the hallway.

Garrett stood there frozen, not knowing what to expect from me. Probably another disappointed person coming to let loose on him. We hadn't talked since all this went down. I'm sure he had his hands full and calling me wasn't at the top of his list of things to do. Besides, I'd been too wrapped up in my own heartbreak to even consider his, until right now. Swallowing back my own sadness, I walked up to him and said, "Mystery meat for lunch today, but I've got an extra sandwich. You guys make sure to sit with me."

I didn't have an extra sandwich. Garrett and I both knew it. But when he smiled at me, the fear in his eyes was a little less.

I WAS PERMANENTLY grounded that entire school year. My parents couldn't control who I walked the halls with at school. They couldn't control who I sat with at lunch, but I was under lockdown at home. Only school activities were permitted. All because they found out I'd been hanging out with Garrett. Sheena was always there, too. Garrett only left her side when he was forced to. I wanted to take out a billboard that said, "Teenage pregnancy is not contagious." But Eden Valley has a ban on billboards. Just my luck.

And I had to wonder if our English teacher assigning The Scarlet Letter *that year was just a coincidence. After all, we were having our very own interpretation in our own town. Hopefully, no one burned at the stake this time.*

When I heard Sheena had the baby, I had to get creative. I snuck out my bathroom window, took the car without permission or a license for that matter, and drove myself to the hospital. I wanted to be there for Garrett. Most everyone had continued to keep their distance, so I knew that no one would be there for him other than his family.

That little stunt had me washing dishes and scrubbing the floors of Biscuit Girl for the entire summer. It was worth it, though.

To get to meet little baby Mia. I was grateful that Sheena was in the bathroom getting ready to go home. It gave me a few minutes with Garrett. He placed the baby in my arms.

I looked up at Garrett, bags under his eyes, his hair all crazy. He looked older somehow. It was as if overnight he became a man. "I'll help you."

His head shook. "I'm sure your parents won't . . ."

"I don't care," I said.

"DD, this isn't like sitting with us at school when no one else would."

"You think I care what people think?" I asked, motioning down to my orange shorts and pink frilly top.

Garrett chuckled, and I wondered when the last time he laughed was. "Thanks, Devlyn," he said, and it was the first time I heard him use my real name and not DD. Apparently, I'd grown up, too.

My visit was cut short when Sheena came out of the bathroom. Something about the way she looked made Garrett send me away. If I'd known what that look meant, I would've stayed.

Sheena left him.

That day.

Instead of going home a family, Garrett took Mia home without her mother.

That left me and the whole town in a state of shock.

I didn't talk to him for what seemed like forever after that, but really it was only a month. I wanted to talk to him. My parents took my phone from my room, so I couldn't call. I managed to get one letter sent to him, but I'm not sure he got it or whether he responded. If he did, my parents never gave it to me.

I've watched him coming and going from the hardware store—he's still working there. It must be hard to balance work, being a dad, dealing with what Sheena did. I tried to wave, but his head's always down.

Wiping down a table at Biscuit Girl, my mother walked by, giving my shoulder a little pat. It was summer break. I should be happy, but I wasn't, and I didn't have it in me to fake a smile for my mother.

"That poor boy," I heard a customer say and looked out the window.

Garrett was sitting in the gazebo in the town square, a little baby girl in his arms—alone. Like she read my mind, my momma yelled out my name, but it was too late. I was already out the door.

I was already grounded, so what did I have to lose? I didn't care how it looked. I didn't care what anyone thought—a young teenage girl hanging out with a teenage single father. I know my parents were worried I'd be next. The only thing I was worried about was Garrett.

"Hey," I said.

He jumped slightly, the dark circles under his eyes coming into view. "Wow, she's getting so big," I said, smiling down at the baby.

He looked over my shoulder, my mother standing outside the diner watching us. He and I both noticed others beginning to appear as well, coming out of the diner or filing out of other stores to catch a better view, all standing and watching us like my mother.

"Sorry," he said, getting to his feet. "She's been up all night. Won't take her bottle. I thought maybe a walk, some fresh air. I don't want you to get into trouble."

"Let me try," I said, reaching for the bottle.

"You sure?" he asked, eyeing my mother.

"I'm already grounded for life for taking the car and coming to see you at the hospital."

"God, Devlyn, I'm sorry."

"Shut up," I said, holding out my arms. "Let me try."

He slipped Mia into my arms, and just like with her father, I fell in love at first sight. She was beautiful just like him. And stubborn just like him. And just like him, she missed Sheena.

I tickled her little baby mouth with the nipple of the bottle, causing her to open wide. It had to be beginners' luck, because I had no experience with babies—none, nada, zilch.

Mia went to town, and Garrett looked like he'd won the lottery. I wanted to know if he'd heard from Sheena. I wanted to know why she left. Instead, I said, "You know you look like complete shit."

His laugh was so loud I'm sure it raised the eyebrows of our onlookers. I loved that I could make him laugh. I didn't have much I could offer him, but I could give him that.

He wiggled his daughter's hand, and she wrapped her hand around his finger, gripping tightly. "Mia doesn't care how I look," he said sweetly.

I leaned over, close to his neck. All I wanted to do was lean my head on his shoulder, kiss his neck. Inhaling softly, I breathed him in. We were in Eden

Valley, not the Garden of Eden, but he was my very own forbidden fruit. Now, more than ever.

Playfully, I took a big whiff. "What about how you smell?" He smiled at me like he was thankful, so grateful that I was treating him the same way as always. Smiling at him, I asked, "How are you?"

He shrugged and nodded his head. "We're fine."

I hate the word fine. What the hell does that word mean? It sounds so ordinary to say, "I'm fine." Unless you're talking about fine wine or fine china, then it sounds classy and important. Garrett was a lot of things, but "fine" wasn't one of them—unless you were referring to his body, then the boy was FINE, with a capital F.

Rolling my eyes, I bumped his shoulder. "How about we get something to eat for you, too?"

"I'm good, really."

Like all teenage boys, Garrett was an excellent liar, but he wasn't going to fool me. I got to my feet, Mia in my arms, and we headed toward the diner. He followed along, both of us acutely aware of all the eyes staring, and none more harshly than my mother's.

As we made our way, the patrons filed back into the diner, but my mother stayed outside. She blocked the door to the diner. "Garrett, I'm sorry for what happened," she said. "Truly I am, but you brought this on yourself, and I'm not going to let you drag my daughter into it. She's not some substitute mother for that baby."

That baby!

I'd be damned if she used Mia as a cuss word. "Mom! I . . ."

Garrett touched my arm. "It's okay." He took Mia from my arms then looked at my mom. "I know you want what's best for your daughter." He looked down at his own. "I get that."

He turned to walk away, and I looked to my mom, seeing her heart soften. "He's my friend, Mom. I won't stop trying." She glanced at Garrett. He made mistakes, but he was doing the right thing. He loved his daughter just like she loved me. That was enough of a common ground to make a start. She gave me the slightest nod then disappeared inside. "I just made fresh biscuits," I called out to Garrett. "Want one?"

He turned back, and I opened the door. "I appreciate it, Devlyn, but . . ."

He looked over my shoulder into the diner, the patrons still gawking at him. "I promised my parents I'd be responsible. You know, with money and stuff."

"Never got you a baby gift," I said. "Breakfast's on me."

With that, a tradition was born. Garrett walked through that door for breakfast that day and most every day since.

That morning changed everything. It only takes one person to change things.

The town started to rally behind him and Mia. How could we not? A sweet little baby like Mia. The more people that saw Garrett and Mia together, the more people realized he was still the same boy they cheered for at football games. It helped that Garrett was so utterly devoted to that baby girl. Hard to hate a guy who walked around town with a baby strapped to his chest. Soon his "mistake" turned into the town's daughter. Everyone loved seeing them together. People sent over diapers, clothes, offers to babysit. There was no town treaty, no oath, but silently everyone in Eden Valley adopted Mia in their hearts.

And it all started with a biscuit.

CHAPTER FOUR

GARRETT

"YOU REALLY SHOULD be taking her to dinner," Mia scolds me. "Lunch is so . . . lunch."

Date one is today, and I'm going in blind. I figure if these women pass the Mia Test, then they've been through the wringer. I must've missed the newsletter that dating is now a damn audition process.

Mia has strict age requirements. They can't be too young or too old. She doesn't want them to have other children; they must be educated, financially independent, spiritual, no history of serious illness, have good fashion sense. The list goes on and on. And true to the spirit that is my daughter, there isn't one thing on the list about the woman's looks or physical appearance. I know beauty's on the inside and all that shit, but I may be meeting a woman for lunch that has three heads, and that's just not going to work.

I don't get the same courtesy. Mia's been giving me tips on what to wear for the past three days. "You should put on a suit, like for my graduation. You're always in jeans and a white or black t-shirt."

"It's lunch. Jeans and a shirt will work just fine." She rolls her eyes. "No spying," I say, giving Mia a quick peck on top of her head as I head to meet the woman by the town's gazebo.

I see a woman standing there waiting. She's tall with dark brown hair, very attractive. Good job in that department, Mia. Maybe this won't be as bad as I think.

A quick hello, and we're walking to my truck to head to the restaurant. I'm taking her to a place one town over, knowing there's no chance at privacy with the rumor mill in Eden Valley working overtime. I reach for the handle of her door when her hand quickly beats me to it. "I can get my own door!" she bites out.

Christ, not one of these women that thinks chivalry is the opposite of feminism. The way I see it, chivalry and feminism go hand-in-hand. I know she can get her own door. I know she can pay her own way. I get the door out of a sign of respect for her, not a sign of weakness. Chivalry is a sign of respect, not an insult.

"Well, then you can get your own lunch, too," I say, grinning, and turn and walk away.

She yells a few cuss words my way as I head back towards my hardware store. If that's any indication how dating is going to go, then you can count me out. I don't need that shit. I know I said I thought all love is hard, but I'm beginning to wonder if it's damn near impossible.

Almost back to my store, I spot Devlyn beside her SUV with her arms full. Hurrying her way, I open the door for her just before she drops everything. This time I'm greeted with a bright smile and a thank you, not a dissertation on the history of female rights in this country.

As I take the boxes and sacks from her, she starts to load up the backseat. "I thought you had a date?" she asks.

Must have my dating schedule up on the town's Facebook page now. "Don't ask."

"You're going to be in big trouble with Mia," she teases me.

"Think I've humored that girl long enough."

"You're going to miss her craziness when she goes off to school."

She's absolutely right. I will. "You've got a lot of deliveries today," I say.

We don't have homeless people in Eden Valley. If we did, I'm sure Devlyn would feed them, too. Instead, she takes food to those in town that are sick, housebound, or have lost a loved one. She doesn't charge them one cent, either. She'll tell you it's just leftovers that she'd have to throw out, but I know better. All anyone in town has to do is call the diner, and Devlyn guarantees them a hot meal.

"Want to help me?" she asks, raising an eyebrow. "Or would you rather go explain to your headstrong daughter why you bailed on your date?"

This time it's her who opens the door for me. Grinning, I hop in. "Who's the first stop?"

A DOZEN HOUSES, and the same question to me every time. "Found a girlfriend yet?" Apparently, even the sick and elderly have a vested interest in my love life. Devlyn pulls up in front of her diner. "It's really sweet of you do this," I say.

"It tickles my heart, you know?" She shrugs. "Thanks for the help."

"Anytime," I say.

Devlyn unbuckles and turns to me. "Can I ask you something?"

"Why the hell not? Everyone else in town has."

"Why haven't you . . ."

"I've dated. It's . . ."

"A regular Thursday night hookup with that nurse two towns over isn't dating."

My eyes fly to her. "How'd you know about that?"

"I know everything there is to know about you, Garrett Hollis."

Struggling for what to say, I feel my jaw tense. Can't really argue with the truth, but that's been over for a long time. How does Devlyn know about that? Mia had a couple hours of dance class every Thursday. I didn't set out to make that my hookup night, it just sort of happened. I'm not going to apologize or explain it. I'm a grown fucking man, but that doesn't mean I would want my daughter to get wind of my extracurricular activities.

"Don't worry," Devlyn says. "I'm the only one that knows. I was taking a class and saw you walking into her house. Your truck was there week after week."

"It's been over for a while."

"Figured as much," she said. "So why no real relationships?"

"Couple of reasons," I say. "Women my age want kids, and

frankly, I'm not sure I want to start over with all that. Babies are hard work."

"You were alone with a kid last time," she says.

"Even if I could get over that," I say, "I've never met a woman who understood that Mia comes first. They all say they do until Mia gets sick or I have to spend money on something Mia needs instead of on dates or gifts. Things tend to go south pretty quick when your daughter needs new uniforms for dance team, so you can't take your girlfriend away for the weekend." I look over at Devlyn. She's helped me so much with Mia over the years. "The thing is, I don't think bad about these women. They deserve those things. Hell, someday I want Mia to have a guy that loves her so much he makes her the center of his world. I could never offer that to any woman because the position was filled."

"Mia," she whispers, and I nod my head. "You had to be lonely."

"There's no time to be lonely. There are tutors and dance lessons and . . ."

"Still, at night when you're alone."

"I wait up for her at night."

"When she was little, then."

"You mean during fevers and bad dreams and bedtime stories."

She gives me a look. Women have a lot of damn looks they throw around. Us men need a damn translation app to figure them out. "Are you sure it's not more than that?" she asks.

"Like what?"

"Like Sheena. She did a real number on you."

She said *her* name. No one in town brings up Sheena, ever, and if they do, it's to refer to her as *that woman*, or the woman who gave birth to Mia. They don't even call her a mother. It's like the name Sheena has been permanently ruined for the entire town of Eden Valley. It's as though her name has become associated with everything wrong in the world. So for Devlyn to use her name—well, it's sort of like calling out to Voldemort in Harry Potter.

No way am I dredging up all that shit. "Look, it's simple, there's no use looking for something I can't have, so I stopped looking."

She opens her car door. "I should get back to the diner."

Suddenly, I feel like I've done something wrong. "Devlyn?"

She turns to me, giving me a little smile. "Good luck on date number two." Then she disappears through the door to her diner.

THEY SHOULD REALLY make bedroom ceilings more interesting to look at. I've been staring at mine for hours. It's not one of those terrible popcorn ceilings, but at least if it was, I could try to count the bumps to make myself fall asleep. As it is, I'm just staring up at the blank space above my head.

Sheena.

I don't think about her too much anymore. Sometimes Mia will do something that reminds me of her mother, but otherwise, I've buried that all away. Being busy raising our daughter made it pretty easy to not think about how she left. Why she left.

It does no good to think about it. She left me. She left Mia. I have her signature on a piece of paper saying she wanted nothing to do with our daughter. Actually, my father has it. He was a lawyer. He drafted it. I've never actually read it. That was the last time I saw Sheena, just days after Mia was born.

Wonder what made Devlyn bring Sheena up?

I know she wasn't just being nosy. That's not Devlyn's mode of operation. She must think my bachelorhood has something to do with Sheena and not single fatherhood, which I blamed for my lack of dating. If she were wrong, I'd be fast asleep by now, but I know she's right—at least a little bit.

Fucking hate admitting that.

I hate that I'm losing sleep. I hate that I give one ounce of thought to that woman. I doubt Mia and I get the same space in her mind. I doubt she's ever lost a night's sleep over us. Last I heard, she had some big life over in Europe. She's probably married, has more kids. She probably has everything she ever talked about. I'm sure we aren't even on her radar.

So I'm pissed that she's also robbing me of my sleep.

I know what my dad would say, what my mom would say, what Devlyn would say.

Don't let her rob you of anything else.

Fuck, fuck, fuck! I throw the sheets off and sit up, my head lowered to my hands. I've been fine alone all these years. I have been. I tried to date. Okay, so I didn't try that hard, but I'm good. I didn't need the romantic hassles of dating someone. When I needed a warm body, I found one, but I didn't need all the other stuff that comes with being in a relationship.

Especially the risk.

I had more on the line than myself. My daughter was already growing up with a huge handicap, not having a mother around, and I wasn't going to set her up for more disappointment.

I wasn't going to set myself up, either.

Letters to Mia
Fifteenth Birthday

Dear Mia,
At fifteen, I was boy crazy. I'd already had my first kiss. Have you? Most moms probably wouldn't tell their daughters some of things I write about, but since you'll never read these letters, I figure I'm safe.

The first time your father kissed me was two days after we met. I was in the library pretending to read and escaping the Georgia heat. Garrett was beside me, not even pretending. I remember I had the biggest smile on my face and elbowed him slightly to try to get him to stop staring at me. When I did, he lightly took hold of my chin, tilted my head up and kissed me. It was sweet and, like everything else that summer, totally unexpected.

He didn't cop a feel for two more weeks. It wasn't until the Fourth of July that the real fireworks happened.

It wasn't something we planned. It wasn't something we even talked about before it happened. Looking back, I should've known it was coming. I'd had sex one time before, on my sixteenth birthday with my boyfriend at the time. It was just once. It wasn't great, and we broke up shortly after.

I never told Garrett about that. He probably assumed I was a virgin like him. I bet all the girls he knew were. I was the big city girl with more experience, but the thing was, everything felt new with Garrett.

Everyone was at the Falls to celebrate, but Garrett and I snuck away. Between my parents, his parents, and small-town life, privacy was hard to come by. We'd found our own secret hideaway in his grandparents' old house, spending afternoons there making out. That night was no different.

Before either of us realized it, we were at the point of no return.

I remember I cried myself to sleep that night. I never told Garrett that. I never told him how lonely I felt after we untangled ourselves, and he took me home. I didn't want him to feel bad. It wasn't his fault we were kids, playing as adults.

But once you cross that line, have a taste of the forbidden, it's hard to stop, so we didn't. As you get older, remember that.

I was on the pill. It's not foolproof. Every girl back home was on it. Our mothers justified it by saying we needed to regulate our periods, but we all knew it was to avoid the shame of having your daughter get pregnant.

Shame I would bring on them sooner than I could've imagined.

Labor Day came, and I left. We promised a whole lot to each other in those final minutes together. For a girl who went to Eden Valley kicking and screaming, I was leaving a huge part of me behind—love.

Every slow minute of that summer was spent with Garrett, but somehow it all went too quick.

I left how I came, looking at the window, watching him—a strawberry blonde girl I now knew as Devlyn smiling at him.

Happy Birthday,
Until next year,
Your mom

CHAPTER FIVE

GARRETT

SENIOR YEAR OF high school is a busy time. Actually, it starts junior year. I missed out on most of it. There's prom, ACT's, confirmation class if you're Catholic, college tours, college applications, senior rings, senior class portraits, graduation. The list is endless. For Mia, ending her senior year also means her very last dance recital.

I've had her in dance lessons since she was a toddler. My mom insisted. They used to love to twirl around together. My mom gave Mia a charm bracelet the year she started dance, and she added a new charm every recital. Her bracelet is nearly full with fifteen charms. Some are dance related, like a pointe shoe. Some are special to that time in Mia's life, like the polar bear charm for the year she loved polar bears and a wand for the year she loved Harry Potter. When mom passed away, I kept the tradition alive. Of course, this year's charm is a graduation cap.

Grabbing the box with the charm bracelet and a bouquet of flowers, I start walking to the small town hall where they have the recital each year. Mia's been here all afternoon. She's got a solo performance tonight. It's tradition that all the seniors get a solo their last year. My phone rings, and I grab it from my pocket, seeing my dad's calling. "I'm almost there."

"I'm saving you a seat," my dad says.

"Why do you need to save me a seat?" I ask. It's not as though the dance school recital is a big-ticket item.

"You'll see," he says. "Hurry up. I don't know how long I can keep this seat saved. It's worse than Christmas Mass."

"Dad?" I say, but he's already hung up. Picking up the pace, I notice a lot of cars parked on the streets. The streets of Eden Valley are never full. Parking is not an issue here. Tonight is the exception. As soon as I walk into the town hall, I know why.

A sea of women fills the room.

Some are sitting, some are standing in the lobby, others are lining the walls. I wonder what the occupancy limit of this building is. We are probably breaking a dozen fire codes. A wave of whispers starts, and I realize I'm the reason why. The smiles, hair flips, and batting of eyelashes are all for my benefit—not to mention the cleavage, short skirts, and bare midriffs. It's as though these women have entered a beauty pageant, and I'm the only judge. How did they even know I'd be here?

"Garrett?" I hear my name being called and see my dad waving at me. Great, Dad, create more of a scene.

Giving him a nod, I try to cut my way through the crowd. "Excuse me, excuse me."

"Hi, I'm . . ."

Each woman I pass gives me her name. One kisses me on the cheek, and I swear at least three grabbed my ass. "Garrett Hollis!" A finger finds its way to my face. The very pointy finger of the principal's wife. "This is all your fault," she scolds me. "I can't find a seat to save my life."

"I'm sorry. You can have my seat," I say, pointing to where my dad is saving my spot.

"No, no," she says. "This is Mia's big night. I'll find a place."

We shuffle past each other, and I continue my trek towards my seat, thankful when my ass lands in the chair and that it's located safely between my dad and Mia's best friend, Penny. I blow out a deep breath, and my dad lets out a hearty chuckle.

Looking down at the bouquet of flowers I bought for Mia, now crushed, I huff, "This is not funny."

"Oh, it is," he says, laughing even harder.

Scanning the room, a few women give me little waves. "How the hell am I going to get out of here later?"

"Don't know," my dad says. "But I'm going to stick around to watch."

There's not one part of me that's enjoying this attention. Actually, I'm downright pissed off by it tonight. It's making me crazy. It's my daughter's night. It's not the night for this. I want to focus on her, but that's damn hard with more tits in the room than tutus.

That reminds me. I pull out my phone to send Devlyn a text. Fathers aren't allowed in the dressing rooms, and Mia needed help with her hair, so Devlyn volunteered.

How's my girl doing? Is she nervous?

I should've expected Devlyn's sassy response.

Thanks for asking. I'm not nervous at all. I've done a bun a thousand times.

A couple seconds later, Devlyn's next text arrives.

Don't be nervous, Garrett. Mia is ready. We are having fun. She looks beautiful.

I write a quick thanks in reply, put my phone away, then sit facing straight ahead, my eyes focused on the stage. There's nothing happening. There's nothing to look at. Nothing to do but sit here and ruminate over my predicament. How the hell did I get here? I had a nice little life in a small town with my daughter, and suddenly I'm the center of attention. That hasn't happened since news of Sheena's pregnancy hit town. I didn't want the attention then any more than I want it now.

"Mr. Hollis," Penny says from beside me. "Um . . . You remember my aunt, right? You went to high school together."

"Of course," I say, having some vague memory of her. "She got married and moved to . . ."

"She's divorced now," Penny says, flashing me a smile. "She saw the video and wanted me to . . ."

"Not you, too, Penny!" I laugh. "Not you, too."

"Sorry, Mr. Hollis," she says. "I told her I'd try."

Shaking my head, the lights flicker on and off, the sign that it's almost time to start. With each passing year, Mia's in more and more numbers. I think she's up to about eight now, not counting her solo.

Every year, there's one little girl who cries through every routine of her first recital. Fifteen years ago, it was my daughter on the stage bawling. Fifteen years ago, it was me who rushed the stage to rescue her. Tonight, I'll keep my seat, no matter the chaos surrounding us. The spotlight is all hers.

I hear a lot of dads and grandpas complaining about recital night. That it's boring. That it's too long. I'm not one of those dads. Maybe because I never had a son. I never had the excitement of a home run or a touchdown to compare this to. Instead, I hold my breath when Mia does a spin or leap in the air, hoping she lands just right. I can't scream out loud, I can't wear crazy face paint or make a sign to hold up. Instead, I hold those precious seconds in my heart.

She is my whole life. Most parents face their kids going off to school together. Most parents probably look forward to the day that their life becomes their own again. As the spotlight finds Mia on the stage, I glance around the room. There is no doubt that my life is about to change.

The reason for the past eighteen years of my life is about to be gone.

As usual, Mia is smarter than me and figured that out before I did. The music starts, and some boy in the crowd yells out my daughter's name. I see her smile, just slightly. A subtle reminder that I'm not her whole world anymore, either.

She's refused to show me the whole routine. All I know is that it's choreographed to some rap crap that her and her friends all seem to love. That hardly seems appropriate for a ballet routine, but Mia insisted it would be "epic."

The music seems to be taking forever to start. I know my daughter. She's freaking out on the inside. I see her fingers tap the side of her thigh. Just like that, Sheena pops into my mind.

The beat of her fingers tapping the side of the bed like a metronome when she was in labor with Mia. I watched those fingers land—one, two, three, four, one, two, three, four—over and over again. She refused an epidural, even though I begged her to get one. Sheena was petite and still a teenager when she had Mia. The doctor had expressed concern about Sheena being able to deliver Mia naturally, but Sheena did what she wanted—like always. Twenty-two hours of labor, two hours of pushing and a constant drumbeat of her fingers.

I'd read all the books, so I was expecting Sheena would want to walk, move around, soak in a tub. That's what all the natural birthing books said. Hell, I was even prepared to dance with her. More than one book suggested that.

That twenty-four hours was the scariest of my life. The mother of my child was in pain, and I was helpless. Helplessness is the worst fucking emotion. Watching someone you love hurting, and being unable to do something, is there anything worse?

I look up at Mia on stage, knowing she's scared, standing there still except for the tapping of her fingers, just like her mother. I couldn't do anything for Sheena and I can't do anything for Mia. Wish I could fire the audio guy right now.

The music starts, but in my head I hear the sound of my daughter's first cry. I was a dad. Her dad.

From screaming infant to rap crap ballerina, that's my girl.

CHAPTER SIX

GARRETT

DATE TWO, TAKE two.

At least I made it to the restaurant with this one, which is a miracle considering this woman stopped and took selfies every ten steps or so. The ride over to the restaurant wasn't terrible, if you don't consider small talk torture.

Walking into the restaurant, I didn't hold her hand or place mine at the small of her back. Instead, she walked one step in front of me. She's a pretty woman—tall, slender, dark hair and eyes, but she's trying way too hard—too much makeup, too much hairspray, her dress giving everything away. I prefer a more homegrown girl—someone comfortable in her skin, whose eyelashes aren't going to fall off or whose hair I can actually run my fingers through.

The restaurant sits on the edge of a lake, and we got a table by the window. It should be a great spot to watch the sunset. My date didn't even sit down before heading to the ladies' room. I really hope she's not applying more makeup. She already added lipstick twice in the car, every fifth selfie or so.

Quickly, I check my phone before putting it away for the night. I don't plan on taking any pictures and even though I'm not a big dater, I know it's rude to be on your phone. Flipping open the menu, I glance at the options. I'm not at all nervous, which I figure is a bad sign. Shouldn't I have those little butterflies everyone talks about in movies all the time? There's nothing going on in my stomach besides being hungry as hell.

"I'm back." I hear my date's voice.

I look up, finding her standing by the table, on my side. Before I know it, she's taken the seat beside me. Dear God, she's turned me into one of those couples that sits beside each other instead of across from each other. This seating arrangement makes perfect sense if you are out with another couple, or have kids with you, but for two grown ass people on a date to sit beside each other with no one across from them . . . well, it's just fucking weird.

She holds her phone up. "This way we can take some pictures together," she says. "With the pretty view behind us."

This just went from bad to worse—threat level red. She wants me to take selfies with her. Okay, so I admit that Mia has roped me into doing this a time or two, but she's a teenager and my kid. Before I can object, she's holding the phone out and snapping a picture.

"Oh, that one's not good," she says, deleting it. "You had this weird look on your face."

Yeah, like I want to get the hell out of here. She holds the phone out again and snaps another. She gets the most disappointed look on her face and suddenly, I feel like I'm being judged on my ability to take a good selfie—like her perfect partner should be able to snap a perfect pic and if I can't then I'm out. Honestly, that's fine with me.

She reaches over, playing with my hair a little, and not in a sexy, flirty way. She's literally positioning the strands of my hair in a perfect selfie pose. "The natural light from the window makes for a good picture," she says, holding up the camera again. "Watch me."

Am I getting a selfie lesson?

"It's best to hold the camera up and to the side a little, but not too far out. That way you can look up towards the camera."

Yep, that's what she's doing, and she seems totally serious about it.

I don't think most guys have a checklist on what we want in a woman. We know it when we see it. Trust me, this isn't it.

She pinches my cheeks and says, "A little pout is always cute."

"I think that only works for women," I say, inching away.

She giggles then scoots closer, pressing her cheek to mine with the camera ready again. "Try smiling," she says. "Like you've got a naughty little secret."

I'd like to toss your phone in the damn lake. Click, the flash goes off. She pulls up the picture, squealing a little bit.

"See, it's perfect," she says. "We look perfect together."

Perfectly insane! The waitress comes over to take our orders, and this time it's not Devlyn here to rescue me. I'm trapped. When the shrimp from my appetizer becomes her next selfie partner, I draw the line and mentally check out.

BARELY NINE O'CLOCK at night, and I'm driving back home. Eden Valley is dead at night. There's no real nightlife, unless you count old movie nights in the town square or school functions, like the annual spring play and sporting events. So I'm surprised when I see Biscuit Girl's lights are still on. Devlyn usually closes by seven.

I pull into a parking spot right out front and hop out of my truck. Suddenly, I see the front door of the diner open. Devlyn comes rushing out, a string of cuss words following her as she pulls a trash can behind her. She's not dressed in her tutu, just torn jeans and her usual t-shirt. "Hey," I say.

"Hey," she says, her voice strained from pulling the garbage.

I take over for her, pulling it to the curb, then look over at her, her eyes wet with tears. I take a step towards her, but she holds up her hands. "Shit day."

"You okay?" I ask.

"The dang freezer decided to go out, and everything is melting, and the repair guy said he can't get here until tomorrow. I'm going to have to throw everything out and . . ."

She stops and takes a deep breath. This isn't like Devlyn. She doesn't stress about small stuff or get worked up like this. "Let me take a look."

"What do you know about freezers?" she asks.

"Not much," I say. "But I know a lot about Devlyn Drake, and she's upset about something more than an appliance."

She gives me the best smile. The smile that comes through tears.

I open the door for her and head towards the back of the diner, through a swinging door. I've been here enough times to know my way around the place. Devlyn doesn't follow me.

The damn freezer is massive. I say a little prayer to the appliance gods that I can help her out. I know I'm going to have to pull this sucker out from the wall to get a look at the condenser in the back. I open the door to try to get a good grip when I notice something. She's going to be so pissed.

I stick my head back through the door, seeing her sitting on a stool at the counter, a far-off look on her face. "Fixed."

"What?" she cries, leaping off the stool towards me. I hold open the door for her then open the freezer door, pointing to the culprit.

"Your thermostat was way up. Someone must have bumped it accidentally."

Her lips land on my cheek. "I'm so stupid."

Has she ever done that before? I can't remember. I'm sure she didn't mean anything by it. We're friends. My eyes catch hers as she pulls away. "Could happen to anyone."

"It's just been one of those days," she says.

"Me, too."

"Date two was that good?"

I just huff. That's the best I can do.

She bends down and reaches into a cabinet, pulling out some whiskey. "How about a drink?"

"You've been holding out on me!" I say, snatching the bottle from her.

Smiling, she grabs two glasses. A couple drinks in, and she knows all about the selfie queen. Drinking with Devlyn in her diner is a lot more fun than either of the dates I've been on. Devlyn and I already know each other, there's no awkwardness, no having to make a good impression. I've seen her crying, she's seen me covered in baby puke. We can just be us.

Her finger slowly traces the rim of her glass, the alcohol becoming a truth serum. "This isn't how I thought my life was going to go," she whispers.

I know what she means. When you're a kid and you envision your life, you don't envision being a single, teenage father.

"How'd you want it to go?" I ask.

She shrugs, giving me a little smile, the kind that's polite and full of complete shit. The kind that are for other people's benefit, to make them feel better. "When's the next date?" she asks.

"Few days. Devlyn, what's wrong?" I ask, placing my hand on top of hers.

She lowers her head to my hand. "Did you know the boy I dated my senior year of high school turned out to be gay?"

I'm doing my best not to laugh at her, but she's an adorable drunk. "Everyone in school knew he was gay."

She rolls her eyes. "And the guy I dated after him broke up with me on my birthday."

"Didn't know about that," I say.

"Oh, and there was the guy who I met on vacation who stole my wallet. He was a real gem."

"You don't have to tell me how shitty dating is."

"Or how about the one who broke up with me because he said he liked women who were thinner," she says.

"What fucker said that?"

"It doesn't matter," she says. "You know, every single one of those guys is married now. Even the gay one."

"Is this about Scott?" I ask. They have a long-distance relationship. They met when he came into town for a wedding almost two years ago. Ever since, they've had a long-distance thing.

"He talked about me permanently moving to Florida to be with him."

All the hair on the back of my neck stands straight up. "What?" Her forehead wrinkles up. I'm a selfish bastard. She's moving? She can't move. Who will I . . . Where will I get my coffee? No one makes coffee like Devlyn. Yeah, that's the reason I want to slam my fist through the wall. "Mia would miss you so much."

She rests her head on my shoulder. "He video-chatted me today. He was in Harry Winston, the jewelry store." She breaks down in tears. "He was down on one knee. He had all these rings. He wanted me to pick."

She buries her head in my neck. Tightly, I wrap my arms around her. My heart is thundering in my chest. What the hell? Devlyn's my friend, I should be happy, but happiness is not the cause of the twisting in my gut. Gently, I lift her chin with my fingers, but she doesn't look me in the eye. "Devlyn," I say, unable to think of anything else.

"I said no," she whispers.

Thank God! Fuck, I shouldn't be thinking that. I'm a terrible friend. She's hurting. It's selfish, but I don't want her to leave. "Why?"

Her mouth opens, she shakes her head, like she's searching for the answer. Maybe she doesn't know. Maybe she doesn't want to tell me.

"We were just so . . . Business, you know? I think we only worked because we didn't see each other much. I think I probably always knew that. I mean, if I really loved him, I would've moved. I would've just wanted to be with him. That's the way it should be. But now, I've really hurt him."

I get the feeling there's more to it, but don't want to pry when she's so upset. I want to think of something to say, something to help her, make her feel better, but I'm drawing a blank. I get up from my stool, so I can better pull her into my arms. It's the only thing I know to do, and something about holding her close feels so natural, so right.

She's just tall enough that my head rests on top of hers. My arms coil perfectly around her waist, and her head lays right over my heart. Something stirs in me. It's like waking up after a long sleep—a little confusing. Where am I? How long have I been out?

Holding her shouldn't make me feel this way. She's Devlyn, the girl I've known forever. We grew up together. She's crying over her boyfriend, for Christ's sake. That should be enough to make my dick stand down, but it's not. I have to let her go, but I don't. I'm now awake, and there's no going back to sleep.

I run my fingers through her long, strawberry blonde hair, breathing her in. I'm a jerk. A huge ass jerk. If she knew what I was thinking right now, she'd knee me in the balls so hard. Focus on her, not on my cock.

Okay, I got this.

She sniffles. I'd like to make her moan.

She cries harder. Wonder how loud she'd be crying out my name.

Her hands grip the fabric of my shirt. Wish it was her nails down my back. Or better yet, a firm grip on her curvy ass.

Like they have a mind of their own, my hands slip down her back. She pulls back slightly, her eyes downcast. "I'm sorry. I got your shirt all wet."

Wish it was your panties that were wet.

I look down at her. This is better. Giving my dick some space to breathe is helping me focus on what she needs, not on what I want. I reach over the counter for a napkin, handing it to her so she can wipe her eyes.

"If only I'd figured things out . . ."

"Don't do that. Don't play the *if* game. It's a game you'll lose every time. Don't set yourself up for that."

Her blue eyes lift to mine, and the game shifts.

What if I kissed her right now?

"Tell me the truth," she says, looking me right in the eye. "Did I do the right thing?"

Without hesitation, I say, "You did," and I give her a little grin. "Want some more truth?" I ask, and she nods. "It's not just Mia that would've missed you."

CHAPTER SEVEN

DEVLYN

"YOU KNOW, YOU took your first step right over there," I said. Mia looked up at me with her big, toothless grin. Most six-year olds could care less where they took their first step, but Mia wasn't like most kids. She was precocious with an understanding way beyond her years.

"Daddy says my first step was more of a sprint," she said with a sweet giggle.

I nodded. "I was there, and I'd say it was more like a dash."

Looking over at the spot of said marathon, I had to smile. Almost everywhere in this town holds a Mia memory. She lost her first tooth in the diner, eating an apple. Took her first step by the gazebo. Vomited all over the Reverend at the town's Christmas play.

As the sun began to set over Eden Valley, everyone in town started setting up their picnic blankets and lawn chairs. That is, unless you're a Hollis. Their tradition has always been to bring out this old, worn out sofa, set it up in the back of the crowd, and watch the movie. It's what Garrett's grandparents did, what his parents did with him, and what he continued to do with Mia. For as long as I can remember, me and my family sat in front of them, which meant I ended up on the sofa with them. First with his folks, then with Mia and Garrett. Every other day of the year, the sofa lived in the storage closet of the hardware store.

"Daddy says the movie tonight is good," Mia said, plopping down on the old sofa with me.

Garrett was finishing up at work, so I offered to get Mia settled in for the movie. Liking Indiana Jones *seemed to be built into the male DNA. Watching Harrison Ford for a couple hours worked for most women, so it was a win-win.*

"It is," I said, running my fingers through her hair. It was the last movie night of the summer. There wasn't a chill in the air yet. Instead, groans from all

the children having to return to school filled the night sky. "So how are you going to wear your hair the first day of school? You know, the teachers always take pictures the first day. Maybe a bow or a cute headband?"

Her head hung low, and she shrugged. "I always wear it down."

I pulled her closer. "It's very pretty down."

She looked up at me, her brown eyes rippling with tears. "Granny's got something wrong with her hands, so she can't do my hair."

I knew she was referring to arthritis. "I'm sure your daddy . . ."

"Daddy can't do a ponytail," she whispered then broke down in tears, burying her head in my lap. "Please don't tell him I told you that."

"Shh," I whispered. "I won't tell him."

She looked up at me. "He tried, but it was lumpy."

"Hey, what's wrong with my girl?" Garrett asked, tossing a blanket on the sofa and sitting down beside us.

My heart did this weird leap in my chest, wishing he was referring to me. Mia jumped in his lap, kissing his cheek, and he tickled her. He had the father thing down to a science now. Sure, he still had his rough days, but he loved that little girl so much you could see it a mile away.

His blue eyes landed on me. "She just bumped her knee. She's fine."

Mia smiled at me, and I gave her a little wink. Our first secret. Just one of many to come, I thought. Girls have to have a little mystery. Of course, I would never keep anything big from Garrett about Mia.

"Thanks for watching her," he said.

"Anytime."

"You should come have movie nights at our house," Mia said, bouncing up and down. "I've got all the Disney movies."

"Mia," Garrett said with an apologetic tone, "Devlyn is busy. She doesn't . . ."

"You got *The Little Mermaid*?" I asked.

"Uh huh, I have that one! And *Beauty and the Beast* and . . ." Mia continued to rattle off the entire Disney collection. "Daddy doesn't let me watch them every night, but maybe if you come over. . ."

I laughed. I was a pawn in her game for more screen time. "Would you let me do your hair if I came over?" I asked Mia.

Her eyes grew huge, and her head was nodding so fast she looked like a little

Mia bobblehead. "Daddy, please," she said, making sure to draw out the e sound.

"Maybe," he said, tossing me a look like he knew I had better things to do—but I didn't. Nothing could hold a candle to movie night with Garrett and Mia.

I reached into my purse. "I think I've got a comb and hair elastic. How about we start tonight? I can braid it for you."

She looked to her dad for permission, which he gave with a smile. Mia then moved to the ground in front of me, and I ran the comb through her hair. I looked over at Garrett, watching us, a sad look in his eyes. I bumped his elbow. "Why don't you follow along? I can teach you a thing or two."

"OVER, THEN UNDER," *I said, watching Garrett's hands trying to craft a braid in his daughter's hair, which was difficult considering one of his hands was about the size of her head. I had to continually remind him not to pull too hard, but he was used to wielding a hammer, not a brush.*

Still, over the course of a few movie nights at their house, he got it. He could now do a ponytail in five seconds flat. A bun. A basic braid. A French braid. I even taught him how to do a fishtail braid, although that one did take him all of Finding Nemo *to master.*

He twisted the elastic into Mia's hair. "All done."

"Thank you, Daddy," she said, jumping up and running off to the bathroom to take a look.

I started to gather my things when Garrett touched my arm, and my toes curled. "Thank you, Devlyn. She's so happy. You did that."

I shook my head. "I just ate popcorn and bossed you around. It was fun."

His fingers stroked my skin, giving me goose bumps. I wondered if he even knew he was doing it. "She misses having a mom around," he said softly.

"Garrett, you are doing a great job with her."

He grinned at me. "Thanks, DD."

His childhood nickname for me. That's how he'd always think of me—his childhood friend.

Two simple letters that could break a girl's heart.

CHAPTER EIGHT

GARRETT

"WHAT ARE YOU doing?" Mia asks, rubbing her eyes as she walks into the kitchen.

"Making breakfast," I say, pointing to the coffee pot.

"But we go to Biscuit Girl for breakfast," she says.

I can't tell her that I think Devlyn probably has a hangover from hell. I can't tell her that I'm feeling our little binge drinking session myself. I *absolutely* can't tell her that I beat off in the shower this morning thinking about Devlyn. I don't dare tell her that I walked Devlyn home and tucked her safely into bed. Or that I stayed most of the night just to make sure she was alright.

"Won't Devlyn wonder where we are?" Mia asks.

Shit, she's right. A woman's mind can come up with some off-the-wall shit. I can't tell you the crazy scenarios Mia has come up with. It never ceases to amaze me how one benign comment from five years ago can still sit in the forefront of her mind. I can't tell you where I was five days ago. If we don't show for breakfast this morning, Devlyn might think it has something to do with what she told me last night. I won't do that to her.

"Besides, her coffee is better than yours," Mia says, kissing me on the cheek.

Her everything is better. What the hell? Maybe it was just last night. The crazy date, the confession, the drinks. Maybe my dick was drunk. A drunk dick is not an honest dick.

"You got me there," I say. "Go get dressed."

She rushes off, which means I've got less than five minutes to clean up this enormous mess I've made. I've never mastered the whole cooking thing. It's a wonder Mia didn't starve to death. I guess I have Devlyn to thank for that. We've eaten more meals in the diner than we have in our own kitchen.

I hear a little rap on the back door right before it opens. I don't even glance up, knowing who it is. "Morning, Dad." When he doesn't answer, I look over. Slumped against my doorframe with a bloody rag against his head, my dad holds his hand up. "Jesus!"

"I'm fine," he says. "Just need a Band-Aid."

"A Band-Aid?" I say in disbelief. The man looks like he was in a bar fight and lost. I try to help him inside to sit, but he shoos me away. "Let me take a look."

"It's fine. Knew I shouldn't have come over here. I just didn't have any bandages in the house."

"What the hell happened?"

"Your mother happened."

If Mom wasn't dead, I could totally believe she'd whack my father in the head—playfully, of course.

"You know that old box she has in the closet with pictures and such?" Dad asks.

"Yeah," I say, trying to remove the rag to take a look.

"I always told her not to put it up there. Anyway, I went to get it down. I wanted to take it with me to visit her this morning. When I went to get it, I fell off the chair and knocked my head."

"I'd say you did more than knock it. This needs stitches."

"Oh, don't make a big fuss," he says.

"Granddad!" Mia cries.

It's not me he has to worry about making a fuss. Mia will have that covered in spades. "I'm fine," he tells her. "Can you get your old granddad a Band-Aid?"

She looks up at me, obviously in complete agreement that the old man has lost it. "How about stitches and a CT scan instead?" I ask.

EDEN VALLEY ISN'T big enough to have its own hospital. There's one about twenty minutes away, though. Dad insisted the entire time that he didn't need to go, that I was wasting my time. He even tried to convince me that I was helping to destroy the environment with the gas I was wasting on the trip. Sorry, ozone, my dad's head injury is more important.

My dad is not a grumpy old man. He's quite the opposite, but he hates being the center of attention. His job, as he sees it, is to take care of his family, not the other way around. The fact that he's getting older and roles are shifting a little doesn't sit well with him.

Two hours into the emergency visit, the scan of his head came back clear, and he's been stitched up. We are just waiting on the discharge papers to go home. I give Mia a quick call to let her know I'll be home soon then hand my dad a cup of coffee from the hospital cafeteria. "Take you by to see Mom on the way home?"

He pats my hand. "You know what I talk to your mother about every day?"

I shake my head, taking a sip of my own coffee. It's really terrible. "Mia."

"Well, yes, but mostly you."

"What about me?" I ask.

"Mia will be gone soon," he says. "And so will I."

"Dad . . ."

He holds his hand up, stopping me. "Your mother and I were real hard on you after Mia."

"No, you and Mom were . . ."

He stops me again. "We were happy to watch her so you could work, take classes, but we weren't going to watch her so you could go out, party, date."

"Dad, that was only fair. Mia is my responsibility."

"Yes, but I'd like to see my son in love. I'd like to see you have what I had with your mom."

Releasing a deep breath, I say, "Why is everyone so concerned about this all of a sudden?"

"It's not sudden," he says. "I've talked to your mother about this for years."

"So you agree with this dating hunt Mia has me on?" I ask, lifting my cup to take another sip.

His grin covers his whole face. "Nah, I think the woman for you is right under your nose."

RIGHT UNDER MY *nose.*

I stare out the window of my hardware store across the square at Biscuit Girl. I haven't seen Devlyn since last night. I'm sure she's heard about my trip to the ER with my dad, which explains my absence this morning. The town rumor mill can be useful. There's no reason for me to go over there, none at all. Nothing except this ache in my chest that won't seem to go away.

"Garrett?" I hear Trudy, the local postwoman, say.

"Yeah?"

A stack of mail waves in front of my face. "Got at least twenty more letters in there." She holds one up. "This one smells like perfume."

I snatch it from her and say, "Pretty sure you aren't supposed to snoop through my mail."

If you pictured a nosy person in your mind, that's Trudy. A little older, a mysterious glint in her eye that matches the smile permanently etched on her face.

Smirking at her, I toss the letters in the trashcan.

"Daddy," Mia cries, starting to dig them out. "Don't do that. The love of your life could be in there."

"It's true," Trudy says. "One time a letter got delivered to the wrong man from this woman. He wrote her back. They ended up writing every week. They got married."

"Who was this?" I ask.

"Well, I don't know. Happened down in Atlanta."

"Uh huh," I say.

Trudy heads for the door, calling out before she leaves, "Mia, make him open the perfumed one."

Mia starts to rip open the letters. "You never told me how your date went last night."

"I suppose 'none of your business' isn't going to work for an answer."

Her mouth goes right into a pout. "Guess that means it didn't go well." I watch her eyes scanning the letter in front of her. "This lady . . ."

"One more, Mia. That's what we agreed. One more."

"But . . ."

"No. I have that date on Friday afternoon. Then that's it."

"I just think . . ."

I give her my best serious Dad Look. Mothers may have all kinds of looks, but I only need this one. I perfected it years ago. I spoil Mia, overindulge her, but she knows when to back down. This look is her warning.

Her shoulders slump, as she slides all the letters into the trashcan. I can tell it's killing her.

"How about we focus on your birthday?" I say. "Eighteen is a big one."

She nods, but her eyes cast down. "Do you think my mother remembers my birthday?"

We don't ever really talk about her mom. I didn't design it that way. It's simply a side effect of my hatred for Sheena. I tried my best to hide it over the years, but I guess I didn't do a very good job because Mia learned from an early age to avoid the topic. "I'm sure she does."

Mia looks up at me with those big eyes of hers, and I try my best to hide any discomfort I'm feeling. "Do you know where she is? What she does? Anything like that?"

"Last I heard, she was living in Europe somewhere. That was years ago, though."

"What about kids? Do I have any half-siblings or . . ."

"Mia," I say gently, pulling her into a little hug, praying she doesn't ask me to help her get in touch with her mother. I'd do anything for Mia, but I'm not sure how I'd handle that. "What's this about?"

"It's just, certain times I wish I had a mom around. Not even necessarily her."

"I get it."

She looks up at me. "You do a great job, Daddy."

"Mia, you don't need to do that. I understand. I do my best, but shopping for prom dresses isn't my strong suit."

She smiles. "Some of the girls from my class were talking about the stuff they've done with their moms to get ready for college."

"A trip or something?" I ask. "We can do that."

"No," she whispers. "Birth control."

Fuck me! Okay, stay calm. She *is* almost eighteen. I'll pummel the guy who . . . No, calm. Mia needs me to be chill, cool. I can do this.

"Some of the girls' moms took them to get on the pill."

"Penny?" I ask.

"I'm not telling you names," she says.

That's a yes! For fuck's sake, my daughter's best friend needs birth control. "Mia, do you need birth control?"

She takes one look at me and busts out laughing. "You should see your face. You look like you're about to vomit."

"I'm doing the best I can here."

"No, Dad, I don't need anything. I'm waiting until at least I'm out of college."

"Thank fuck!"

"Daddy!" she scolds. "I just figure if I'm going to have sex, then I need to be able to deal with the consequences of having sex. Like having a baby. I'll be ready to have sex when I'm ready to take care of a child, if by some chance I end up pregnant. So when I'm out of school and stuff."

I'd prefer she say never or not until she's married, but I'll take after college. That gives me four more years. Still, I know her logic is going to go right out the window when hormones come into play. "So what does this have to do with your mother?"

"I get jealous of the other girls sometimes. They talk about their moms, or complain about them, and I don't know . . . It doesn't usually bother me."

"But sometimes it does," I say, squeezing her tighter.

A TRIP TO the emergency room, a talk about birth control, a nosy mail carrier plus working all day—add those up to equal one long damn day. Mia and the rest of my employees went home already, but I stayed to get payroll and some other paperwork done. Turning off the lights, I step outside and lock the door.

"So glad I caught you," I hear the mayor say behind me.

Not bothering to turn around, I say, "Closed for the day."

"I know, I know," he says. I turn around and see him with a pretty blonde by his side. "I met this poor gal earlier today. She came all the way here to meet you, but her car broke down. So she never got a chance to . . ."

"Garrett," I say, reaching my hand out to shake hers. This girl looks like she's closer to Mia's age than mine, and the mayor looks like he's damn proud of himself. I'm not the least bit sorry to disappoint him. This whole thing is ridiculous.

"We need to get together and talk about Eden Valley's Fourth at the Falls," he says. "I'm thinking the town would like to hire you to build some sort of gazebo or pavilion for the festival."

"Great," I say, my eyes going right over his shoulder to the diner across the square, my mind on the woman inside. The woman I haven't been able to get off my mind. I didn't see this coming. She is the one woman I didn't see coming, and God knows, there have been a lot of women coming into my life lately.

But why now? After all these years? I've literally seen Devlyn almost every day of my life, so why now am I thinking about her as someone other than a friend? It's true, I've had a strict policy about not dating women from Eden Valley, not that the dating pool is extensive here.

Devlyn's been single on and off, mostly off, so why haven't I ever gone there? I mean, she's hot as hell. It's not like I didn't notice that.

Why her? Why now?

The mayor urges the young woman forward. "Maybe you should go to the Falls . . ."

There's only one place I want to go. It's not to the Falls. It's not home. I've got to see Devlyn and figure out if last night was just a fluke or something more. "I've got something I need to do, but you go on ahead," I say then nod to the woman. "It was nice to meet you."

I hear the mayor fumbling for something to say, apologizing for my behavior, but I just keep walking. It's only a few feet to the diner. Is my dad right? Could the woman for me have really been just steps away all these years?

I've balked at Mia's silly dating experiment, but maybe in a weird way, it's worked. Made me realize what's right in front of me.

Unfortunately, I'm not going to find out tonight. She's not here. There's only a waitress closing up. "Did Devlyn head home already?" I ask.

"No," she says. "She went out of town for a few days."

"Where?" I ask, hoping it's not to make up with that Scott. Maybe she went to see her parents, needing some downtime. Her parents retired from the diner several years ago and moved to the coast, but Devlyn didn't mention a visit. Not that she tells me her every move.

"To see Scott," the waitress says. "Think they are having problems."

Well, shit! I step back out onto the sidewalk, pulling out my phone. What would I say if I called? A warm summer breeze blows through the streets. The sun is low in the sky, but the heat still lingers. Even in the dead of night, the heat is there, buried under the shadows, waiting for its chance to scorch our skin. Heat like that you can't escape from.

There's a warmth to Devlyn. Always has been, even when we were kids. I always thought that was it—a friendly warmth. I wrack my brain wondering again why now, after all these years? Is it that Mia's older? Is it that her dating experiment worked? Is it that I'm more settled? Is it . . . In the end, it doesn't matter why. It only matters that *somehow* things are different.

Last night, the heat was kicked up a notch or a hundred. Did she feel it, too? Is that why she left town? Did it scare the piss out of her? Or maybe she doesn't feel the same way? Or maybe she's gone to fix things with Scott? No phone call is going to answer those questions. So instead, I send Devlyn a simple text.

You're missed.

CHAPTER NINE

DEVLYN

"DON'T ANSWER IT," my date said, kissing my neck, trying to move his hand up my shirt as the phone rang.

Maybe if he'd been a better kisser, I would've let it ring, but he wasn't that great. I shoved him away. "What if it's an emergency?"

I was a single twenty-something, and it was close to midnight. The only guy who would call me for a booty call was already in my house, so no one should be calling me. I picked up the phone.

"Holy fuck!"

"Garrett, is that you?" I asked.

"Who is Garrett?" my date asked.

I waved my hand at him. "Shit, now I'm bleeding."

"You're bleeding?" I cried, jumping to my feet, straightening my clothes, and grabbing my purse and keys. He was always messing around with that old motorcycle of his. The thing probably decided to finally fight back.

"My finger," Garrett said. "If I get blood on the satin of these pointe shoes, I swear to God . . ."

"What?"

"These things were over a hundred bucks," he barked. "They should come finished. I mean, why do I have to sew in elastics and straps?"

"So you're not bleeding to death?" I asked, feeling my chest relax.

"No, but I'm about to murder the asshole who invented these things. You used to dance, right?"

"Yeah," I said.

"Could you just walk me through how to sew . . ." he begged. "Mia needs them for tomorrow. I know it's late. You weren't sleeping, were you?"

I looked at my date, the rock-hard erection in his pants. Too bad, I wasn't feeling the same way. "Give me ten minutes. I'll come over."

It took me twenty to get to Garrett's doorstep, because my jerk date couldn't even dump me quickly. Totally surprising, since he did everything else too quickly, if you know what I mean.

Garrett opened the door, sucking on his finger. Two fingers already had Band-Aids on them. What the hell was the man doing? It's a sewing needle, not a hatchet. His eyes scanned my body. I hadn't changed out of my date clothes, so my skirt was short, my heels were high, but everything else was covered up. You can't give everything away.

"I was on a date," I said.

"You're dating someone?" he asked.

"Not anymore," I said with attitude.

He cocked a smile. "Must not have been that great of a date if you offered to come over here."

He had me there. I rolled my eyes. "Where's the pointe shoe emergency?"

He held his arm open for me to come in, his entire kitchen table littered with needles, thread, thimbles. No way he knew what half that stuff was used for. I kicked my heels off and sat down, grabbing a ballet shoe. "Come on," I ordered. "Sit down. I'll do one, and you'll do one."

He looked at me with puppy dog eyes. He could give me that look until the cows came home, but no way was I going to do both. I was annoyed all of a sudden, and his pleas for help were getting no more sympathy from me.

He sat down next to me, pulling his chair close enough that he could look over my shoulder. God, he smelled great, like a man should—rugged and earthy. I threaded both our needles with a pale pink thread then handed him one. His fingers grazed mine as he took it. "I'm sorry about your date. I never intended for you to . . ."

"It's okay," I said, turning my attention to the shoe. "Now, the first thing you want to do is bend the back of the shoe over. That lets you know where to sew the elastic on."

He followed along with me step-by-step. I moved, he moved. In those moments, everything from our bodies to our breathing fell into a rhythm. We barely spoke. He simply followed the cues of my body, knowing exactly what I was telling him. It was perfect.

It passed too quickly. Soon, we had both shoes done, and he held them up.

"Yours still looks better than mine."

It did, but I wouldn't rub his nose in it. "Mia won't know the difference."

He eyed them again. "How can you even tell left from right in these things?"

I couldn't help but laugh. "There are no left and right in pointe shoes."

"You're fucking kidding me."

"No," I laughed at his cluelessness. "But I suggest she mark them for each foot. They are made to soften up and mold to your feet as you wear them."

"Got it," he said. "Why couldn't Mia play basketball? That I could help with."

"Maybe because she's not even five feet tall yet?"

He huffed a little. "Short like her mother."

Garrett rarely brought up Sheena, although I could always tell when she crossed his mind. His blue eyes changed—turned darker, almost black. "You ever hear from her?"

"Not a word in twelve years," he said. "Not since the day she left."

"I never did like her," I snarked.

"You were always nice to her," he said.

"I was nice to you," I corrected. "She was just a bystander of my kindness."

"Fuck, that's hardcore," he said.

"People think because I'm nice that I don't get mad, get my feelings hurt, feel used, or . . ."

"Devlyn," he said, concern in his voice. "Have I . . . I hope I've never made you feel that way. Over the years, I know you've helped me out a lot with Mia."

I held my hand up. "If I ever feel wronged by you, you'll know it."

He nodded. "Still, you know if you ever need anything, you can call me?"

"I know," I said, winking at him. "And since you own the hardware store now, I expect all the free nails . . ."

My hand flew over my mouth, and I could feel the heat in my cheeks. Garrett busted out laughing. "Devlyn, are you telling me you need a good banging?"

My hand flew to my hip. "You offering?"

"Consider me your own personal handyman," he said.

The smile on his face let me know he was only playing around. He didn't think of me that way. I could fall on my back, naked, with my legs spread, and the man would probably ask me if I needed help getting up. I'm not sure why. Maybe because we grew up together, and he remembers me as a kid? Maybe because he just closed himself off after Sheena? Maybe he doesn't like strawberry blondes? "What are your qualifications besides nailing and banging?" I flirted.

"I'm pretty good at screwing," he said, raising an eyebrow at me.

My legs clenched together. One look from Garrett Hollis could do what going to first base with my date hadn't done. Garrett wasn't even touching me, and my panties were wet. I inched closer to him. I couldn't help it, my body took over. I knew it was going to hurt like hell when he stepped away, but there was still hope in my heart. "I'm pretty good at . . ."

"I thought I heard voices," Mia said, coming down the stairs, rubbing her eyes. "Woke me up."

I stepped back from Garrett. "Sorry, baby girl," he said. "Devlyn was just helping me with your pointe shoes."

Mia nodded sleepily, and I headed toward the door. Garrett flashed me a grin, and I gave him a little wave as I opened the front door to leave. The cool night air did nothing to soothe the heat radiating off my skin. The short drive home didn't, either.

I plopped down on my bed. For the first time in my twenty-eight years on the planet, I couldn't control the desire in my body, slipping my hand between my legs. I wondered if Garrett ever jerked off thinking about me. Probably not.

I closed my eyes, thinking about his big, strong hands, how they moved. I wanted his hands on me, working me. I wanted my fingers to be his. Just once, I wanted to know how he kissed. A life full of wanting that man, and all I had to show for it was an ache so deep not even I could reach it.

Unsure whether there was anything more frustrated than a horny woman, I stopped touching myself. I was sick of having no control over my feelings for Garrett. Damn it, I was going to find some control. I might have been the only young woman on the planet that didn't own a vibrator. My eyes scanned my room for something, anything for me to be on top of. I still had my favorite stuffed animal from childhood, but I couldn't bring myself to defile him that way.

I'd read all the articles, heard enough girlfriends, watched enough late-night television to know women used some interesting things to get themselves off. But I didn't have a fancy shower head, the laundry machine was too far, I refused to go so far as to use my electric toothbrush, I didn't have one of those back massagers that everyone knows are undercover vibrators, and the cucumbers in my fridge were for my eyes, not my vagina.

Another night of my life ended in frustration, thinking about Garrett Hollis.

New plan—Eden Valley had a lot going for it, but it wasn't the hub for vibrators. I could've ordered one online, but who wanted to wait seven to ten business days? I knew a nearby town where I could get one, which worked out well since my weekly exercise class just so happened to be in that town.

So the next day, after closing up the diner, I headed off, proudly walking into the sex shop wearing my darkest sunglasses and a hat, and purchased two. I couldn't decide between pink or purple, so I got both. A girl has to have choices.

Liberated and determined to be a woman in charge—well, as charged up as my two vibrators, at least—I headed back to Eden Valley. That's when it happened.

A simple trip to the not-quite-local sex shop crushed my heart. Along the way, I spotted Garrett's truck outside a blue house, a woman wearing scrubs kissing him on her porch before tugging at his jeans and pulling him inside. I didn't stop. Tears fell down my cheeks.

He sure was good at screwing, all right. Screwing with my heart.

CHAPTER TEN

GARRETT

OPENING THE DOOR to my house, I'm met with laughter. I'm going to miss that beautiful sound.

"In here," Mia calls out. Stepping to the den, I find Mia and my dad on the sofa, two pizza boxes on the coffee table and an old episode of *Friends* on the television. She smiles at me. "Granddad's staying the night."

Looking to my father, he just shrugs. Mia is so used to having men wrapped around her little finger she may never get married. "She's worried I have a concussion."

"You hit your head hard," Mia says, planting a kiss on his cheek. "So we ordered pizza and are going to binge watch *Friends*. Can you believe Granddad's never seen it?"

Trying not to laugh, I grab a slice and sit down with them. "I just want to know if that Ross fellow ever gets up the nerve to ask out Rachel," my dad says.

"You haven't even made it to the break part yet?" I ask, having watched all two hundred and thirty-six episodes more than once. Comes with the territory of raising a teenage girl, I guess.

"Shh!" Mia says. "You don't want to ruin it."

"What do you mean *break*? Somebody going to break something on the show?" my dad asks.

"Not that kind of break," Mia says. "A relationship break."

"No such thing," my dad says. "You're either in it, or you're not. Can't have it both ways."

He glances at me. Another coded message from my father. Or maybe it's my daughter giving me hidden messages. We are watching a show where friends date each other. I've avoided dating anyone from Eden Valley. It's been a rule of mine, so why am I considering breaking it now? The same nosy people live here. That's why I have the rule about not dating local women in the first place. Plus, it would be harder to protect Mia when things went south. The logic is there. It makes sense to stick to my rule.

Maybe I've been sticking to the rules too much lately? I broke enough as a teenager. I look over at my daughter and smile. That didn't turn out too bad.

I really have to figure this out.

"I like that Phoebe girl," my dad says, elbowing Mia a little. "She's my favorite."

TWO MORNINGS AT the diner, two mornings without Devlyn. No response to my text, either. Must've all been in my mind, or rather in my dick.

"Lucky number three," Mia says, referring to my third and final date this afternoon.

"Why is three so lucky?" I ask her as I hand a customer some change. "They say bad things happen in threes, too."

"Genies always grant three wishes. Three is considered divine in a lot of religions, like the Blessed Trinity," Mia says.

"Isn't three in the morning also the witching hour? That doesn't seem so lucky."

"Fine. Three's not lucky, but it is a crowd," she says, giggling. "So I'll stay at Granddad's tonight. We can finish watching *Friends*."

"Mia," I say, a certain tone in my voice. I've never, and I mean never have I brought a woman home, whether Mia was there or not. Maybe that's her fascination with all this. She's never actually seen me with a woman on a date until all this started. There haven't been many girlfriends, but the few there have been were kept hidden from Mia. Sure, she'd know I had a date, but she's never come face-to-face with that reality. No matter her enthusiasm now, I have to wonder how long that will last.

"Get going," she says, shoving me out the door. "I think I see her waiting by the gazebo."

I head that way, ready to be done with all this. My eyes go the Biscuit Girl, wondering when Devlyn will be back. I need to see her, but there's another woman I have to focus on right now.

This woman doesn't fit the mold of the others. She's not dressed up. She doesn't have on any makeup. Her hair is pulled up in a simple ponytail, and she doesn't smile when she sees me approach.

"Are you . . ."

She holds her hand up. "Look, I'm here because my Nana wrote a letter. I didn't know anything about it until Mia called. I only came out of respect for my grandmother."

Honesty, thank God. "Well, I'm only doing this for my daughter."

She smiles slightly. "How about we take a walk? I'd like the see the Falls. Then I can tell Nana I met you, and you can satisfy Mia. We both get out of this unscathed. Deal?"

I need to scope out the Falls for the Fourth of July project anyway, so that sounds good to me. Kill two birds with one stone, so to speak.

A short walk from town square, there's a series of bridges with streams running through and an old water mill. The path cuts through a wooded area, which hides the Falls. The waterfall itself isn't large. We aren't talking Niagara or anything. You can't hear it from town. Town folklore says if you kiss someone at the Falls during a rainbow, they will be yours forever.

On one side, there's a huge meadow where weddings, picnics, and the annual Fourth of July Fest is held. We might be the only town in America that doesn't light fireworks on that day. Fireworks and trees don't mix well. Sparklers are about it. The whole town potlucks together. There's music, and if the sun hits the Falls just right, a rainbow becomes the only light show we need. It's Mia's favorite town event. A downside is that it's also the day I lost my virginity with her mother, which makes it my least favorite.

We look out to the Falls together. "It's beautiful," Date Three says. "There's some legend about it, right?"

"I've heard the story so many times growing up. It's said that during the Civil War, there was a beautiful Southern girl who fell in love with a Union soldier. In secret they would meet here," I say, looking up at the rush of water, no rainbows out today. "Night after night, they would meet. The waterfall their guardian, holding all their secrets."

"If you tell me one of them killed themselves here, I'm going to be so upset. This better end happy," she says.

I grin. "One night, her brother, a Confederate soldier, followed her, worried for his sister's safety and wondering where she disappeared to every night. He found his sister in the arms of the enemy."

"He killed him, didn't he?"

"He drew his weapon, ignoring the cries of his sister, begging him not to shoot, promising she'd never see him again if he just let her love live. Moved by her pleas, he let him go. Her brother pulled her away. Her soldier's final words to her were that he'd find her. She came to this spot every day, and every day the only thing she found was a rainbow."

"That can't be it," she says, smacking my arm. "That's a terrible story."

"Supposedly, he was killed in battle, and the young girl never married. It's said she came here every day of her life. She believed the rainbow was his spirit, keeping his promise."

I see her wipe her eyes a little. "Why do loves like that only happen in stories? I mean, in real life, we get set up by our grandmothers and kids."

She giggles, causing me to smile. We start the walk back. As far as dates go, this one has been good. I like her. She's attractive, funny, smart, seems to have her head on straight. All the boxes are checked. This should be the point where I kiss her, ask her out again. I should be devising ways to get in this woman's panties, but instead I'm thinking more about yanking down the tutu of one very sexy Biscuit Girl. I should be thinking about how to get this woman to fall for me, but it's me that's fallen. I should have one thing on my mind, and I do—Devlyn.

There's just one big ass problem. She's my friend. I can't go there. There are so many reasons why I can't go there. The town would have a field day. We'd have no privacy. Everyone would have an opinion. If we broke up, where would I get a decent cup of coffee? How would Mia react to this? Then there's Scott, who's actually the least of my concerns. Devlyn seemed pretty sure it was over, and if it's not, I plan on convincing her.

I don't want to lose Devlyn.

Staying friends guarantees her in my life. Dating her doesn't.

Love doesn't come with a guarantee.

Love is a risk. I used to be a risk taker, but teenage fatherhood buried that part of me. Stability became the name of the game. It had to. I look towards her diner, wondering if she's back.

Love is a risk.

I realize that all these women who've written me letters, called, travelled here, have all been risk takers. Some of them batshit crazy risk takers, but risk takers all the same. I've been annoyed by it all, but these women are brave. They put it all out there, some of them literally. I should've been more appreciative of that.

"I had fun," Date Three says.

"Me, too."

She stands there, waiting. I can see the hope in her eyes. She wants me to ask her out again. I need to let her down easy, but I know if I tell her she's great and that it's me, she won't believe me. Drawing a deep breath, my mouth opens, but she shakes her head at me.

"It's okay. I know your heart is with someone else," she says.

All I can do is nod.

"Does she know?" she asks.

"No. We're friends."

She shakes her head at me again. "Maybe she's like the young girl at the Falls. Maybe she's waiting for you to find her. Maybe she's been waiting years, too." She leans up on her tippy toes and kisses my cheek, then starts to walk away.

"Thank your grandmother for me," I call out.

"I will," she says, and she's gone.

THE THREE-DATE EXPERIMENT is over. Most of the women in town have gone home, the emails and phone calls are waning. My daughter's viral video has been replaced by the latest cat video. It wasn't a complete waste of time. I learned a few things. Mostly that I'm an idiot and the right woman has been across the street from me my whole life.

Heading towards the diner, the lights are low inside, but I can make out the shape of her moving around, hear the faint beat of music she has on while she cleans up.

There it is again. That same feeling from the other night. The dick hardening, heart pounding, can't wait to be near her feeling.

She catches me watching her and waves me inside, turning the music down as I walk into the diner. "That looked like it went well," she says, nodding towards the town square.

Shit, she saw the kiss on the cheek. I guess from a distance it did look like a beginning instead of an ending.

"Why, were you watching?" I ask.

"I wasn't," she says, her forehead wrinkling up. "So is she the one?"

No, you are, I think, but don't say it. My feelings for her are coming out of nowhere. I can't just whack her over the head, but standing here looking at her, I'm not just looking at my friend anymore. It's like I'm seeing her, really seeing her, for the first time. I knew she was sweet, smart, funny, and sassy. I knew she was beautiful, but I don't think I appreciated it before. Right now, I'm fully appreciating the curve of her waist, the tiny bit of cleavage showing, how perfect her ass is.

"Garrett?" she says. "You're acting weird."

"Sorry," I say. "No, I won't be seeing her again."

She puts down her rag. "I feel like I need to explain. About the other night. I was a mess, and I shouldn't have laid all that on you."

"Consider us even," I say, seeing relief cover her face. "For teaching me how to braid hair."

She smiles. Damn!

"And how to sew the damn elastics on ballet pointe shoes. Remember that?"

"The middle of the night string of cuss words is burned into my brain."

I step a little closer to her. "And for being my friend when no one else would."

"That was a long time ago," she whispers.

I shake my head. "It's something I'll never forget."

"It was the right thing to do."

"Do you always do the right thing?" I ask, stepping closer until my body is against hers.

"I try," she says, her blue eyes a mix of confusion, unsure if she's reading me right.

She steps back slightly, moving to turn off the music. "Leave it," I say, offering her my hand. "Dance with me?"

"Here?"

"Here." She rubs her palms on her pants then slides her hand into mine. I give her a twirl before pulling her to me. She laughs, and my heart skips. Even though I know, I still ask, "Where have you been the past few days?"

"Florida," she says.

I know I shouldn't ask, but fuck it. "Did you and Scott work things out?"

"No," she says. "I believe in clean breaks. None of this back and forth stuff. I had some of his things. Plus, I just thought I owed it to him to see him one last time."

"And you're okay?"

"I am." Her head finds my shoulder as we sway.

I bury my nose in her strawberry blonde hair, breathing her in. This is the same feeling from the other night. She has to be feeling this, too. Why is she so hard to read? I guess it's like I told her—hard love is the only kind I know.

Her hands slide up the muscles of my back. I'm a man, we don't analyze things like women do. Her hands on my back mean one thing—sex.

The song stops playing, and she leans away slightly. My hand slips to her neck, her cheek. She can't look me in the eye. She knows if she does, I have her. Lucky for her, I've got other tricks up my sleeve, and tilt her chin up, her eyes landing on my lips.

It's not an invitation. It's a decision. If we do this, there's no going back. Things won't ever be the same. At this point, it's a no-brainer for me, but the decision doesn't look so easy for her. I'm more than happy to help clear that indecision right up, leaning in.

The phone rings, causing her to jump right out of my arms. "I need to answer. It might . . ." she stammers, walking backwards towards the phone, her eyes gluing me to my spot. "Hello . . . Of course . . . I'll be right over . . . No problem . . . All five kids have it?"

She covers the phone with her hand. "You know Mrs. . . ."

I just nod, listening to her explain how she has to take some food over to this family. It can't be helped, and she'll see me tomorrow. So many excuses are spilling out of her.

Another place, another time—story of my life.

Letters to Mia
Eighth Birthday

Dear Mia,

Happy Birthday! For the first time since you were born, I've seen you. The Eden Valley paper went online this year. I check it daily for any sign of you. I've seen your name listed under "A" honor roll. I've seen you listed as a Girl Scout, but the best was a picture of you on your dad's shoulders during some town Christmas event. You were looking down at him, and he was looking up at you. The both of you wearing the biggest, goofiest smiles. You're happy.

All these years, that's all I wanted to know. That my baby is happy.

Garrett's happy.

I hoped he was. There was no one else in the picture. I can't lie. Over the years, I've wondered if Garrett married, if you call someone else Mom.

I don't allow myself to stay in those thoughts long. I can't.

I printed that picture out. It's framed by my bed. You and your dad—happy.

Until next year,
Your mom

CHAPTER ELEVEN

GARRETT

MIA'S AT MY dad's for the night, so I finish up sending out the email invitations for her eighteenth birthday, which is coming up fast. I got everything she wanted. She's going to love it. It's amazing how much I can accomplish when I'm trying to avoid something. I left Devlyn a couple hours ago and planned a whole party in the wake of that disaster. Reminds me of the time after Sheena left, I was super dad for months and months before I even uttered one cuss word over her.

I can't curse Devlyn, though. She's coming off a breakup. Plus, our friendship is important. I'm sure she wants to protect that. I can't fault her for that, although I wish she'd ignored the phone and let me lift her up on the counter, wrapped her legs around me . . .

Nope, not gonna think about it. I'm not gonna think about her tits in that tight little t-shirt that dares me to "butter her biscuits" every fucking day. Nope. I can start drawing some sketches for the pavilion at the Falls instead. I know the mayor wants something covered, but that defeats the purpose of being at the Falls. You're there to admire it. So whatever I build either has to be set far enough back not to obscure the view or have a roof you can see through. Or maybe there's another option to consider. . .

The doorbell interrupts my thoughts. Mia and my dad wouldn't ring the bell. I'm not sure who it could be. When Mia was younger, I used to have these nightmares that Sheena would ring the bell in the middle of the night, showing up to take Mia from me. There was no going back to sleep after one of those.

I open the door. Devlyn's on my porch dressed in what look like her sleep clothes—pink and green striped shorts and a bright pink tank top. Her hair is wet, hanging down, slightly dampening her shirt, and she's barefoot.

"Are you alright?" I ask, reaching out for her.

"Is Mia here?" she asks.

"No, she's staying the night at Dad's house. What is it? What happened?"

She doesn't come inside. Her eyes roam my face like she's searching for something. "Was I imagining earlier?" she asks. "I mean, at the diner. It was all in my head, right? I was imagining it?"

Taking her by the waist, I bring her inside, shutting the door behind her. "Depends on what you were imagining," I say.

"Don't do that," she snaps. "Don't you dare flirt with me."

"No, you weren't imagining it," I say, stepping closer, my chest pressed against her. Her breasts are rising and falling, her skin is a rosy pink color, and her lips are slightly parted. I whisper her name.

"We won't ever be able to undo this," she says softly.

"I know," I say, my eyes on her full, pink lips. "I can't lose you."

Her hand slowly raises, but she doesn't touch me. It just hovers in the air by my face like there's a line she's not sure she wants to cross. It's the friendship to lovers line.

For me, that line has already been obliterated. There's no way I could go back to the way things were. I take her hand, moving it to my cheek, her soft skin against the stubble of my face. I inch closer, taking her cheek in my hand.

We are one choice away. One choice away from changing everything. I'm one choice away from her. Perhaps we've always been that close. Right now, this moment, she's the easiest choice I've ever made.

I kiss her and know deep in my soul I'm in trouble.

A lifetime of repressed desire I didn't ever realize was there takes over. There's no denying it anymore. Usually a first kiss is soft, slow—a get to know you. How the person moves, tastes—an exploration, but there is nothing soft or slow about this.

Her hands wind in my hair, our tongues battling, our bodies

grinding against each other. Her head tosses back, a loud moan falling from her perfect lips. She reaches for the bottom of my shirt and I take over, pulling it over my head. She follows my lead, removing her tank top. I make quick work of her bra, tossing it to the floor. She tries to pull me closer, but I step back. I need a second to look at her. She's too damn beautiful to rush and not stop and appreciate.

"Christ, you're perfect," I whisper.

Her body trembles, blushing. Stalking towards her, I slip my hands under the waistband of her shorts, giving her hips a gentle squeeze before pushing them to the floor, making sure to take her panties, too. My dick pulses against the zipper of my jeans, but he's going to have to wait. There are too many parts of her to taste, suck, and explore.

I run my finger across her red, swollen lips, down her collarbone, to her tits. Then I make the same path with my mouth, kissing her. When I pull her nipple between my teeth, she starts to beg, yanking on my zipper. "Please, oh please," she begs.

Guess we're skipping the foreplay. She frees my dick, her soft hand working me over. Grabbing her ass, I pick her up, and her legs wrap around my waist. I can feel the warmth between her legs calling me, begging for me. My dick is heavy and aching and desperate for her.

"Look at me," I order. Her blue eyes open, holding me hostage as I glide myself deep inside her. Her body immediately starts trembling, on the edge of her orgasm, but I don't want her to come too quickly, and slowly start to slip in and out. Fuck, she's tight and warm and clenching around me. Her nails dig into my shoulders as I hold her ass.

Her eyes catch mine as our hips thrust against each other. "Hard," she whispers. "Love me hard."

She flashes me a smile, remembering my words to her that all love is hard. At the time, I wasn't referring to sex, but this works, too.

Fucking hard has been my mode of operation since Sheena. Then I was young, inexperienced, and completely in love with her, so things were slow, sweet, and tender. After her, there was no time for slow, sweet, or tender. With my Thursday night regular, I was on a time crunch. I only had the length of Mia's dance class. With other women here and there, it was the same. I fucked those women for entirely different reasons than I'm with Devlyn.

So instead of going harder, I slip my dick out of her, scoop her into my arms, and carry her to my bed.

Reaching towards my nightstand, she catches my hand. "Just so you know, I'm on the pill."

I've heard those words before. No, I don't think Sheena lied to me about being on the pill, but I've worn condoms ever since. No harm in doubling up. Other women I've been with have been on the pill, but I was never tempted enough to go without a condom. This is different. Having felt Devlyn without anything between us, it's really no decision at all.

Her eyes wander my face. This time when I slip myself inside her, her whole body coils around me. "Garrett," she moans in a sweet whisper.

Moving a strand of hair off her face, I hold her cheek in the palm of my hand, grinding my hips into her hard, watching her eyes close, her mouth drop open.

"Mmm, right there," she says, her hands slipping to my ass.

I know as soon as I find any rhythm at all, she's going to go flying over the edge. I give her one more hard thrust, and her eyes flash open, seeing my mischievous grin and catching on to my game.

"We've waited too long for this to be quick," I say.

Smiling, she pulls me to her mouth, slowly stroking my tongue with hers. My dick takes over, and going slow is not a priority for him.

"I don't care," she begs. "I just want to come."

Never one to like disappointing a woman, I start to pound into her. The muscles of her pussy tighten over and over with each thrust. Fuck, she's good. Her body tightens underneath me, her back arching up, and I see her bite her bottom lip.

"Let me hear it, baby," I order. No way is she going to deny me hearing her orgasm rip through her.

I thought I knew everything about this woman. I was only kidding myself. Her touch, her kiss, the way she moves—I realize I knew nothing, because nothing has ever felt like this before.

She's a mystery. Guess she always has been. I'm about to solve a little piece of her. Witnessing someone orgasm is seeing their vulnerability. They are letting you see them naked, without defenses. For those few moments, their guard is completely down. It's a rare and beautiful thing to see someone completely without inhibition, completely raw.

Watching her hair spread out on my pillow, feeling her hands on my back, hearing the moan of my name from her lips, tasting her sweet skin—I memorize it all. Her body quakes, her arms and legs wrapping around me as her body relaxes beneath me. That little piece of her is no longer a mystery to me.

Stroking her cheek, her eyes flutter open. She doesn't shy away from my gaze, but reaches for my face, this time without hesitation. "You're so beautiful," I whisper. Her response is to tighten her muscles around my cock. "Oh, fuck." She laughs. "So that's how you want to play?" I say, pinning her arms over her head.

"Dirty," she says, pulling free and slipping me out of her. A naughty glint in her eye, she pushes me to my back, slowly crawling over me. "I want to play dirty."

There really is nothing like the sight of a beautiful woman straddling you—their hair wild and loose, their tits on full display, the warmth of their pussy taunting you. There's not a more beautiful view in the world than this. Holding her hips, I slip back inside her. Christ, how is it possible she feels better than she did a minute ago?

Some women feel self-conscious in this position, not liking their tits bouncing or some shit. Devlyn doesn't suffer from that affliction. Thank God, because I don't think I'll be able to live without this in my life. I always say we don't often want what we really need. Well, Devlyn riding my dick is both a want and a need for me from here on out.

Holding her ass, I encourage her to go faster. My cock pulses inside of her. I see her biting her bottom lip again, her little orgasmic tell. A good man never lets his woman lose her orgasm. What a waste that would be. Slowly, I slide my hand across her thigh. One little flick to her clit, and she's calling out to the Big Man upstairs. As her muscles clench, she forces my orgasm.

She collapses on top of me, her hair fanning out across my chest, and I let my hands wander—her soft skin, those killer curves, her perfect ass. She lifts her head, resting her chin on my chest. I look down at her, expecting to see questions in her eyes.

What does this mean?

What will we tell Mia?

Are we a couple?

Are we still friends?

But I don't see any of that. Instead, she leans up, kisses me softly, then cuddles into my side.

CHAPTER TWELVE

GARRETT

BELIEVE IT OR not, I've never actually woken up with a woman in my bed, never spent the entire night with one. I don't think I've ever actually fallen asleep with a woman after sex, either. So when I feel Devlyn's fingers playing with my hair, I startle awake.

Mia?

I glance at the clock. It's too early for Mia to be awake and up. I'm sure she's still fast asleep at my dad's house. Devlyn leans up on her elbow. Looking down at me, she smiles and says, "I can't believe I'm in Garrett Hollis' bed."

"Well, I can't believe I get to have Devlyn Drake for breakfast," I say, flipping the sheet up and disappearing between her legs.

"Garrett," she giggles out. "I have to . . ."

She can't finish the thought once my tongue finds her. One lick, one suck, and I know I'm going to love doing this to her. Holding her thighs open, I work her over.

"Oh, God," she moans. "The diner. I need to go."

"Come first," I tease.

"I can't," she says, flipping the sheet back to look down at me. Lifting my head slightly, I look up at her. "Cause then I'll have to return the favor. Then that will lead to sex, and then we will never make it out of bed." Laughing, I just shake my head. "And I don't believe in sixty-nine."

Now I completely raise my head. "You don't believe in it? Like on principle?"

She laughs. "No, I mean I'm bad at it. I get too distracted and forget my part."

I lower my head, laughing. Have I ever laughed in bed with a woman before?

I kiss her inner thighs. She's been feeding me for years, now's not the time to change that. Even if now the only thing on the menu is her. "You wouldn't deny a starving man," I say.

Her head tosses back laughing, her legs falling open a little more. Thank God. The thing about giving oral sex to a woman is you've got to go all in. You can't be tentative. If you don't love doing it, then you probably shouldn't. You'll just end up disappointing her.

Lifting her thighs to my shoulders, I bury myself between her legs. Last night was sex. Straight up, hardcore sex. This morning, it's time to get into the finer points of making a woman come. The dick is great. Fingers work, too, but there is absolutely nothing like making a woman come with your mouth. My cock throbbing, I want nothing more than to feel her shuddering as my tongue slips in and out of her. I could come just from the taste of her, she's that good.

"Right there, oh God, yes, don't stop," she begs.

As much as I'm not ready to stop, I give her what she needs. Her legs tighten then fall open. Planting light kisses along her folds, I feel the last tremors of her orgasm. Silently, I promise her pussy I'll be back. We will be seeing a lot of each other.

Devlyn motions for me to come to her. I get to my knees, and her eyes go wide, my erection heavy and hard. Like she knows it's going to hurt like hell if we leave him that way, she straddles me, sitting in my lap—face-to-face.

Some positions are just more intimate than others. Taking a woman from behind is fun as hell, but I wouldn't call it intimate. On the intimacy scale, this is off the charts. Facing each other, direct eye contact, no hiding.

Taking hold of me, she slips me inside. Good to know that last night wasn't all in my head, she really does feel that good. Holding on to each other, our hips rock back and forth slowly, deliberately—my orgasm their only goal.

Devlyn moves her hair behind her shoulders, granting me access to her full, gorgeous tits. Placing one hand behind my neck, she urges me to her, never stopping the rocking of our hips. Lightly, I outline her nipple with my tongue, then suck, making sure my teeth barely graze her. The pleasure shoots right between her legs, making her even wetter.

"What are you doing to me?" she moans. "I need to come again." Taking hold of her hair, I lift my head, forcing her eyes to me. "Please, Garrett."

"Fuck," I groan, on the verge myself.

Lifting my finger to her mouth, I say, "Suck." Her eyes waver, but she slips my finger between her lips, sucking. Jesus, what I wouldn't give for that to be my cock, but I can't think about that right now. "Get it nice and wet."

Her eyes close, her tongue circling my finger. Slipping it out, I move my hand to her ass. She stops moving. "What are you . . ."

"Making you come," I say.

Her blue eyes study me for a second before she gives me a little nod. Pulling her close, I slip my finger just inside. She tenses. Her eyes close, tightly. For a second, I wonder if she's going to stop me. I tilt my head, kissing a path down her neck, feeling her body relax a little more with each kiss, letting my finger sink deeper and deeper.

"Good?" I ask, slipping my dick in and out. Her mouth drops open, her head nodding. Damn right it feels good. A little anal play never hurt anyone. I plant a kiss behind her ear and whisper, "Let me know if you need me to stop."

Her head shakes, and I bite the inside of my mouth so I don't laugh at her. She's totally shocked and surprised about how good it feels to have my finger and dick filling her up at the same time.

"I'm gonna come," she says, her hips moving faster. "Oh, God, I'm going to come like this."

"Get there, Devlyn," I say, about to lose it. "Get there."

Two seconds after her orgasm rips through her, I follow along. I lower her down to the mattress and gently kiss her forehead, pulling her into my chest, waiting for her ragged breath to slow. I let my hands roam. The curve from her tits, to her waist, to her ass is perfection. Her body is the perfect blend of soft and strong.

She looks up, pouting her lip at me. "I don't want to go."

"I don't want you to," I whisper.

"I have to."

"I know," I say.

One more kiss and she sits up, looking around for her clothes. I watch her. With each piece of clothing she puts on, she moves slower and slower, like she's being weighed down.

"Devlyn," I say, taking hold of her waist. "Just because the night is over doesn't mean this is over." She's biting that bottom lip again, only this time it's to hold something else in, her tears. "You know how hungry I can be."

She laughs, and I hope it carries her all the way to work.

"ARE YOU SERIOUSLY still sleeping?" Mia cries out, like she's caught me breaking the law.

Shit, I must've fallen back asleep after Devlyn left. God knows I didn't get much sleep last night. I sit up, the sheet pooling at my waist.

Mia walks closer, her head tilted. "You have a shirt on? You never sleep with a shirt on?"

Shit! I put a shirt on when I walked Devlyn to her car. We're going to have to be more careful. Her car can't be parked at my house until the early morning hours, and I can't change my habits.

She reaches out, trying to feel my forehead. "Are you getting sick?"

I shoo her away, having not showered off my night with Devlyn. "No."

She steps back a little. "Was there a woman in here?"

"What?" I bark. "Mia, you cannot . . ."

"You had a date with the third woman," Mia says, her voice growing quiet. "Was she here?"

My after-sex high deflates. As much as she's pushed me dating, the reality smacking her in the face isn't what she expected. "I took her out, but she didn't come here." I take her hand. "And I'm not sick, either. I planned your birthday last night."

My gut twists a little bit. I'm not technically lying to her, but her reaction to the thought of another woman being here has me worried.

She kisses me on the cheek. "Out the door in five."

"That's my line," I tease her.

She playfully snaps her fingers at me, and I grab some clothes to go take a quick shower. Turning on the water, Devlyn's arching back flashes in my mind. I head to my nightstand and grab my phone, pulling up Devlyn's number. She's still programmed in as DD. Quickly, I type.

Next time, I need to shower with you.

Her response is immediate.

It's a date.

DEVLYN IS WITH a customer when Mia and I walk in and find our usual table. Mia gives her a little wave, and Devlyn smiles, her eyes barely glancing at me. It's funny, I can't remember how we usually greet each other. All I can think about is wanting to grab her, kiss her, lift her on the counter and . . .

"Dad?" Mia says. "Are we . . ."

"Hmm . . ."

"You aren't listening."

"I've got the plans for the pavilion on my mind."

She frowns at me. "I was asking if we're going to the movie in the square tonight."

"Of course," I say.

Our coffee mugs appear under our noses. I look up, Devlyn doing her best not to make eye contact with me, a little smile on her pink lips. "And how are things with the Hollis clan this morning?"

"Not good," Mia says. "Daddy failed dating."

Devlyn looks down, her lips pursed together. "That right?"

Mia nods, winking at me. "It's alright. I decided I like having him all to myself, anyway."

Devlyn's downcast eyes glance at me. I'm just as unsure as she is whether Mia's serious or not. I doubt Mia even knows. Her father dating has to be strange for her. Her graduation joke turned into something she never intended, and as much as she pushed me to date, I don't think she's one hundred percent ready for there to be another woman in my life. Maybe she'll never be ready. I look at Devlyn. Maybe it shouldn't matter.

"Guess I'm his date for movie night tonight. You coming?" Mia asks.

"I'll be there," Devlyn says, glancing at me. We've sat together for movie nights for as long as I can remember.

Mia begins ordering for herself and for me, but I don't care, too busy trying not to stare at Devlyn. "Just the man I wanted to see," the mayor says, coming up behind me. "Any ideas on the pavilion?"

"I'll just get your order," Devlyn says, starting to walk away. Damn, that ass. How am I not supposed to stare?

"Devlyn," the mayor calls out. "You hurt? You're walking kind of funny."

Oh shit, I cover my mouth to contain my laugh.

She throws me a look and tells the mayor, "Pilates. Really stretches the muscles."

One last look and she's off behind the counter. Half listening to the mayor droning on and on about the project, I keep stealing glances at Devlyn. Most of the food is prepared out front by Devlyn or her short order cook. There's an additional kitchen in the back that's Devlyn's territory. It's also where she does all her baking. When I see her disappear to the back, I excuse myself.

Making sure Mia's not looking, I slip through the door to follow her. Jumping slightly, Devlyn turns around, her back up against the freezer. "What are you . . ."

I let my kiss shut her up. Is there a better way? "Good morning," I whisper, moving to her neck.

Her moan is damn near intoxicating. I no longer care where we are, who could walk in, how this might look. I only care about the little sounds of pleasure she's making. Letting my hands roam the curves of her body, I flip up her tutu.

"Garrett!" she whispers in a little giggle. I cup her, feeling her heat through her leggings. She's soaked through. There is no greater compliment than knowing I can do that to her. I slip my hand underneath her waistband.

Her eyes flash wide, forcing my hand away. "I'm going to burn your toast!" Grinning, I play with a strand of her hair. She looks up at me and whispers, "I lied to you about something."

I've been lied to enough by women. Sheena took care of that by the time I was eighteen. Devlyn knows that. "What?"

"Scott," she says, looking down, her skin turning red.

"Devlyn, if you didn't really break up with him, you are now!"

She looks up, a tight-lipped smile on her face. "I lied to you about why we broke up."

"You said you guys were all business."

"That's true, but there's more to it."

"Okay, so what's the real reason?"

Lightly, she places her hand on my cheek. "He's not you."

She gives me the most adorable little smile. That's the kind of lie that's easy to forgive. Leaning in, I let my mouth hover over hers, and her lips part.

"Dad?" Mia calls as the door opens, causing Devlyn and I to jump away from each other. "What are you doing back here?"

Devlyn's eyes dart to me. Good thing my lying skills are well-honed. "Devlyn had a problem with her freezer the other night, and I fixed it. I was just making sure everything was still running smoothly."

LUCKY FOR ME, Mia bought the freezer bullshit, but she's been by my side all day. There's been no time to sneak a phone call to Devlyn, or a kiss for that matter, and I doubt there will be time tonight. Movie night in the square is a tradition for Mia and me, and Devlyn, too, so there's no skipping out.

I look towards the diner. The lights are off already, but Devlyn's not here.

Sometimes she brings cookies or brownies or something, but I don't see any tonight. Only the old popcorn machine the local Boy Scout chapter sets up to raise money for their troop. I throw a blanket and pillow on the sofa. It's summertime, but ever since Mia was a baby, she always ended up curled in a blanket—sometimes with her head in my lap, sometimes with her head in Devlyn's lap. Devlyn taught me how to braid Mia's hair right here during a showing of *Indiana Jones*. Yeah, that's the other thing about movie night. The movies aren't from the last two decades. Perfect example is tonight's movie, *Weekend at Bernie's*.

"Hi."

Devlyn's voice stirs me from the past. Looking over at her, she's dressed in cutoff jean shorts, sandals, and a white t-shirt tied at the waist. Tonight, her outfit is simple. No crazy patterns, no tutu, no bright colors—nothing to distract from the real her. All her hair is pulled up into a bun, and every bone in my body wants to pull her into my arms.

"Does Mia know?" she asks. "I worried all day that she . . ."

"No," I whisper, stepping a little closer. She freezes me to my spot with her eyes. I motion for her to sit, and we both take a seat, angled toward each other without touching. "Still sore?" I tease.

She raises an eyebrow at me. "I have one particular ache that needs some attention."

My dick twitches. He's the man for the job. "How about after the movie we . . ."

"What's the movie tonight?" Mia asks, plopping down right between Devlyn and me.

Exhaling, I scoot over. This is the way the past eighteen years have been. Mia between me and the entire female population. Now it's just more literal.

Devlyn looks over at me, her eyes telling me we'll figure it out.

She knows what she's getting with me, and she's okay with that. "So tell me about your roommate?" Devlyn asks Mia. "Your dad told me she's from . . ."

Mia excitedly starts talking a mile a minute about her roommate, their plans to decorate their dorm, the matching headboards she wants me to build for them, the bedding they have picked out. Devlyn listens, seemingly just as excited as Mia. She glances at me a few times, smiling. I look around at all the families here. To an outsider, Mia, Devlyn, and I could pass as a family. There's just one problem. We're not. I'm not going home with Devlyn. She won't be falling asleep in my bed or be there for me to kiss good morning.

"Evening," my dad says, walking up to us. "Got room for one more?"

"Granddad!" Mia says. "I can't remember the last time you came to one of these."

He just smiles. We both know he hasn't come since my mom died. Some things are just harder to do as a widower. Movie night was always special to him and my mom, so when she passed away, he just couldn't bring himself to come without her. Wonder what brought him here tonight?

"The smell of the popcorn called to me," he says, showing us the extra-large tub he bought. He motions to Mia. "I'm going to need some help eating all this."

Mia moves beside him. My dad gives me a knowing glance as I scoot closer to Devlyn. He couldn't possibly know, could he? He tosses the blanket on top of my lap, making sure it covers my and Devlyn's legs. Yep, he knows!

He extends his arm, cuddling Mia into his side, and I slip my hand under the blanket, taking Devlyn's hand in mine. Her fingers curl around mine, and from the corner of my eye, I see a little smile playing on her lips. It's the simplest thing—holding her hand—and I can't remember the last time I just held a woman's hand and watched a movie.

In that moment, I realize exactly how much I've missed. When Sheena got pregnant, I had to grow up fast. I went from sixteen to like forty in an instant. Suddenly, I had to worry about taking care of someone else when I didn't even know how to take care of myself. School, work, bills, insurance—I became an adult before I could vote, but there is a part of me that stayed stuck. Yeah, I had side pieces of ass through the years, but I never had this. There's lots of things I never had—waking up with a woman, showering with her, making her breakfast in bed. The list is piling up.

I stroke Devlyn's hand under the blanket. She turns to me, her blue eyes shining through the darkness. She's always been here. How did I not see it? She yawns a little. We both smile, knowing why she's tired. What I wouldn't give to be in bed with her right now. Instead, I cock my head toward my shoulder. That's all I can offer her right now.

Devlyn glances at Mia, and I mouth to her, "It's okay."

But Devlyn shakes her head at me. We've known each other our whole lives. It's not as though she's never laid her head on my shoulder, hugged me, but it's different now. Now those small acts have big meaning even if we're the only ones that know it.

Devlyn leans a little closer and whispers, "Think I'll go home."

I try to squeeze her hand tighter, but she stands up, the blanket falling to the ground and forcing me to release her hand. She kisses Mia and my dad on the cheek, making some excuse that she's tired then quietly walks away. Shit! What the hell just happened?

I keep my eyes on the screen but feel my father's stare. He pats Mia's shoulder. "Could you help an old man out and go get a refill on the popcorn?" Smiling, Mia takes the bucket, heading for the popcorn machine. My dad continues to stare at me for a second then he leans over. "When you get old, you don't sleep much. I think it's nature's way of letting you know that your time is running out."

"Don't talk like that," I say, unable to picture a day without my dad.

"I get up early," he says.

He lets the words linger, and I don't know what he's getting at. Then it hits me, and my head whips around.

"I saw Devlyn's car," he says.

It doesn't matter that I'm a grown man. Getting caught with a woman at your place by a parent—who knows you were having sex—immediately makes you feel like a teenager again. My dad is completely old school about this stuff, too. He and my mom were each other's only. Premarital sex and my father don't mix. I get it. I'm a hypocrite, but I get it. I've preached to Mia endlessly about waiting, even though I didn't. Correction, I don't.

"Mia didn't see anything," he says. "I made sure of that."

"Thanks, Dad. It's . . ."

He holds up his wrinkled hand. "Long overdue, if you ask me." He nods toward the diner. "That girl has been like a mother to Mia. She's been a lot to you, too."

"She has," I whisper, staring at the dark windows of the diner, wishing this could all be easier, but there is nothing easy about dating and being a single parent.

"Just love her," my dad says softly. "Love her crazy. Everything else you're worried about will work itself out."

Love? Sheena is the only woman I've ever said those words to, other than Mia and my mom. And I'm not sure it was true when I said it to her back then. Sure, my teenage hormone-fueled brain thought I loved her, but how real could it have been if she just left like she did?

Patting my shoulder, he says, "You need to be careful."

"You don't need to worry about another surprise . . ."

"Not that," he says. "Mia! What if she'd seen you two? This is a small town. You don't want Mia to find out from anyone other than you."

"I know."

"Good."

"Devlyn and I haven't had a chance to really talk."

"I can help with that," he says, nodding toward Mia walking back.

Letters to Mia
Thirteenth Birthday

Dear Mia,
You're a teenager! I have a teenage daughter. No one knows that. I feel so guilty about that. My parents are the only people in my life that know about you. I wonder if that makes me horrible.

I guess everyone who gives up their child feels like this. You never stop thinking about them. They are always there. You are always here. Always with me. That's the part you don't realize when you give your child up. There is no "giving" them up. Children stay with you. You've stayed with me.

I wonder who you are. Are you funny or quiet? Did you like to play with dolls or in the mud? Do you eat vegetables or like only sweets? I suppose you probably wonder those things about me, too.

What will you become? Will I ever know? Do I deserve to know?

So many questions. Questions are all I have.

I hope you understand why I did what I did. I pray that you know I love you.

I wonder what you wish for when you blow out your birthday candles. I wonder . . .

That sums it up. Mia—you are wonder.

Until next year,
Your mom

CHAPTER THIRTEEN

DEVLYN

I'VE HEARD STORIES about waking up and not knowing whose bed you're in, an unfortunate side effect of one-night stands and random hookups. I hope last night with Garrett wasn't just for one night, and there was nothing random about it, but the shock of waking up in his arms, in his bed, is still very real.

I gave up on us having a shot years ago. I can't pinpoint when it happened, exactly. It happened slowly, which is odd considering how fast I fell in love with him. I think I was about five. It was the first day of school, and I got separated from my parents during the school tour. I was crying when Garrett found me. He walked me back to my classroom, holding my hand. I went home and told my mom I was going to marry Garrett Hollis. It was silly, but no less real.

It took me a lot longer to give up on the hope I had for me and Garrett. Teenage pregnancy didn't do it. Sheena herself didn't do it. Other guys didn't do it. It wasn't just *one* thing. It was a combination of everything, I guess. I'm not saying I ever really fell out of love with Garrett, I know I didn't. I just sort of accepted it wasn't ever going to happen.

But now it has.

Perhaps I'm overthinking this. I tend to do that when Garrett is involved. Like the time he called me in the middle of the night. I answered the phone thinking it was a booty call or he was drunk dialing me, ready to confess his love. Instead, Mia had the flu, and he needed me to bring over chicken soup. I get it, kids get sick, but a booty call would've been better.

Maybe that's what last night was—the standard nail and bail. I wanted him too much to stop and ask. Even if it was just sex for him, I will forever remember our night. Even if it's all we ever get.

The man is one solid piece of hard muscle—the definition in his abs, that delicious little trail of hair from his belly button, the feel of his arms tight around me. His abs are nice, his ass is even better, those blue eyes can melt any girl's heart, but it's his arms that slay me—tan, rock hard biceps. Being wrapped up in them was everything I imagined it would be. It's the feeling that there is no safer place in the world. I hope that's true.

Garrett's burned me before. He doesn't even know it. That's the thing about unrequited love—it hurts, and the other person doesn't even know they are hurting you. Every glance that you read too much into. Every touch that you think is leading to more but doesn't. Every time he leans in and you think he's going to kiss you. Every phone call, text, email. Every laugh you share. Every time you see them and want more, and they have no idea.

I think that's why I gave up on us. The alternative hurt too much. Our friendship became enough. From kids to teenagers to Mia, our relationship has lasted longer than most marriages these days. Last night, we risked it all.

I've been at every one of Mia's birthday parties. Heard her first words, watched her first steps. I've made that girl breakfast more times than even Garrett has. It seems like just yesterday I was helping Garrett feed her mashed-up banana and peas for the first time in a high chair at Biscuit Girl.

Now I could not only lose him, but I could lose Mia, too. I don't know what last night meant to him. If I know Garrett, I doubt he even knows, but I couldn't sit at movie night, holding his hand. I certainly couldn't put my head on his shoulder. Until I know where his head is, I have to protect myself a little bit.

So I lied and told Garrett I was going home when, instead, I walked to the Falls. Probably stupid to come here alone in the dark. I could trip, hit my head, and die. That would be my luck. Just when I bed Garrett Hollis, I have a freak accident and die.

I come upon a few teenagers walking through the woods, laughing. Guess the movie is over, and it's time for the extracurricular activities to begin. What's supposed to be a romantic spot has long been the town's make-out point.

The moonlight bounces off the rush of the waterfall. No rainbows promising forever love tonight.

Maybe Garrett's right. All love is hard. Especially when you suspect you love the other person more than they love you.

I know that's not entirely fair. Garrett just figured out I was a woman, so he needs a little time to catch up. After all, I've loved him my whole life.

My phone rings, lighting up the darkness. I see Garrett's name. Drawing a deep breath, I answer.

"Wish you were in my bed," he says quietly.

"Is this Bryan? Or Steven? Or Mark? Or that fella I was with last night, whose name I can't remember? Starts with a G, I think."

"That's me, the one from last night," he says, and I can hear his grin through the phone. "I was wondering if you might want to do it again sometime. Like maybe for three nights straight?"

"What?" I cry out.

"Where are you?" he asks. "I hear . . . Is that water? Are you at the Falls?"

"Yeah," I say. "What's this about three nights?"

"Why are you at the Falls?" he asks. "You said you were tired, going home."

"I needed to think."

"So you're not with Bryan, Steven, or Mark?"

I laugh. "No, I'm alone. I was just about to walk back."

"Good, talk to me while you walk back. That way I'll know you get home safe."

"It's Eden Valley. What could happen? I could die of boredom."

"I don't like the idea of you alone in the dark," he whispers.

"I'm walking back," I say. "So what's this about three nights?"

"My dad's decided to take Mia on a little trip."

"Just like that?" I ask, walking the bridge.

I hear Garrett exhale. "Don't freak out, but he saw your car at my house until the early morning. He knows."

"I'll never be able to look him in the eye again," I say.

"He's happy for us."

Us? Two little letters—only these two don't crush my heart.

"So I was thinking, the hardware store is closed on Sundays, and Monday is my scheduled off day. Maybe I could get Tuesday covered. You're all mine for three nights."

I'm speechless. All his? Three nights? Us?

"Devlyn," he says. "Sorry, guess I should've asked if you . . ."

"My place or yours?" I ask, letting him know my answer.

He laughs quietly. "I don't care as long as it involves you naked."

"Well, we've already christened your place, so how about my house?"

"Not sure how I'm going to make it until Sunday."

"It's only one more day," I say, smiling so wide my cheeks hurt.

"Why'd you really leave the movie tonight?" he asks. "Why'd you say you were going home?"

Lying to Garrett is the crust of my relationship with him. I've been lying to him about how I feel about him my whole life. Now I'm just supposed to spill it all out?

Loving Garrett is kind of like pounding on a locked door. No matter how hard you love or how hard you pound, he's not going to open the door to his heart until he's ready. Is he now?

My legs start moving faster, not wanting to have this conversation, scared of what he'll say. I forget he knows me as well as I know him. When I don't answer, he softly says my name, urging me to respond. My pace stays fast, as my words come out slow. "Now I'm the one that doesn't want to freak you out."

"I won't."

Taking a huge breath, I say, "I wasn't sure if last night meant anything to you other than sex."

"Are you sure now?"

"I'm sure I need to hear you say it."

He chuckles. "Devlyn, last night was not just about sex."

"And you're not just saying that because I asked you to?"

"Women are insane," he says, laughing. "Devlyn, even if you had a bizarre accident and your pussy had to be sewed permanently shut, I'd still want to be with you."

I start laughing. "That's because I'd still have my ass and mouth."

"Even if those are gone, too," he says, laughing. "In fact, assume you have no holes. Not even in your ears or nose. Nothing."

"You'd still want me?" I ask, giggling.

"Still," he says.

CHAPTER FOURTEEN

DEVLYN

THREE NIGHTS ALONE with Garrett—how will we spend our time?

I can't seem to stop smiling as I walk toward the hardware store. His father is taking Mia to the beach for a few days. They're leaving tomorrow, which means I have less than twenty-four hours to wait. I want things to be perfect, so once the lunch crowd died down, I decided to duck out early (perk of being the owner) and do a little shopping.

Three days alone with Garrett calls for some new lacy panties, maybe even a sexy corset or bustier. Although he certainly didn't seem to mind me showing up in my pajamas, fresh from the shower the other night. The local shopping scene isn't going to do. There's not a lingerie store in sight. Antiques we've got by the dozen. A bookstore, a couple clothing boutiques, an old-fashioned toy store, but nothing in the realm of ladies' underwear unless you want some granny panties.

Eden Valley prides itself on not having any big chain stores. That's good for small business owners like myself, but bad when you need a thong.

I peer through the window of the hardware store. Garrett's by the register, leaning over, sketching something. I'm sure it's the plans for the Falls. I know the look in those eyes. Before, I'd only seen it when he was working, but the other night the intensity was focused right on me. My skin covers in goose bumps remembering.

I walk inside, and he looks up. Dear God, the smile he gives me makes my heart flip-flop in my chest. Feeling my skin heat, I want to say something sexy, something mysterious, something that will have him thinking about me non-stop until tomorrow, but his blue eyes have me dumbstruck.

"I'm going shopping," is all I can manage to say.

He gives me the funniest look. I obviously sound like an idiot. Just because we slept together, that doesn't mean I have to give him a play-by-play of my movements. I try to recover, lowering my voice and flashing him a smile. "I mean, I'm going shopping for . . ."

His eyes dart to the floor behind me, his head shaking a little.

My head whips around. "Oh, Mia," I say, finding her sitting on the floor, piles of paint samples in front of her, sorting them into correct piles. "I didn't see you there."

She looks up at me with the same puppy dog eyes her father can give. "Dad has me sorting paint colors. Little kids come in and like to play with them, then I have to fix it."

I wrinkle my nose up, letting her know that doesn't sound like a great way to spend a lazy Saturday afternoon in the summer. "Shopping sounds better, huh?" I ask.

Her eyes light up. "Totally. I can go with you?" I cock my head towards her dad. She leaps up. "Dad, can I go with Devlyn? I really want a new swimsuit for my trip with Granddad." Garrett smiles, and Mia runs over, planting a kiss on his cheek. Guess that's a yes. "And can I have an advance on my paycheck?"

He chuckles and reaches to his back pocket, pulling out his credit card. She goes to take it, and he snatches it back. "Don't go crazy."

"I won't," she promises. "One swimsuit, I swear."

"Don't forget the shoes," I tease her. "You'll need new flip-flops."

Giggling, she turns to Garrett, who shakes his head at me like I'm in big trouble. I'll be more than happy to take that spanking later. He gives Mia a little squeeze. "Let Devlyn get her shopping done, too."

"I will," Mia says, turning to me. "What are you shopping for?"

One look at Garrett, and he knows his daughter just blocked my lingerie surprise. He mouths the word "fuck" to me, and a big smile covers my face. "Well, I actually was going to shop for your birthday, so it's good you're coming with me. You can give me some ideas."

Mia's face blossoms into a huge smile, then Garrett places his hands on her shoulders. "Before you leave, could you go in the back and grab me some more paper for the register?" She nods, throws me a smile, and heads that way. When she's disappeared, he holds his hand out to me and says, "Come here. It won't take her long to find it."

He pulls me behind a cabinet away from any windows. His lips sweetly brush mine—once, twice, three times. I feel his body start to tighten, wanting more, but he gently cups my cheek, looks right into my eyes then pulls me back into the main part of the store just as Mia reappears.

She places the paper on the counter then says, "I'm ready."

She kisses her dad goodbye. Garrett and I exchange a smile then Mia and I head for the door. "Be good," Garrett calls out.

I flash him a look over my shoulder. "Never."

TEENAGE GIRLS AND shopping require a snack for energy and the Supreme Court to make a decision. It took Mia three trips to the dressing room to decide on the perfect swimsuit. If she liked the color on one, she wished it came in a different style. If she liked the style, she wished the color was different. Thank God she's relatively modest, and it wasn't up to me to talk her out of anything too revealing. I really wouldn't want to have to face Garrett and explain why his daughter was in a thong.

I wasn't able to sneak any lingerie shopping in, but Mia gave me some great ideas for her birthday, mostly practical things like a new backpack or shower caddy. That's no fun, so when I saw her eyeing a pair of pearl earrings, I snatched them up while she was in the dressing room. Every college girl needs a pair. It was a great afternoon.

Driving back, Mia plays with the radio in my car. Apparently, she doesn't have satellite radio, and it seems to have her fascinated. She played with it on the ride to the mall, and it looks like she's going to do the same on the ride home.

"There's literally any kind of music you could want," she says, flipping the channel again. She lands on the Beatles. "Granddad loves the Beatles," she says. "I told him they were the original boy band."

I bust out laughing. "I bet he loved hearing that." She giggles, holding out a bag of trail mix, offering me some. "No, thanks," I say. "That's basically M&M's with obstacles."

Taking a handful, she asks, "You didn't go off to college, did you?"

"No, I lived at home and commuted."

"Why?" she asks. "Dad told me you were valedictorian like me."

"I was," I say, hoping for a change in topic. "But my parents needed my help with the diner." I don't add that Garrett needed my help with her, and I couldn't bring myself to leave him. He'd watched so many of his friends go off to school. He always wished them well, but I knew it must've hurt. "Besides, I always saw my life in Eden Valley."

She looks out the window, tapping her fingers on her leg. "So you knew my mom?"

This is not the change of topic I was hoping for, and she already knows the answer to that question. So there must be something else she's searching for. "You know I did."

"What was she like?" Mia asks softly. "Daddy doesn't talk about her much, and for some reason, she's been on my mind a lot."

"Probably because of all the big changes in your life," I say. "That's understandable."

She turns to me. "So what was she like?"

"I think this is a conversation you need to have with Garrett." God, I see her whole body deflate, sinking into the seat. Reaching for the button, I lower the music. "You look just like her when she was your age."

"I know," she says. "But what was she like? You know, was she into books or sports or dance? Did she like chocolate or vanilla ice cream? Was she a good dancer? What was her favorite holiday? Could she cook? Or was she good . . ."

"Mia," I breathe out, looking down the road. "Sheena and I weren't close."

"But you knew her."

Sheena brings up some painful shit for me. She was everything I wasn't. Beautiful and sexy, and she knew it. Worst of all, she had Garrett's full attention. When she was around, I was always second best. Pushing my own issues aside, I search my mind for something to tell Mia, something that Garrett wouldn't mind me sharing. "Want to know one thing I remember about your mother?" She nods, angling herself towards me. "She ate avocado every day. Said it would help make you smart." I pat her leg. "Think she was right."

Her head falls back to her seat. "I don't like avocado."

I know what she really needs to hear, but it's not me she needs to hear it from. I say it anyway. "She loved you."

"I know."

"Talk to your dad," I say.

"I can't," she says. "Daddy's the best, and I don't want him to feel bad like he's not enough."

"Mia, he knows that," I say. "He'd be more upset knowing that you are upset and not confiding in him."

She nods. "He really loved her, didn't he?"

That's a knife to my gut. "Yes, he did."

"It wasn't just puppy love?"

"I don't think it was," I say.

"Thanks, Devlyn," she says.

I want to say anytime, but I wouldn't mean it. "I remember this one time your mom got sick at school. Threw up all over the place. Your dad picked her up and carried her out of the lunchroom." Mia's head turns to me, and she smiles. "Then there was this time that you wouldn't stop kicking, and he sang to her belly right in the middle of the school parking lot."

"He sang?"

"Yep," I say. "Want to know the best part?" She nods. "He sang your mom's favorite song to you. A show tune. All I Ask of You' from *Phantom of the Opera.*"

"I love that musical," Mia says. "That's my mom's favorite song?"

"Was when she was your age." I reach for the nob on the radio. "Think there's a Broadway channel on here somewhere. Maybe we'll get lucky, and they'll play it."

Mia flings her seatbelt off, leans over, and hugs me as I drive. I get the feeling that little piece of information meant more to her than the earrings will.

HUMMING, MIA OPENS the door to her house. Garrett appears from the kitchen wearing jeans that hang just right from his hips and a white t-shirt, his hair wet like he just got out of the shower. Mia does a little spin, her shopping bags twirling with her.

"What's the damage?" Garrett asks, grinning at us. She hands him his credit card and the receipts. He looks down, seemingly impressed by our restraint. "Looks like you had fun."

Mia tosses me a smile. "We did," I say. "I should get going, though. Big day tomorrow."

Mia misses my comment, but Garrett doesn't, giving me a dirty smile. "Why don't you stay for dinner? It's the least I can do for you saving me from the mall."

My eyes go straight to Mia. I'm not sure Garrett or I will be able to keep our hands off each other to make it through dinner. "Yeah," Mia says. "We can watch a movie like we used to. Just maybe not Disney. It will be fun."

"Stay," Garrett says. "I'll cook."

"That's not a selling feature," Mia teases. "I can run out and pick up food."

My eyes go to Garrett. That will only take about ten minutes depending on how long she has to wait for the food. Eden Valley has two choices for takeout—pizza and Chinese, neither of them more than five minutes away. This is how things will be if Garrett and I stay together. Dinners and movies with Mia when she's home from school. It's the prequel of what could be coming.

"Sold," I say.

Garrett tries unsuccessfully to convince Mia to just order the food when she gets there, but she insists we call it in. I like how he was trying to extend how long she'd be gone, but no dice. Once she's out the door and pulling out of the driveway, he pulls me into his arms. Placing my hand on his chest, I hold him at bay. "I have to talk to you about Mia."

"Something happen?" he asks.

"She asked me about Sheena."

He turns away from me, the muscles in his back so tight they look like they'll rip his shirt. "I'm sorry she put you on the spot."

"I thought you should know she asked me. I didn't want to keep it from you," I whisper. "I told her a few things."

"She asked me about her a few days ago."

"She's curious, and she knows it's a sore topic for you," I say.

"What am I supposed to say about Sheena?" he asks. "It doesn't matter what I tell Mia. The story ends with her mom leaving us."

He's done a really good job with Mia. I should know. I've had a front row seat for the whole thing. Placing my hands on his broad shoulders, I plant a little kiss. "You raised a great kid. You did that. All by yourself."

I feel his chest inflate. "But there's not a damn thing I can do to take away the pain of her not having a mother around."

"Maybe not," I say, stepping in front of him. "But you've done everything to make that pain as small as possible."

His blue eyes find mine, the pain in him seems like a giant, and I wonder if I'm the one that can shrink it down to size.

He kisses me.

It's just a kiss.

The kind where you know you aren't going to end up naked, but the kind that you know is taking you somewhere.

CHAPTER FIFTEEN

GARRETT

MY FATHER'S GRAND plan was an impromptu road trip with Mia. The promise of a few days at the beach was an easy sell for my teenage daughter. They'll be back just a few days before Mia's big birthday party. Dad laid it on pretty thick with Mia, talking about how much he's going to miss her. She ate it right up.

So this morning, they got an early start. I have to say, it gave me a little anxiety, as Mia was the one doing the driving, but the thought of three days alone with Devlyn made it easy to get over. I've probably only had a fraction of the sex most men my age have experienced. It's time to make up for that.

Leaving my truck parked at the store, I walk to Devlyn's house. It's not far, and I don't want any nosy neighbors talking, so it's best that my truck not be in front of her house all night. It's only been a few days since our night together, but it feels like months. I hope the next few days go by slowly.

Devlyn's house, like the rest of Eden Valley, looks like it was ripped from the pages of a fairytale. A winding path of flowers leads up to a stone cottage with huge front windows and a slate roof. The double front door is painted white to match the window trim. I'm not sure how old the house is, but Devlyn has kept it immaculate. I doubt I could find so much as a broken flower stem.

Before I step to the door, I give one more glance over my shoulder. All clear. I lift my hand to knock, but the door opens. A smiling Devlyn pulls me inside and jumps in my arms. Her arms and legs wrap around me, my hands on her ass, and she kisses me hard on the lips.

"Guess you missed me," I tease.

She pulls back, looking into my eyes. "I've been missing you all my life."

"We only just . . ."

She runs her fingers through my hair. "All my life."

She's had these feelings for me that long? She has to be exaggerating. "I had no idea."

"I'm a good liar," she says, wiggling free.

"Why didn't you ever say anything?" I ask. She gives me one of those woman looks where you know they are internally rolling their eyes. "Garrett, I know you. You love hard. There was only room for one woman in your life. Mia."

"My life, Mia, we wouldn't be where we are without you. My life doesn't happen without you. I know that," I say.

Softly, her lips land on mine. Unlike the other night, there's patience behind her kiss. Apparently, she's been waiting years for this moment. Years for my dumb ass to figure out how I feel about her, which also means she's played out this moment a thousand times in her mind. The female mind is vastly different from the male, so I doubt seventy-two hours naked is what she has in mind. So I do what any gentleman would and ask, "What do you want to do today?"

"A lot of this," she whispers, kissing me again.

I SNATCH HER panties out of her hand. "Nope."

Her laugh fills the room. "I'm not sleeping naked."

"Who said anything about sleeping?" I say, holding them over my head.

"Give me my panties," she says, smiling and reaching for them, but I capture her in my arms. Her body is still warm from our shower together, her hair still pinned to the top of her head. "I need those."

"No, you don't."

"Yeah, I do. What if there's a bug or a spider or something? It could bite me or crawl up in there and make a home in my vagina."

I just stare at her. She has the craziest mind in the history of women. Who the hell thinks of these things?

"Besides, I could get cold," she says, yanking the panties from me.

I snatch them back. "Is your story that you have an arachnophobic vagina or a hypothermic vagina?"

She's laughing and shaking her head at me, and there is nothing better than this. Nothing better than being with her. "Today's been the best day," she giggles out.

Anyone else looking in would think we didn't do anything special today, besides all the sex. We watched a movie together, cooked together, showered together—all the things that other couples probably take for granted. It's business as usual for them to crawl into bed together, and I hope to God I never feel that way about sharing a bed with Devlyn.

Grinning, I hand her panties back to her. She slips them on then pulls the sheets back on her bed, holding them up for me. I slip in beside her. She lays her head on my chest, her hair fanning out, and I wrap her in my arms. You always see couples in movies sleeping like this, and I've always thought it was ridiculous. Who can sleep all tangled up with someone else? Sleep or not, I'm not letting go of her. I can go without sleep if it means she's in my arms.

"Garrett," she whispers, and I hear her voice crack.

Moving her hair, I look down at her face, a few silent tears glistening in the moonlight. "Baby, what is it?"

"It's . . ." she stammers. I sit up, pulling her with me, getting concerned now. Devlyn Drake is seldom without a witty comeback. "I'm having a hard time believing this is real."

"I wouldn't play with you."

"I know that. It's just . . ." She shakes her head. "I gave up on you, on us, a long time ago."

Having your woman cry is the worst. As much as I want it to stop, I know she's got years of shit she needs to get off her chest. "Don't give up on me again," I say. "No matter what stupid shit I do."

She giggles through her tears. "I'm being silly."

"You don't cry for silly reasons," I say. "You have some things you need to say?" She nods. "And you're scared to say them?" She nods again. I give her a little kiss on the forehead. "We've had non-stop sex with the promise of more. Aside from the panties you insisted on wearing, you're naked in bed with me. There couldn't be a better time to lay some deep shit on me. I'm liable to give you anything you want."

She sits up, looking me right in the eye. "Kids?"

Well fuck, she couldn't start with something little, like do you keep the ketchup in the cabinet or refrigerator?

"I want them," she says. "It's a non-starter."

"Devlyn, we haven't even had a real date yet. I think . . ."

"That's not going to work with me. Look, if you are certain you don't want any more kids, you need to tell me."

"How am I supposed to tell you? You basically just said it's over between us if I do."

"I'm thirty-three years old. My clock is ticking away."

"The truth is, I don't know," I say. "You have to understand that while everyone else was partying in their twenties, I was raising a kid. I never got a chance to do a lot of stuff other guys did. I can finally . . ."

"Party?" she asks snidely. "Sleep around?"

"No," I say with a huff.

"Then what?"

"Travel. Maybe get my degree." I tilt her chin up. "Find the right woman, fall in love."

"Oh."

Giving her a halfway smile, I say, "So honestly, I just don't know."

"But it's not a hard no?"

"No, but it's not a soft yes, either. Can you live with that for now?" I ask, holding my breath. She nods a little, and I sense there's more. A lot more she needs to say, but she glances away. "Let's get something straight." I tackle her down to the bed and kiss her. "You might have known longer how you feel about me, but that doesn't mean what I feel for you isn't as strong. In fact, I think what I feel is stronger."

She giggles. "Oh really?"

"Yeah, I'm the man." I tease. "So by nature that means . . ."

She rolls over, and I let her pin me to the bed. Staring up at her, it's so clear how she feels about me. How I missed it all those years, I'll never know. She hasn't said it—it's too soon—but I can see it in everything about her. She loves me—her eyes say it, the sound of her laugh says it, the way her body moves, the taste of her lips. Everything down to her curling toes tells me how she feels. I just had to stop and pay attention.

She's loved me in her own way—quiet, secret, soft. She didn't ask me for anything, she knew I couldn't give it. Her love is unselfish and pure and given without ever knowing if I'd love her back.

It's fast, but that's the thing about falling for your best friend. The love is already there. You just have to add the sex and boom! It happens, and there's nothing you can do about it.

CHAPTER SIXTEEN

DEVLYN

"OH GOD," I groan.

I'd come into the kitchen to make us breakfast and somehow ended up hoisted on my countertop with the sexiest man alive between my legs.

Sex with Garrett is amazing. Everything about it. The man is a god between the sheets. And he is the absolute king of cunnilingus. His tongue is a gift, and lucky for me he's a very generous gift giver.

"Not yet, baby," he groans.

But it's too late. Does the man really expect me not to finish when he's working me over like a machine? My orgasm shudders through me. Most guys would take that as their cue to exit, but not Garrett. He rides the wave with me, sucking, kissing, and licking every last ounce of pleasure. I know he's also hoping for any sign I've got more in me.

If he keeps lightly kissing me, then he may just get his wish. Running my fingers through his hair, he rests his head on my thigh, wanting more. I've never seen a man look so disappointed over giving a woman a mind-blowing orgasm before. It's the sweetest thing.

I smile down at him, and his finger lightly traces a circle on the bare skin of my thigh. He senses the clenching of my muscles before I do, a devilish grin on his face. Reaching for him, he gets to his feet, and I draw him to me. There's more than sex in the way he's looking at me. I wish I knew what he was thinking. I wish I knew what all of this means.

Are we dating? Are we a couple? I'm trying my best not to over-analyze it, but it's not working. He hasn't mentioned telling Mia about us. That's not a good sign, and I'm afraid to ask. He didn't freak when I brought up wanting kids, and frankly, that was a lunatic thing for me to bring up, but it was better than yelling, "I love you."

I told myself a lot of lies over the years, trying to convince myself to let go of Garrett. A perfect example is I used to tell myself that if Garrett and I ever slept together, it would be awkward and weird because we were such good friends, but it's quite the opposite. We are so comfortable with each other, and not in the lazy kind of way couples can get. None of the lies ever really worked, and now I'm convinced I'd never be able to let him go. Maybe now, I don't have to.

Scooting off the counter, I let my fingers trace the muscles of his chest. He's got boxer briefs on, but nothing else. I had him pegged as a boxer briefs guy years ago. He has Mia, so he couldn't go commando. Regular boxers are too loose. Garrett's too active to fly free, and my father wore tighty-whities, so it couldn't possibly be that.

He takes my hand in his, kissing it gently. How we go from him going down on me to such a sweet gesture in the blink of an eye, I'll never know, but it works.

"Good morning," he whispers. I have to get on my tiptoes to kiss him gently. He lowers his forehead to mine.

I whisper his name, and that seems to be the key to unlocking his thoughts.

"I've never had this," he says softly, bending down slightly to look in my eyes. "The morning after." He must see the confusion in my eyes because he smiles. "I've never spent all night with a woman, much less woken up with one beside me."

All I can manage to say is, "Oh."

"I thought you should know that," he says. "How much last night, how much this morning, means to me."

I pull my bottom lip between my teeth, trying not to cry. I've never thought about the things Garrett lost when he had Mia so young. Simple things the rest of us take for granted like waking up with someone, cooking with them, being lazy on the sofa together—

he never had. I guess I was too caught up thinking about what I didn't have to consider what he lost.

I flash him my naughtiest smile. "In that case, let's make this morning even more memorable," I say, slipping my hand under the waistband of his boxer briefs and sliding to my knees.

If I had a Bible, I'd place my right hand on it and swear this man is hard twenty-four seven. At his worst, he's sporting a semi. Freeing him from his boxer briefs, I glance up at him, smiling. Impatience shows in his eyes. He's thought about me doing this. I can tell. I vow not to disappoint.

I will not rush this moment, but Garrett has other ideas, reaching down and taking hold of himself. Can't say that I blame him. He's rock-hard and huge, the thing must be heavy as heck.

"Let me," I say, taking him in my hand. Hot and hard, I feel him grow longer and heavier in my hand. Slowly, I run my hand over him.

"Fuck," he groans. I've had him inside me, touched him, but I've never had my mouth on him. When he starts to leak, he begs me, "Devlyn."

"Not yet, baby," I tease him like he does me, and the man actually growls.

Still stroking him slowly, I plant light kisses on his inner thigh, seeing his toes curl under. It's hot to have a man want you so much. As I give his balls a gentle tug, his hands fly to my hair, encouraging me.

I pull back, looking up at him. "Hold my hair back," I say. "Like it's in a ponytail." We both smile, knowing I'm the one who taught him how to do one. He pulls my hair all back, holding it in one hand. "I want you to watch," I say, giving him one long, slow lick up his shaft.

"Christ!"

This is the best tip I've ever gotten about giving a blowjob. Ask the guy to watch. Something about watching your lips slide over their dicks makes them go crazy and gets them there quicker. Let's just be honest, when you're on your knees—quick is best.

I slide him into my mouth, getting the first taste of him. The sound he releases makes my thighs tighten. I really need to work on my sixty-nine attention deficit because right now, I want nothing more than to be straddling his face.

Got to focus.

I use one hand to pump him while he slides in and out of my mouth and gives my hair a little yank. I can tell he's desperate to move. Some guys don't care and will immediately ram themselves down our throats, but not Garrett. Placing my other hand on his ass, I encourage him to thrust.

I didn't think it was possible for the man to get harder, but he does. He starts off very slowly. It's all I can do not to roll my eyes. His dick is almost down my throat—now is not the time to be a gentleman. I increase my speed, letting him know it's okay to thrust harder, faster. He gets the message.

The taste of salt hits my tongue as he moans my name through gritted teeth. He sinks to his knees beside me on the floor, pulling me to his chest, cradling me. Just takes one little ole blowjob to bring a big, strapping man to his knees!

I peer up at him, his eyes closed, completely relaxed. I know every edge of his body, every feature of his handsome face. His eyes open, catching me staring, and the corner of his mouth turns up in a cocky little smile. "Wish I would've known you . . ."

My mouth drops open, and I playfully push away. He starts laughing, tickling me. I spend a lot of time in the kitchen, but never on the floor, naked, in a tickling match. "If you would've known I could suck cock like that, then what?" I tickle his abs. "You'd have been with me sooner?"

His laugh is so loud. "That's not what I was going to say."

"Oh really?"

He pulls me to him, his hands in my hair. "I was going to say, I wish I would've known earlier how you felt about me. We could've had a lot more mornings like this."

"I don't think it would've mattered," I say.

"Of course it would have mattered," he says, a bite to his voice.

Reaching for his cheek, I say, "I wanted you to want me first."

He says my name tenderly. Years of pain and hurt bubble in my chest. I wish it didn't. It doesn't matter anymore. We're together now, in this moment.

"I want . . ." His phone rings from the other room, and his eyes dart that way then back to me. "It might be Dad or Mia. I really should get it."

Nodding, I say, "Answer it. I'll finish breakfast."

He helps me to my feet, taking my hand. "I want to make you breakfast this morning. Just give me five minutes."

Smiling and nodding, I watch him snatch his boxer briefs off the floor and hurry to my bedroom. Garrett is a great guy, but there's a reason he eats in the diner most of the time. The man can't cook to save his life. It's sweet that he wants to make me breakfast, but I'd rather not end up with food poisoning, so I throw some bread in the toaster then head to my room to get some clothes. I don't think it's very hygienic to cook sans panties.

Garrett's voice stops me at the door. "Mia, please don't cry."

I rush to his side, sitting beside him on my bed. He covers the phone with his hand and whispers he's sorry.

"She alright?" I mouth back.

His head does this weird thing, sort of like saying yes and no at the same time. "I'm sure it will turn up." There's a short pause, and his eyes close tightly, hating to hear her cry. "I know we'd never be able to replace it." Another pause. I assume more sobbing. "Mia, baby, please. I'm not at home right now, but . . . It doesn't matter . . . I'll check to see if it's at home . . . Yes, I'll call you back."

A few seconds later, he hangs up. "Mia alright?"

"Yeah," he says, standing up and starting to get dressed. "She thinks she lost her charm bracelet. You know, the one from her dance recitals?" I nod. "She swears she was wearing it when they left for the beach, but now she can't find it. My dad doesn't remember. I told her I'd go look at home."

"You have to go?" I ask but already know the answer.

He exhales deeply. "I can be back in . . ."

I shake my head. "It's fine. I should go check on the diner anyway, since I took those few days off last week."

He captures my hand, a worried look on his face. "Mia tried to call the house a few times. She . . ."

"Garrett, I understand."

I'm not sure he believes me, but it's true. "Pack a bag," he says. "Pack a bag to stay at my place. I'll take it with me. Then just come over after you've checked on the diner."

I smile. The man wants a guarantee I'll show. Guess having my toothbrush gives him security that he can hold it hostage.

CHAPTER SEVENTEEN

GARRETT

CRISIS AVERTED—THE CHARM bracelet was resting on top of Mia's dresser.

Some things are chick magnets—like dogs and babies. My daughter is a repellent to the opposite sex. Even from a couple hundred miles away, she can cock block me.

Rain batters the windows of my house. Summer showers are not uncommon in Eden Valley, but this is a full-on thunderstorm. The wind is howling, the rain coming down in sheets, the sky blanketed in darkness. Some rain can be refreshing, some can be romantic, but this storm isn't either. It's ominous.

I'm worried. Devlyn hasn't shown up.

I'm not a worrier by nature. Some people are genetically predisposed to worry, I think. Mia is one of them, so I get it. I'm not. It's not that I don't ever worry. I do. I have a teenage daughter, so worry comes with the territory. By nature, I think women are more likely to be worriers than men. My mom was the worrier between her and my dad. Maybe it's because the female brain is a multi-tasking machine. Men tend to focus on one task, complete it, move on to the next. Women's attention seems to always be divided among a dozen different things. Seems to me that kind of thinking would cause more stress. Still, I've been around Mia long enough to know that child can actually worry about getting worried.

The terrible rain and Devlyn's absence are messing with my worry-free attitude. I don't want her out in this weather. Time to go get her.

Grabbing my keys, I open the front door, the sideways rain blowing right in my face, but I still spot her. Devlyn is walking down my street, her bright orange umbrella has been flipped the wrong direction by the wind, and she's carrying two canvas bags on one arm. Yes, she's the woman who brings her own grocery bags with her to the store. She is just all-around good.

"What the hell are you doing?" I call out, rushing to meet her.

"We said we shouldn't park in front of each other's house," she says, giving me a wry smile.

"That didn't mean you should walk here in the rain," I say in disbelief and take the bags from her, guiding her up to my porch. I take her umbrella, examining it. It's shot, so I toss it on my front porch before heading inside with her.

Her teeth are chattering, her skin is covered in goose bumps, and there's not a spot on her that's dry. She motions toward the bags. "I went to the grocery store. It was bright and sunny when I walked inside then I'm standing at the checkout, and it just starts pouring. That always seems to happen to me," she says, smiling.

I start stripping her wet clothes off. "Why'd you even go to the store? I've got food here."

"Since we can't really go out, I wanted to make you a nice dinner and . . ." she says, a little sneeze cutting her short.

Scooping her into my arms, I say, "Let's get you in a warm bath. You're ice cold."

"I'm fine," she says. All I can do is shake my head at her. She starts playing with the material on my shirt. "You're wet, too."

"I'll join you in a minute," I say, carrying her into my bathroom. "I want to get you something warm to drink first."

She kisses my cheek as I place her down next to the tub and turn on the water. I show her where I put the bag she gave me earlier in case she needs anything then head to the kitchen and start to rummage through my kitchen cabinets.

Mia's told me enough how bad my coffee is, and I don't have any hot tea in the house. There's no cans of soup, either. What the hell was Devlyn thinking walking in the storm like that? Someone seeing her car in my driveway isn't worth risking getting sick or worse. She could've called me to come get her. I shove the box of cereal to the side, spotting some hot chocolate mix. It's the peak of summer, but I don't care.

Pouring some milk in a mug, I pop it in the microwave for a minute, mix in the powder, and it's almost done. I reach into the refrigerator for some whipped topping I know is there, spray a generous amount on the top, then head back to the bathroom.

The door is open. Guess I've seen her naked enough that she's not shy. I see her leg come up out of the water, turning the faucet off with her foot, her toes painted a shiny pink. She's filled the tub with bubbles.

I'm frozen, watching her. The way her hand comes up out of the water, the gentle stroke of the washcloth across her skin. She reaches down to her leg, feeling the length of her skin.

Do all women look this sexy when they're taking a bath? I can't take my eyes off her. The subtle way she moves, the bubbles sliding down her skin, I wonder how many men would walk right past their wives or girlfriends and not even pay attention.

Suddenly, she sinks under the water until she's fully submerged. When she comes back up, she smooths her hair back, and I bend down next to the tub. Her eyes open, and she gives me a bright smile, taking the cup from me. She doesn't drink it. She simply holds it in both her hands, using it to warm them more.

"Did you find Mia's bracelet?" she asks. I nod, tucking a wet strand of her hair behind her ear. "Where'd you tell her you were this morning?"

"Working on my motorcycle."

"I'm sorry you had to lie to her," Devlyn says, taking a small sip.

I feel a heaviness hit my chest. "I've been thinking about how to handle this with her."

"You have?" Devlyn asks.

"As much fun as it is to sneak around with you," I tease, "I don't want Mia to find out we're seeing each other from anyone but me."

"She's not a baby," Devlyn says, sitting up. "She and I have a good relationship. You really think she's going to flip out?"

"No," I say. "But I want to make sure I tell her at the right time, in the right way."

"Are you thinking of waiting until she's at school?"

I can tell by her posture my answer better be no to that question, and lucky for me it is. "She'll have enough new things to deal with being away from home for the first time. I don't want to add to that. I was thinking about after her birthday party."

"That's next weekend," Devlyn says, unable to hide the shock in her voice.

"Did you have something else in mind?"

Her head shakes. "You haven't mentioned telling Mia until now, so I'm surprised you've got this whole plan."

"It's not fair to her to hide it, and it's not fair to you, either," I say. She leans over the tub, gently kissing me. "There's something I need you to understand, though."

"Okay."

"It's not going to be like this. At least not until Mia's away at school. I won't be able to stay at your place, and you can't sleep here."

"I knew that," she says.

"And you're okay with it?" I ask, having had more than one woman complain when I had to leave after sex.

"A little bit of you," she says, leaning up and kissing me sweetly. "I only need a little bit of you."

"I'll have to remember that," I say, flashing her a grin. "You only need the tip."

"Garrett," she laughs, playfully swatting my shoulder.

Planting a kiss on her lips, I say, "You have all of me."

CURLED UP IN one of my t-shirts, Devlyn's fast asleep on my sofa, her feet in my lap. I adjust the blanket covering her. It was another great night, making dinner together. Well, Devlyn attempted to teach me how to cook. When she caught me grabbing the sugar instead of the salt, I was relegated to chopping things and cleaning up.

When I finished cleaning up, I found her curled up asleep on my sofa. Might have something to do with the fact that I had her for dessert. I lifted her feet up, placed them on my lap, and have been here ever since. We had the Mia talk, which went perfectly, but we only have one more day together, tomorrow.

I'm thinking we need to get out of town, a little day trip. She hasn't complained, but Devlyn deserves better than hiding out in my house and cooking for me. My cell phone dings, and I look down, finding a few pictures from Mia—a selfie with my dad, a shell she found on the beach, the view from their room.

I type a little response and hit send. I'm expecting Mia to type something back, but instead my phone rings. Devlyn stirs a little, and I quickly accept. Declining the call isn't an option. Mia knows I'm awake and have my phone, so I answer.

"Granddad let me drink this thing called a Bushwacker," Mia says. "Don't worry. He had them make it without alcohol."

"What?" I ask.

"A Bushwacker," she repeats.

I'm not one for fruity little cocktails. Give me a beer or a whiskey any day over that shit, and who the hell thought that was a good name for a drink? Thank God, Mia doesn't seem to make any correlation between bush and a woman's pubic hair, or at least she's not acting like she does. I guess my father didn't, either, or he would've bought her a virgin piña colada instead.

"So you're having fun?" I ask quietly.

She tells me about the beach, the boys, the junk they've been eating, how nice the condo is, all the stuff she didn't tell me about this morning during the charm bracelet crisis.

"You're not giving your grandfather any problems, are you?" I ask, although I know she's not.

"Why are you whispering?" she asks.

I look down at Devlyn. Not wanting to wake her, I try to slip her legs off my lap and get up, but she moans a little. Shit. "I'm not," I say. "Must be a bad connection." I realize if I want to whisk Devlyn away for the day tomorrow, I've got to have an excuse for my daughter. I don't want her calling the store and being told I'm not there. "I might do some work on the pavilion site tomorrow, so if you need me, call my cell."

I'm getting really good at sneaking around and lying. I haven't lost my touch since my days with her mother, I guess.

"Okay," she says. "I can barely hear you."

I'm caught between having a real conversation with my daughter and waking up the half-dressed woman asleep in my lap. Gently, I give Devlyn's foot a little rub. Her lip pouts, and she kicks her leg a little. Note to self, she's grumpy when sleepy.

"Mia, hang on. We've had some bad storms here today. Maybe if I go outside."

I hit the mute button on my phone and move to get up, but Devlyn throws the cover off and flips herself around so her head's now in my lap. I run my fingers through her hair. "Okay, baby, you win," I say, and Devlyn responds by nuzzling down deeper.

I try to talk a little louder. "Mia, is this better?"

"A little," she says, starting to tell me about their plans for tomorrow. Listening, I look down at Devlyn's face asleep in my lap. It's the first time I've seen her like this, soft and sweet and sound asleep in my arms. Mia's the last girl I held in my arms sleeping.

"Garrett," Devlyn mumbles, sleepily.

I hold my finger up to her lips, and her eyes pop open. Luckily, Mia didn't hear her, still chatting away. Sometimes the self-centered nature of teenagers can come in handy. Devlyn moves to sit up, but I shake my head at her, encouraging her back to my lap. I like her using me as her own personal mattress.

She lays there, smiling up at me. Grinning, I play with her hair. If someone saw us right now, we'd look like two lovestruck idiots. She doesn't rush me off the phone. She doesn't interrupt. She just waits patiently, smiling.

Apparently, that's what Devlyn does for me. She waits and smiles. I'm one very lucky son of a bitch that no other guy snatched her up while I had my head stuck up my ass. She could be married with a houseful of kids of her own by now.

"Okay, goodnight, baby girl," I say then toss my phone aside and pull Devlyn on top of me.

Her laugh fills the room as she grinds into me. "Are you hard twenty-four seven?"

Flashing her a wicked smile, I say, "Are you wet twenty-four seven?" I lean in close, letting my hand slip to her ass. "In fact, I bet you're soaking . . ." Giggling, she tries to wiggle free, but my finger finds her. "Looks like I was right."

She glares at me. "Cocky." I take her hand, placing it on my bulge. She's trying hard not to laugh, biting her bottom lip. "That's where that word comes from. Because you arrogant guys all have big ole cocks."

Pulling her tighter, I say, "And you love it."

Her eyes leave mine, and she moves to get up. "How about some dessert? I can make you . . ."

Capturing her hand, I ask, "Why are you always cooking for me?"

She shrugs, looking down at our joined hands. "I don't know. I guess for the longest time it was the only thing I had to offer you. If it wasn't for the diner, you bringing Mia in for breakfast . . ." Her voice trails off. "I don't want to talk about this."

"Devlyn?"

"No," she says. "It makes it sound like I've been sad and miserable for years, and that's not the way it was."

"I feel like I should apologize."

She busts out in an angry laugh. "You don't need to apologize for not loving me, Garrett."

"That's not fair."

"Sometimes feelings aren't fair," she cries. I reach out for her, but she steps away. "You think it was fair how I felt about you? You think all these years that was fair?"

"I'm sorry. Or should I thank you?" I ask, throwing my hands up. "I don't know what the fuck you want me to say."

"That's why I don't want to talk about this," she says. "There's nothing for you to say."

"All that's over now," I say.

"I know," she whispers. "But those feelings haven't completely faded yet."

"I understand that."

"It's not right to blame you for what you didn't know," she says.

"I know now," I say. "I promise . . ."

"I don't like promises," she says. "They always get broken."

"No promises, no sixty-nine. Anything else?" I tease, and she smiles.

"I didn't say no sixty-nine. I said I was bad at it."

"Well, I'm going to make you a believer," I say. "In promises and in sixty-nine."

She laughs, and I take her in my arms. "My heart broke so many times for you," she says. "It's what my heart expects to happen. Garrett Hollis equals a broken heart."

She doesn't know it, but she just crushed mine. "Come with me," I say, taking her hand and leading her outside. She pauses, dressed only in my t-shirt, the ground soaked from the storm. I motion to a pair of Mia's flip-flops on the porch, and Devlyn slips them on.

Holding her hand, I lead her off the porch. It's late and dark, and no one's going to see us. The air smells fresh and crisp, the crickets are chirping, and the sky is clear. I look back at Devlyn, her eyes filled with questions.

I push open the door to the shop and flick on the light, my motorcycle centering the room. "Is that the famous bike?" she asks.

"Yep," I say.

"It looks almost new."

"You remember when I got it?" She nods, running her hand across the chrome. "It was a disaster. Broken." Her blue eyes peer up at me, knowing why I'm showing it to her. "I've been fixing it for years."

"Garrett, you didn't mean to break my heart."

"It doesn't matter," I say. "Just like with this bike, I'll fix it. No matter how long it takes."

Letters to Mia

First birthday

Dear Mia,

It's your first birthday. I've decided I'm going to write you a letter every year on your birthday. It seems silly since you can't even read yet. Can you talk? Have you said your first word? Was it Daddy? I'm sure it wasn't Mommy. Why would it be? You have no idea what that is, I left. This is harder than I thought. There's too much to say and not enough words. So I'll write the four that have been a constant drumbeat in my heart since I walked out of that hospital.

Forgive me.

I'm sorry.

Until next year,

Your mom

CHAPTER EIGHTEEN

DEVLYN

"READY?" GARRETT ASKS, his hand on the knob of his front door.

It's our last day together, and he wanted to make it special and take me out. Since we aren't public knowledge in Eden Valley, he decided a day trip to Dahlonega, Georgia's very own Napa Valley would do the trick. There are wineries and vineyards, and a quaint little town, and it's the perfect spot for us to have our first real date.

Truthfully, I think Garrett picked it more for me. I don't think I've ever seen the man drink a glass of wine in his life. I grab my purse, checking for my sunglasses. Garrett's mapped out a back way to get there so we don't have to drive through the prying eyes of town.

"Almost," I say.

He just smiles at me. He must be used to waiting on a girl to get ready with Mia. A loud knock on the front door makes me jump. My eyes dart to him. He glances through the peephole. "It's the mayor," he mouths to me.

Another loud knock.

"Bedroom," I mouth back, looking around for any evidence that needs to go hide in the bedroom with me. No bras or panties lying about, I think we're good. Tiptoeing, I disappear into his bedroom, quietly closing the door behind me, but I keep my ear to the door to listen.

"How can I help you this morning?" Garrett says.

"The pavilion," I hear the mayor say. "I was at the site this morning. There's not a board or nail in sight. Fourth of July is a month away."

"It will be done," Garrett says.

"I don't see how," the mayor says. "I stopped by the hardware store, and they told me you've been off. I thought perhaps you were on site, but all I found were the squirrels. If you're no longer interested in the project, then . . ."

Oh no! Garrett can't lose this project. I know he relies on the extra money. My hand goes to the knob of the bedroom door. How dare he threaten Garrett? Just wait until the next time he comes in the diner for coffee, black crap is what he'll get.

"Of course I am," Garrett says. "I'll be out there tomorrow."

"What about today?" the mayor asks.

"Tomorrow," Garrett says with a tone to his voice that says not to mess with him.

Stupid man. I pull out my phone and send Garrett a text.

Go work. I'll see you tonight.

I hear the ding from my hiding spot. His response is quick.

No.

Stubborn! My fingers type quickly.

I'm sneaking out the back. Go to work.

"Shit," I hear Garrett say, knowing that's his response to my text.

"Problem?" the mayor asks.

"No," Garrett says, but his text orders me to *Stay put!*

"So you'll start today?" the mayor asks.

I hear him give an aggravated yes, adding that he'll be out there in a little bit. Once the door slams shut, I open his bedroom door, finding Garrett right in front of me.

"Thought I might find your sexy ass crawling out my bedroom window," he says, with just a hint of irritation.

"You can't lose this job," I say.

"The mayor is a douchebag. He likes to throw his weight around sometimes. He would've backed off."

"Maybe so," I say. "But I couldn't let you risk it for me." He takes me in his arms, swatting my ass. I flash him a smile. "You can spank me later."

I GLANCE AT Garrett as he walks into his store, needing to get a few things before he heads to the Falls. We staggered when we left, but I guess I walk slower than him, probably something to do with the spanking I got before I left. Mental note—don't promise the man ass if you want him to get anything else done.

His smile lets me know he's thinking about the same thing. I head for the diner feeling a tad bit naked without my tutu. I hadn't packed one. I suppose I could've gone home to get one, but I need to conserve my energy. Garrett's a machine.

Opening the door, I step inside, coming to an abrupt halt, the door slamming me in my already sensitive rear end. Only one person does that to me.

"Devlyn," my mom says, raising an eyebrow at me. She's sitting at the counter, wearing a flowery dress, her gray hair up in a bun. She's the type of woman that's always put together, that makes the rest of us look bad. "Running late today?"

I'm twelve years old again, standing tardy in front of class. Only this time it's my customers staring at me. "No, actually I was supposed to be off today, but decided to come in for a few hours. What are you doing here?" I ask, giving her a kiss on the cheek.

"Surprising you," she says. I love my mother, but she and I don't see eye-to-eye a lot. Her blue eyes tend to only pass judgment. "Scott called me."

"Oh, I was going to tell you about that, I just . . ."

"I had to hear from him that you two have broken up."

"Why'd he call you?"

"He wanted to say goodbye, wish your father and I well. He's a nice young man. Why on Earth would you turn down his proposal?"

Everyone in the place seems to collectively lean in a little closer. "Mom, can we not get into this here?"

"Fine, fine," she says, waving her hands. "I just figured I better check on my daughter. Make sure you were alright."

"That's sweet, Mom," I say, not adding that I wish she would've called first. "You didn't need to drive here. I'm good."

"Well, I'm here now," she says. "We can spend some time together before we drive back tomorrow. Your father's around town somewhere."

"You're staying the night?" I ask.

Her blue eyes study me. "Of course, you know it's nearly six hours home."

I know that means they plan on staying with me. Only problem is: I plan on staying with Garrett. My phone dings, and I pull it out. It's from Garrett.

Your dad's in my store!

With my mom's eyes on me, I stuff it back in my pocket. "Devlyn, you're being very rude. You haven't seen us since . . ."

"I'm sorry, Mom," I say, hugging her. "You just surprised me. I had plans tonight. Of course, I'm happy to see you. Let me get you a drink or something."

She watches me behind the counter as I place her favorite cherry danish in front of her. "You certainly don't look heartbroken," she says.

"Because I'm not," I say. "Really, Mom, you don't need to worry."

Picking up her fork, she gives the place a glance. "Business looks good."

Thank God, she's changed the topic. Work is always a safe conversation for us. After all, Biscuit Girl was her baby before it was mine, we both love and cherish the place. "You miss it?" I ask.

"A little," she says with a smile. "There's this little place on the beach just a few blocks from our house. Your father and I walk by it almost every day. We always talk about how it would be the perfect location for a place like Biscuit Girl."

"You and Daddy just retired," I say. "Surely, you don't want to start all over?"

"Well, we were thinking more about you. This place runs like a well-oiled machine. Maybe a new challenge? Biscuit Girl Two?" She raises her eyebrows. "Plus, we'd get to see you more."

"Mom, I really don't think . . ."

"Just come look at the place sometime. I can send you some pictures."

"I'm not interested in moving right now," I say, as the door to the diner opens, the mail carrier, Trudy, walking in.

"Mrs. Drake, is that you?" she says, holding her arms open. "I just ran into that handsome husband of yours. I had to come right over and say hello. Changed my route and everything."

Her route? Town square? She did the stores out of order. Someone call the mail carrier authorities! She places my mail down on the counter, leaning in and saying, "Interesting that you're back at work today, too." My mom's eyes go between Trudy and me. "Same off days as Garrett Hollis."

My heart starts to thunder against my chest. This is exactly what Garrett didn't want to happen. Add my mother glaring at me, and I'm about to have a coronary. I always thought if I had a heart condition, it would be because of my love for anything made from dough, not because of my love of the male species. "Not sure what you're talking about," I say. "Has Garrett been off? He's not sick or anything?"

Trudy smiles. "So it's a coincidence that you two have been off the same days, and the day he comes back to work, you do, too?"

"I worked yesterday," I say, knowing it was only for a few hours, but hoping it shuts her the hell up.

"I must have been mistaken," Trudy says, giving my mother another hug.

Hell almighty, I walk to the back, needing a minute. Placing my hands on the counter, my head is spinning. I've got to warn Garrett. He's going to go apeshit crazy.

"I told Trudy to keep her crazy theories to herself," my mother says, startling me.

Gripping the edge of the counter, I try to steady myself, feeling sure I'm sweating. I swear, I'm going to get Botox under my arms, just so I can look innocent when I'm guilty as sin. "Thanks, Mom,

I'm not sure . . ."

"Please don't lie to my face, Devlyn. I raised you better than that."

She also raised me not to have premarital sex. Guess she failed on both fronts. "Do you think Trudy will keep her mouth shut?"

"She will because I asked her to," my mom says.

"Thank you," I say, looking down at my white knuckles.

"What are you doing?" she says. "Is this why you broke up with Scott?"

I can't answer her. I couldn't marry Scott because I didn't love him. I didn't love him because my heart has always belonged to Garrett.

She sighs deeply. "You're wasting your time with Garrett."

"Mom," I say, my voice as hard as I've ever heard it.

"Your clock is ticking. I'd like to have grandchildren. It's time to find a husband, not be . . ." she waves her hand in the air.

"We aren't just," I say, waving my hand back at her.

"Then why is it a big secret?" she asks.

"We haven't told Mia yet."

"Ah, yes, *Mia*," she says.

"What the hell does that mean, Mother?" I snap.

"It means that Garrett Hollis has no intention of telling Mia anything. She's been the excuse all these years, right? The reason he didn't notice you, date you, have any interest at all. The reason you had to help him, stick around, let him use you, string you along."

My eyes well up in angry tears. "He didn't do that. It was my choice to help, to be there for him and Mia. I wouldn't change that."

"Not even to have your own child?" All the air leaves my chest. My mother releases a deep breath, stepping toward me, her hand landing on top of mine. "I'm sorry, Devlyn. It's just, I've seen you cry over him too many times. It needs to stop." I look up at her, knowing she loves me. Her head shakes. "I'm wasting my breath."

"You are," I say.

My phone dings again, but I don't reach for it. She raises a knowing eyebrow then says, "Better go find your father."

I nod but don't immediately follow her. My mother is exhausting. Is that some kind of rule of motherhood? All mothers have to exhaust their daughters? She's wrong. Garrett wouldn't use me, if for no other reason than we are friends. Unless he doesn't even know he's doing it? Like all those times he hurt me before. He didn't realize it.

I shake my head. I'm not going to let my mother plant little seeds of doubt because if I do, pretty soon they will turn into big weeds. Nothing is going to ruin this. Walking back out into the diner, I smile at a few customers before my eyes find my mother standing by the town gazebo with her finger in Garrett's face.

From the looks of things, whatever she's giving him, he's giving it right back. If we want to keep things private for a few more days, everyone better calm down. Not wanting to make it worse, I stay inside my diner, making small talk with my customers, trying to keep them from noticing my mom and Garrett, but every few seconds my eyes go back outside. I'm sure it was just a few minutes, but it seemed like hours. Finally, my mother walks off, leaving Garrett standing alone, his hands stuffed in the front pocket of his jeans.

I want to run out to him, hug him, tell him to ignore her, but I can't. Pulling out my phone, I see his last text to me. He's wondering if I need to cancel our last night together, telling me he'll understand if I have to because my parents are here, but letting me know how much he's going to miss me.

When I look back up from my phone, Garrett's staring at me from the gazebo. He's a smart guy, he knows he's not my mom's favorite person. I'm just hoping he doesn't give stock to any of her concerns that he's not good for me. Quickly, I type a reply.

Later.

It's vague, but I need a little time to figure out what to do about my parents. I can't exactly say I'm going to have crazy mind-blowing sex with Garrett, so feel free to make yourselves at home! I'll see you in the morning if I can walk!

I look up, hoping Garrett understands. He gives me a little nod before turning and walking away.

EDEN VALLEY HAS a lot of charm going for it, but there is nothing charming about the summer heat. Pulling a wagon, I step onto the wooden walkway that leads to the Falls. I look back at the jugs of water, lemonade, tea, and plastic cups I have packed, hoping the ice hasn't evaporated already. I know Garrett and his crew must be hot as hell out working in the blazing sun, so I packed a little refreshment for them. It gives me a good excuse to come see Garrett.

The wheels of the wagon make a steady beat as they bump against the wood, almost like a heartbeat. The sun beats down against my pale skin. Thank God, I'd put on sunscreen in anticipation of our date today. Otherwise, this short trek to the Falls would've fried me. That's about the only thing that's gone right today.

The mayor, Trudy, my mother—it's one big disaster waiting to happen, and I've got to tell Garrett our little secret could be the town's next headline. I doubt sweet tea and lemonade are going to soothe that blow.

Hearing hammers, I come through the trees and stop. There's a half dozen men out here, but my eyes find Garrett. Like my whole life, I only have eyes for him. If there were a supermarket of men, the only aisle I'd visit would be his.

His shirt is drenched in sweat, clinging to the muscles of his back. He's helping to carry a long, very heavy looking piece of wood, braced up on his shoulder. To be that wood, to have him throw me over his shoulder, swat my booty, and take me to bed. A bead of sweat slowly rolls down my neck, as suddenly it's even hotter.

One of the other guys nods in my direction. Garrett looks over his shoulder, a huge, sexy grin on his face. I roll the wagon out a little further as a few of the guys come over, and I start pouring them each something cold to drink. Garrett hangs back until the others have their drinks and find spots in the shade to relax a minute.

He walks toward me, lifting his shirt up a little to wipe his face. I lick my lips at the glimpse of the muscles of his abs, my legs clenching together. "Got a beer in there?" he asks, motioning to my wagon. My head shakes, unable to speak at the sight of him all sweating and tan and sexy as hell. He bends down, grabbing a cup and pouring some lemonade for himself. I realize I poured drinks for everyone else and not him, and I take the pitcher from him, finishing up. He grins at me. "Thanks for this," he glances around, lowering his voice a little. "You're very sweet."

The way he says it, the look in his eyes, we both know he's referring to something naughtier. I feel the heat rise to my cheeks. "It looks good," I say, eyeing the piles of wood, then feeling stupid because they just got started, and it's basically a floor at this point. I really need to learn how to act around him in public now. He doesn't make it easy when he's constantly looking at me like he can't wait to rip my clothes off. He glances over his shoulder then raises an eyebrow to me. "My mom knows."

"Yeah, I got that while she was screaming at me earlier."

"I'm sorry. I didn't know they were coming," I say, looking at my feet. "Trudy suspects, too."

"Your mom told me that, too."

My eyes dart up. "Crap, she's got a big mouth." He nods in agreement. "My mom doesn't think she'll say anything."

"I think she's right," he says. "Trudy's nosy, always in everyone's business, but she's never spread any gossip to me about anyone else."

"Come to think of it, me, either. Damn, can you imagine what she knows?"

He grins a little. "It's just a few days until Mia's birthday, and then I'll tell her about us."

"It will be okay," I say, looking around at the other guys getting back to work, and reach down for the handle of the wagon, knowing our time is running out. "I should probably spend the night with my parents," I say, not even trying to hide my disappointment.

He nods. "I invited them over for dinner."

"You what?" I cry out too loudly, noticing we're attracting some stares.

"I thought if I invited them over, if they saw us together, it might help calm your mom down."

Garrett is my own personal sun, making me hot and melting my heart. "That's a great idea. I can cook or maybe we could grill something."

His head shakes. "She turned me down." A lump forms in my throat, my eyes watering. His hand reaches out, but quickly he pulls back.

"Why would she do that?" I ask.

"To her, I will always be the teenage boy who knocked some girl up. Not good enough for her daughter."

There's something about his voice that scares me. He can't possibly believe there's one ounce of truth to that.

He glances around. "I've got to get back."

"Sure," I say. "I understand."

That's the thing about me and Garrett. I always understand. I understood when he fell for Sheena. Every guy in town was in love with her. I hated it, but I understood. I understood when she got pregnant, and he stepped up. It broke my heart, but I understood. I understood all those years why we were just friends. He had Mia to take care of. And now, I understand he can't talk, get into it all.

I understand so hard it hurts.

CHAPTER NINETEEN

GARRETT

IS IT BREAKING and entering if you slept with the woman last night? Devlyn didn't technically invite me over, and I don't plan on staying. I know her parents are in town, but I wanted to do something special for her. I helped myself to the key she keeps hidden under the pot in her front flowerbed and came inside to leave her a little surprise.

Yellow and purple wildflowers from the Falls and a bottle of wine. We might have missed our trip to the wineries, but that doesn't mean she can't still have a little taste. I look back at her coffee table where I have everything set up, hoping it makes her smile since she looked so upset over the argument with her mother.

At some point, I've got to fix things with her mother. The only way I know to do that is to take good care of Devlyn and hope that once Mrs. Drake sees that, she'll remove the stick from up her ass. She's not my favorite person, but for Devlyn's sake, I have to try.

I hear the front door open. Not wanting to scare her, I walk to the doorway of the den. I have every intention of calling out to her, but she walks through the front door, drops her purse on a foyer table then does this weird thing and whips her bra out from the sleeve of her shirt, twirling it around.

Instead of saying hello, I bust out laughing. She jumps a little and throws her bra at me like it's a weapon of mass destruction. I only laugh harder. "What if I was a burglar? Your bra is going to stop me?"

She giggles, swatting at me. "What are you doing here? You scared me half to death."

"What were you doing?" I ask, motioning behind my back and

tugging at my shirtsleeve like she did. "Do all women rip their bras off first thing when walking through the door?"

"Yes," she laughs. "You try wearing one of these damn things in the dead of summer. Torture."

I pull her to me, kissing her, not caring that I'm still sweaty from my workday. She doesn't care either, kissing me back. She reaches for my face. "What are you doing here?" I move us a little, angling her toward the den so she can look inside. She leaves my arms, walking toward her surprise, her fingers lightly touching the petals of the flowers.

"Since our date got cancelled," I say, shrugging a little. "I wasn't planning on staying. I know you need to spend time with your mom and dad. I was just going to leave them and go."

She turns back to me, her bottom lip pulled between her teeth. She loves my little surprise. There is nothing high maintenance about Devlyn. The smallest, simplest things make her happy. Makes it easy on us guys, but the thing is, it just makes me want to do more for her. She takes my hand, leading me down the hallway toward her bedroom. Of course, I'm hoping to head straight to her bed, but instead she takes me into her master bathroom, turning on the shower.

Like the rest of her house, her bathroom has vintage touches—white and black marble floor, subway tile, a clawfoot tub. For a second, I wonder where her parents are, but if she's not worried about it, then I'm not going to, either. Without a word, she reaches for the bottom of my shirt. I help her, lifting it over my head, and she drops it to the floor. Then she does the same with her shirt. Soon all our clothes are beside each other on the marble. I'm sure I've never stopped and noticed that before. Our clothes all twisted together, like that's the way they were designed to be.

Holding hands, we step into the shower, closing the glass door behind us. It's just a simple shower, no fancy nozzles or shower heads, but there's nothing simple about the woman standing before me. This is anything but simple. Today proved that.

She's had a hard day.

I need to take care of her, and not just her pussy. Running my hands down her arms, I kiss her forehead, letting my lips linger. I used to kiss Mia's bumps and bruises when she was little. I'm hoping my kiss will do the same thing to soothe Devlyn's mind. Women think too damn much, and I can tell her brain is working overtime.

She leans her head against my chest, the water cascading down over us. We just stand there, hugging each other. Sometimes that's all your woman needs—a hug. Her hands grip my shoulders, pulling me tighter.

I know I'm stabbing her with my dick, but she's naked and pressed up against me. I can't really help it. Who am I kidding? I've been hard since I walked into her house. Thinking about her gives me a boner these days.

She breaks the silence. "I like showering with you."

I grind into her a little bit. "Me, too." She smiles, but I can tell she's not in the mood for sexual innuendo. I know her, and she's only this quiet for two reasons. Either she's sad or she's really mad. If she's just a little mad, she might throw a cuss word around, but when she's really pissed off, she goes quiet. I'm betting tonight she's a little of both.

The last thing I want is her fighting with her mom over me. "Where are your parents?" I ask, running my fingers through her wet hair.

"They left," she says. "It didn't end well."

"Oh, baby," I say, realizing the water running down her face isn't all from the shower. "I know how much they mean to you. I'll call them."

"No," she says. "I just want to crawl into bed with you and not come out until morning."

I WOKE UP alone in Devlyn's bed. Sometimes the diner requires her to go in early, I know that, but I hope she's feeling better. She was pretty quiet last night. We didn't have sex. Instead, she curled up beside me in her bed, and I held her. Her dad called her pretty late, telling her they'd arrived home safely. I overheard Devlyn tell him she loved him, and I assume by the couple tears that rolled down her cheeks, he told her the same.

I got an early start this morning, too, working at the Falls, wanting to beat the heat. Then I came home to shower and meet my dad and Mia. A car horn alerts me to their arrival. She's only been gone a couple days, but it's longer than she's ever been away before. I'm not sure either one of us is ready for this whole college thing.

Opening the front door, I see Mia getting out of the car, waving to me. My dad's a little slower getting out. "That one's got a lead foot," my dad says, stretching his back out.

"I didn't get a ticket," Mia says proudly, cocking her chin up.

"Mia," I say, trying to put on my tough dad voice, but I just end up hugging her.

She squeezes me, looking over at my dad. "Tell him," he says.

She groans then whispers, "I got pulled over." My dad clears his throat. "Twice."

My dad must see the smoke coming out of my ears because he walks over, placing his hand on my shoulder. "Talked the cop out of the ticket both times."

"How'd you manage that?" I ask.

"I had an elderly, sick grandfather in the car," she says, smiling.

My dad fake coughs. "Seriously, Dad? You're encouraging her! You know what you would've done to me when I was her age?"

He raises an eyebrow to me. "Speeding ticket versus . . ." He motions to Mia, who does a little curtsy. "Now I love my granddaughter, but I do believe you tested my abilities as a father more than a little speeding ticket could."

"Fine," I say, "but no car until after your birthday, and if I catch you driving like that again, there will be hell to pay."

She nods, giving my dad a little thank you smile, knowing he saved her ass. I hear another car beep, this one coming from Mia's friend, Penny. Penny's out of the car in lightning speed, and they are chatting even faster. I know they talked, Snapchatted, or some shit while she was gone, so I don't get the urgency in their conversation. It's not like they haven't spoken in weeks.

"Oh my God, I have so much to tell you," Penny says. "There was a kissing booth at . . ."

"You mean mono waiting to happen," Mia jokes.

Penny rolls her eyes. "Anyway, that guy was asking about you."

Mia's eyes get huge, stopping Penny, whose nose wrinkles up, realizing what's she's done. There are a few words that pique any father's interest, and "guy" is one of them. Drugs, sex, and condoms are a few others.

"I'll see you later, Dad," Mia says, shoving Penny back into her car.

"Dinner?" I call out.

"Yep," she says. "Seven o'clock."

"Six," I say.

She flashes me an agreeable smile before they are off. Shaking my head, I turn to my dad and ask, "So do you know anything about this guy?"

"Some," he says. "Don't think Mia realizes that my hearing is still good."

"Well?" I urge, taking the bags out of the car.

"He lives one town over. Mia doesn't want to get involved with someone before leaving for school, but finds him very, very hot, apparently."

"Shit," I say.

"That's not the worst part," he says. "He's twenty."

"What the hell?"

"That's why she hasn't told you about him."

"You got this kid's name?"

"Nope," he says. "But don't worry. I think Mia's flattered more than anything. She's enjoying the attention, is all."

"You sure about that?" I ask.

He nods. "How are things here?"

Suddenly, my dad is being coy. "Good."

Smiling, he starts to walk toward his house. I follow him, carrying his bags. "I need to go see your mother."

Placing his bags down on his porch, I say, "Thanks again for taking Mia. It was nice for you and her to get away together, and Devlyn and I needed the time."

"No problem," he says.

This isn't like my dad. He was an attorney—asking questions is built into his DNA. "Are you not going to ask me?"

"I don't need to," he says, chuckling. "It's written all over your face." He pinches my cheek then gives it a playful slap.

"Dad," I groan, realizing how much I sound like Mia. "I'm going to talk to Mia after her birthday. I want her party to be all about her, not my and Devlyn's coming out party."

He nods in agreement, and we catch up a little bit before he heads out to visit my mom. I watch him as he leaves. She's been gone for years, but he's completely devoted to her still. Maybe Mia should start a dating experiment for him. My gut twists at the thought. I'm a grown man in my thirties and the thought of my father with another woman makes me uncomfortable.

What's Mia's reaction going to be?

Only a few days until I find out, but the truth is, her reaction won't make or break my relationship with Devlyn. It's happening, however Mia feels about it.

I'll help her through it.

CHAPTER TWENTY

DEVLYN

IT'S PARTY DAY, and Garrett's been decorating the backyard all morning, stringing lights across the yard, setting up tables and chairs, a makeshift dance floor. He's gone all out for Mia's eighteenth. It's sweet. I baked a few of Mia's favorites to help him out and came by early to drop them off.

Truthfully, I came by early hoping Mia would be out and Garrett and I could have a little time together, but no such luck. Since Mia's been back, we've shared a secret kiss or two in my kitchen, a couple hours here or there when she's out with friends. Clock watching is not fun, so a part of me can't wait to tell her. Another part of me isn't as excited to become public.

Right now, it feels like Garrett and I have these stolen moments. These little pieces of time that are just ours.

Stolen moments.

That's what each kiss is. Moments we steal from life, from reality. I just hope we don't get caught. I just hope the punishment isn't too great.

If Mia's super upset, then what? What will Garrett's reaction be? Will he give me up? Maybe not right away, but eventually would he cave to the will of his daughter if she can't accept me? Mia and I get along right now, but will that change if she starts to see me as her dad's girlfriend?

"This is going to be epic!" Mia cries, hugging both Garrett's neck and mine. "Everyone's coming."

She's right. It seems like the whole town is coming out to celebrate. This birthday means a lot to Garrett and Mia. They made it. It means a lot to the people here, too. The ones who taught Mia, gave Garrett odd jobs when they really didn't need anything done just to help him out, the ones who left boxes of diapers on his porch just because. It's a happy ending to what could have been a disaster.

"Are you bringing Scott?" Mia asks. "Is he coming to visit? I haven't seen him in a while."

"Umm." I will my eyes not to go to Garrett. It would look weird if he answered for me. "No, we broke up."

"You broke up with Scott? I didn't know," she says, looking at Garrett. "Dad, did you know? Why didn't you tell me? Now I just look stupid."

"I didn't know," Garrett says, and I can tell he's trying to decide if that's the right answer or not.

"No one really knows yet," I say.

She glances at her dad then back to me. "Sorry."

Giving her a smile to let her know I'm good, I'm desperate to change the subject and ask, "What are you wearing for the party?"

"It's between the pink dress or the blue romper," she says.

I reach into my purse, pulling out a little gift box. "Maybe this will help you decide."

Her eyes light up, and Garrett flashes me a smile. "Thank you!" Mia says before she even opens it.

"You're welcome," I say, my palms starting to sweat a little, hoping she likes them as much now as she did in the store.

I watch her slowly untie the ribbon, feeling Garrett's eyes on me. He doesn't know what I got her. When she lifts the lid of the black box, she screeches at the sight of the pearl earrings. "How'd you know?"

She hugs me tightly, and Garrett mouths to me, "Too much."

I shrug. It's a big birthday. She doesn't have a mother to pass down jewelry to her, so I wanted to do something special. Releasing me, she starts to take them out, slipping one in each ear, then she holds her hair up, showing them off.

"Very pretty," Garrett says.

"I love them," Mia says, hugging me again. She pulls back, taking my hands in hers. "Pink dress!"

"Definitely," I say, laughing.

"With my hair up," she says, heading toward the back door. "I'm going to get ready. Tonight's going to be perfect."

She disappears into the house. Garrett steps closer to me but only locks his pinkie finger with mine, glancing back at the house. Damn windows!

God, the way he's looking at me has my panties soaked. "I should go, too," I say, my mouth dry. "Need to shower and get ready myself."

His finger tightens around mine. Is it me that has him wrapped around my little finger? Or is it him that has me wrapped around his?

"You look amazing," he says. "Stay."

I came straight from the diner. I'm a hot mess minus the hot. "What if I promise to come back without any panties on?"

"Thought you didn't believe in promises?" he asks with the cutest little smirk.

"This one I'll keep."

A GUST OF wind blows, and I hold my dress down. This is why promises are a bad idea. It has to be the windiest night in the history of Eden Valley. My knee-length polka dot dress has been whipping around all night. It's only a matter of time before I moon all of Mia's friends.

Looks like there's not a single person who didn't show up. Everyone is here to celebrate. The yard looks great with the twinkling white lights, the music is going, food and drinks are flowing, and most importantly, Mia looks so happy. If only my damn dress would cooperate.

"Problem?" Garrett whispers in my ear from behind me.

"I blame you for this," I say.

"I'm in charge of the weather?"

"No, you're in charge of my recent change in libido," I whisper.

"Hence the absence of underwear." He chuckles, and I glance around at the sea of teenagers dancing like lunatics.

"Wish we could dance," he says quietly.

"Me, too," I say. "Like in my diner that night."

"I left thinking you weren't interested," he says.

"And I thought I was making something out of nothing, again."

His head tilts. "You came to my house, though. What made you do that?" he asks. "You never took that risk before."

"That was pretty ballsy," I say, smiling. "Something just felt different that night. I tried to tell myself it was all in my head, but for once I let my heart win."

"You have no idea how bad I want to kiss you right now," he says.

I smile. I seem to be doing a lot of that lately. I've always been a happy person by nature, but this is different. This is more than happy. It's happy with a side of bliss.

"Dad, can we do the cake?" Mia yells over to us.

He gives her a nod before disappearing into the house. I go to clear a spot on the table, finding Garrett's dad, who has had the same idea. "Mr. Hollis," I say, only making brief eye contact.

He takes hold of my hand in that way that only an old, wise person can, settling me. "Thank you for loving my son and my granddaughter," he says.

My throat closes up. I've never said those words to Garrett. I hope to soon. Well, I hope he says them first. No one's ever thanked me for loving them before, so I'm not sure how to respond. Good thing that he keeps talking. Must be the old lawyer in him—long-winded.

"Warms my heart to finally see Garrett in love again."

"He said that?" I blurt out.

He laughs. "Let's just say I have a hunch."

The backdoor to the house opens as Garrett appears with the three-tiered pink and white cake with eighteen unlit candles on the top. Mia insisted on having eighteen candles and not doing a number eighteen. That, apparently, is cheating.

Garrett places the cake down on the table, and everyone starts to gather around. Garrett stands next to Mia behind the cake, and his father, Edward, off to the side. The rest of the guests, including me, are on the other side of the table.

"Speech," Penny calls out from the crowd.

Mia giggles and looks up at her dad. "Think it's your turn to give the speech. Last time mine caused quite a ruckus."

Everyone laughs, and Garrett shakes his head at her before looking out at everyone. "The day Mia was born . . ." Garrett's eyes catch mine, and I know he's never told her the story of her birth. He avoids thinking of Sheena at all costs, so that includes Mia's birth. I give him an encouraging nod.

He looks at his daughter, who's eager as ever for the information, and begins to describe the day in perfect detail, everything from the weather to the shirt he was wearing to what he had for breakfast. You'd think some of the memory would have faded with time, but it hasn't. It's vivid and clear, and he tells it with such emotion that I feel like I was in the room. Everyone standing in his yard knows how the story takes a sad turn in the days that follow, but right now the only focus is the joy.

"The day Mia was born I fell in love on the spot," Garrett says. "I was so happy to hear Mia cry. No one told me I'd spend the rest of my life trying to make sure she never cried again."

"Daddy," she whispers, and he reaches down, gently wiping a tear from her cheek. "Happy birthday, baby girl!"

She hugs his neck. Her granddad lights the candles as her friends start a very loud, very out of tune version of "Happy Birthday." Mia glances at her dad then leans over, blowing out her candles to a round of applause.

Garrett grabs a knife, examining the cake, trying to decide where would be the best place to start cutting. Finally, he removes the entire top layer, plops it down on a plate, and hands the whole thing to Mia, who just laughs then gives me a wave. "Devlyn, help please!"

Stepping up, Garrett passes me the knife. I swear that simple act is enough to let everyone know we are sleeping together. Garrett hands me a plate, and I slide a piece of cake onto it. Over and over again, we continue. I don't look at him. We don't speak, yet I feel completely transparent.

When everyone has cake and has left the table, Garrett hands me a piece. "What do you think Mia wished for?" I ask.

"I don't know what she wished for," he says, "but I wished that for her next birthday, you'll be standing with us."

My breath catches. I wish that, too. I inch a little closer, but his eyes leave mine. Something has his attention and whatever it is, his blue eyes are dark, cold. Mia walks over to us, her eyes locked over my shoulder, but her eyes look intrigued, hopeful. She touches Garrett's elbow.

"Daddy, who's that?" she whispers.

I go to look over my shoulder, but Garrett grabs my hand. "Take Mia and go inside."

"What is it?"

Mia takes a few steps away from us. "She looks like me."

"Now Devlyn," Garrett barks. "Take Mia inside!"

Turning around, my body immediately freezes. It can't be! The woman is walking right toward her, a wooden box with a red bow tied around it in her hands.

"Is that my mother?" Mia asks, without taking her eyes off Sheena.

"Damn it!" Garrett mutters, glancing around at all the party guests, who've gone quiet, preparing to watch the train wreck. The music stops, too. Garrett grabs Mia by the shoulders. "Inside."

"But . . ." She looks back at her father. She's a complete daddy's girl, but she also knows when not to mess with him. His own father steps to his side, some sort of united front. Sheena's eyes narrow at Edward Hollis, no love lost between them.

"Go inside with Devlyn," he orders Mia again, but my legs aren't working. "Devlyn!" he says my name like it's some kind of warning.

I wrap one arm around Mia, attempting to shelter her, then walk her toward the house. My legs feel like I'm wearing concrete shoes. Mia stops several times, looking back at her mother, but each time, I encourage her forward. I open the door, she goes inside, and then it's my turn to take a look back.

Sheena steps to Garrett.

This is Garrett's nightmare, I know that.

What he doesn't know is that it's mine, too.

Letters to Mia
Eighteenth Birthday

Dear Mia,

I realize these birthday letters have been more for me than you. A way for me to feel close to you on the day you were born. I suppose your biggest question has to be—Why'd I leave?

I'm going to do the best I can to explain. Now that you're a little older, perhaps you can imagine what it was like for me.

This is the letter I've avoided writing. Our goodbye letter.

When you're in the middle of the scariest thing that could ever happen to you, other things don't seem as daunting, like a teenage girl traveling alone from New York to small town Georgia, but that's what I did.

I was pregnant.

I hadn't told your father. In fact, I'd avoided writing or talking to Garrett for a month. He probably thought I hated him. It took me two solid weeks before I told my parents. They were happy I hadn't told Garrett. Their solution was simple. My school had a fall break in October. I'd have an abortion, rest, then go back to school without missing a beat. Except my baby's heartbeat.

I told them I would do it. I promised them, but as the day got closer, I just couldn't, not without telling Garrett. So I ran away. I can't tell you how I did it. It's a blur. And I can't tell you much at all about how I got back to Eden Valley.

All I know is that it was dark when I arrived back on his doorstep. He answered the door in his shorts and t-shirt. Tears streaming down my face, I told him I'd run away, and that I was pregnant.

To his credit, he didn't pass out. He didn't curse. He had to be scared out of his mind, but he pulled me into his arms and held me until I stopped shaking.

I told him my parents insisted I have an abortion, and then I glanced up at him, trying to gauge if that's what he wanted, too. I explained I just couldn't do it without talking to him.

God, did we talk—all night. I'd shown up out of the blue. There was no hiding this from his parents. They yelled like my parents. They cried like my parents. Unlike my parents, they told Garrett how much they loved him.

He told me how much he loved me, how he wanted to keep you.

I told him I wanted to keep you, too. At the time, I didn't know I was lying. I wanted it to be true.

His parents helped us. His mom took me to appointments. I stayed with them. I went to school there. They promised to help Garrett and I finish school. They even tried to help me with my parents, but my parents wanted none of it.

It wasn't easy. Nothing about those months was easy. Kids at school stared at me. I had no friends other than Garrett. I know it wasn't easy on him, either. The town's golden boy, the mayor's son, knocked up some girl. For a long time, the only person that talked to us at school was Devlyn. She'd sit with us at lunch, walk the halls by our sides. Garrett told me her parents warned her to keep her distance, but she never did. Still, she was Garrett's friend, not mine.

We were going to finish out our junior year, have you, then his mom was going to watch you our senior year. That was the plan. No one was insisting we get married, even though Garrett asked me if I wanted to. It was sweet he asked, but I felt too overwhelmed to even consider it.

So a week past my due date, you were born. Garrett picked out your name. I thought it was all wrong. Mia means "wished for child," and you were anything but.

The labor was twenty-two hours of non-stop pain. Despite what everyone said, I didn't get any drugs. I think my subconscious must've known what I was going to do and thought I deserved the pain.

Everyone told me breastfeeding was best, but I refused to try. Just told your dad to give you a bottle. Told him I didn't want you hanging off me. I shut down, blocking everyone and everything out. Then your grandmother told me that she'd called my parents and that they'd come to see me.

I have to wonder now if his mom's decision to call them, my decision to let them in, changed the course of my life, or if it's simply easier for me to blame them for something I wanted. If they simply became my excuse.

Garrett and his family left as my parents walked in. I watched their eyes as they saw their granddaughter for the first time, looking for signs of love. I thought I saw a flicker of something, but it was small, detached. Instead, their eyes quickly landed on me, and they both began to cry.

My mom sobbed as she told me how much you looked like me.

Garrett had told me the same thing. I couldn't see it.

My dad teared up as he told me how much he'd missed me.

There was no apology for how they'd acted. There was no apology from me, either.

My dad told me not to worry, that everyone back in New York thought I'd been sent away to boarding school, that no one knew about my little mistake.

That should've sparked anger in me, but there was nothing.

Mom went on to tell me that they'd had a spot saved for me at a school in Scotland, that I could leave whenever I was ready. We apparently had some distant family there.

I was tired, too tired, and closed my eyes.

Then my mother started again with her "do the right thing" speech. With her "it's not too late to have the life you wanted" speech. She wanted me to give away my baby, but I knew I couldn't do that to your dad. Couldn't do it to your grandparents, who'd been nothing but kind. They loved you.

My dad tried to push the conversation further, but my mother held him off. They'd already planted the seed, they just had to wait for it to sprout.

Just two days after pushing you out of my body, I was supposed to leave the hospital, be a mother. Garrett helped me out of the hospital bed, giving me a long hug. Some of the details have faded over the years, but not that one. That one I held onto. It was the last time I felt his arms around me, the beat of his heart against my cheek, the last time I felt truly loved.

He handed me clothes, and I went into the hospital bathroom. There was one single hook, no shelves, no place to put my clothes unless I wanted to put them on the floor or toilet. There was no mirror, which was a good thing. I didn't want to look at myself. Stripping out of my hospital gown and looking down at my post-pregnancy body was enough of a shock.

My breasts were swollen and now lined with stretch marks. My once tight stomach was squishy like Jell-O. I didn't recognize my own skin. I recoiled when Garrett asked me if I needed help, thinking he wouldn't ever want to see the aftermath of pregnancy. He'd never again be attracted to me, want me. I heard a knock at the door, and your dad announced that DD *had stopped in to see you.*

I couldn't seem to catch a break. I stayed in the bathroom, not wanting to see anyone else. Closing my eyes, I took a deep breath, telling myself I could do this. Women had been doing this for ages. I was a mother. I'd figure it out.

I started to sweat and felt my legs wobble. I forced myself to put on my clothes, slipping the loose-fitting dress Garrett's mom had bought me to go home in over my head. Mom clothes.

Clothes used to make me feel better, but that was gone, too. My head started to spin. My heart raced, and I leaned against the door for support. What was happening?

I wasn't ready to be a mother. I couldn't do it. I couldn't even get dressed.

Needing some air, I started to push the door open when I saw Devlyn holding you, Garrett smiling down at you both. She looked completely natural. She knew to support your head. You weren't crying for her.

It was the first time I realized what I had to do. I pushed the door open all the way. Garrett took one look at me and asked Devlyn to leave.

She passed you to your daddy. I remember thinking that's the way it should be. You two were perfect together—Mia and Garrett.

I looked him right in the eye, my heartbeat strong, my hands steady and told him I couldn't do it. I couldn't be your mother.

I don't think he believed me. Not while we argued. Not when our parents got involved. Not when I told him he could have sole custody. Not when I told him I'd sign anything he wanted. Not when I told him I loved him. Not when I told him I loved you. Not when I told him that's why I was leaving. He didn't believe me. Not until the moment I walked out the door—eighteen years ago today.

I'm on my way,
Mom

CHAPTER TWENTY-ONE

GARRETT

LOOKING INTO HER brown eyes is like looking right into my daughter's. I cling to my hatred for her, but she looks so much like Mia. She's right in front of me, close enough to touch, but we're both just staring at one another. My father is desperately trying to send everyone home. Mia is safe inside with Devlyn, no doubt staring at us from the window. Sadly, this is the first time she's seen her parents together. Worse, she's going to see me send her mother packing.

Sheena rubs the wooden box in her hands. "I've imagined this moment so many times," she says. "Rehearsed what to say, but now I can't remember any of it."

I don't blink. I don't move. I give her absolutely nothing, which is what she deserves.

She licks her lips, glancing down at the box again. "I saw Mia's graduation speech. She's an amazing young woman. I knew she would be with you raising her."

Still nothing.

"I know I've got no right, but I'd like to see her."

Silence.

"Garrett, please," she begs, a tear rolling down her cheek.

Like her, I've imagined this moment endless times. Over the years, I've imagined everything from her coming back saying she loves us and us getting back together (granted that was mostly in the early months), to her falling to her knees begging for forgiveness, to a downright screaming match.

Instead, I turn my back to her and start to walk away.

"Garrett!" she cries. "She's my daughter, too!"

That one makes me pause, and an evil laugh I didn't know I was capable of carries me all the way back inside my house.

Devlyn's by the door like she's guarding it, but Mia flies into my arms. "Is she still here?"

I block her from looking outside. I don't know if Sheena left yet, but I'm not above calling the police to have her forcibly removed if necessary.

"What if she leaves?" Mia cries. "What if this is my only chance to talk to her?"

"She's leaving," Devlyn says softly.

"Daddy!" Mia collapses into tears in my arms.

Devlyn's hand lands on my shoulder, and I flinch. I don't mean to, but my muscles are so tight the slightest touch feels like a threat. Holding Mia, I look over at Devlyn, who, as usual, gives me a supportive smile.

I can tell she doesn't know whether to stay or to go. She wants to give Mia and me space, but she wants to be there for me. The back door opens, my dad walking in. He wraps his old arms around me and Mia. His protective fatherly instinct is just as honed now as it's ever been. He releases us, his hand on my cheek, giving me a look. It's the same look he gave me when Sheena showed up pregnant. The same look he gave me when she walked away.

I know that look. I have it now, too. It's the whatever-it-takes look. Whatever it takes to protect and take care of those we love.

"I'm going to start cleaning up outside," Devlyn says.

Her blue eyes hold the same look. I've never noticed that before. "I'll go with you," my dad says, leaving Mia and me alone.

Alone.

I remember that first night I was alone with her. It was a good while after we brought her home from the hospital. Either Mom or Dad or both had stayed and helped with Mia every night, but that couldn't last forever. That first night it was just the two of us, and we both cried. It was the first time I let myself cry over Sheena.

I'm not sure if it was because I was in shock, too scared, or too busy with a newborn to let myself feel it before, but that first night, I cried. It was the one and only time I've ever cried in front of my daughter. I didn't even do that when my own mom died.

Mia seemed inconsolable that night, just like now.

I doubt a walk in the fresh air is going to help tonight. She's too big for me to swaddle and rock, and words have failed me. I haven't said a word since ordering Mia and Devlyn inside.

Mia pulls away from me. "I know you hate her, but I'm not sure I do."

"I don't hate her," I lie. I read somewhere once that to hate a child's parent comes off to the child like you hate them, too. After all, they are a part of their parent. "I don't want you hurt by her. I'm protecting you."

"She's my mother!" she screams.

"She gave birth to you," I say. "She's never been your mother."

Mia's bottom lip quivers. The truth is hard to hear. "Maybe she wants to be," she whimpers.

"Oh, baby girl," I say, wrapping my arms around her again. I fucking hate this. How dare Sheena show up and do this to Mia! On her birthday, no less! There's no doubt in my mind that Sheena is here for herself, not for Mia. She didn't put Mia first when she was born, and she's not about to start now.

Mia squirms out of my arms again. Somehow, I'm the bad guy in this, the one who's keeping her away from her mother. Silent tears rolling off her checks, she walks to her bedroom. I follow her. She needs to know that nothing has changed, that I'm still here. That I'll always be here. I'm her constant.

Leaning in her doorway, I wait. Her phone is going off like crazy. She picks it up, turning it off, then kicks off her shoes and crawls into bed still wearing her party dress and the pearls Devlyn bought her.

Silent tears are the worst. The amount of resistance it takes to keep from making a sound when you are crying is incredible. That kind of containment is going to do a number on her. It's better to let it all out. She can scream and cry all she wants. I can take it. I can take it all, but this . . .

This silent pain.

Shutting off her light, I take a seat next to her on the bed, my hand resting on her shoulder. My eyes close. This isn't new pain. This is eighteen years of pain. Have there been other nights she cried silently over her mother?

I feel like I've been warped back in time. How many nights did I spend patting her back while she fell asleep? I had a rhythm I used to use, a certain beat. It comes right back to me now. Mia's subconscious must remember it, too, because she soon falls asleep. Probably has more to do with her being mentally exhausted, but I'll take it.

My daughter crying herself to sleep isn't acceptable, but deep in my gut I know Sheena's not going away easily. It's funny. Eighteen years ago, I'd have done anything to get her to stay, and now I'd give anything for her to go.

Slowly, I ease my weight off her bed, careful not to wake her, and pause at her doorway to take one last look at her. When Sheena left me before, my sole distraction was Mia. I couldn't fuck another girl to forget her. I was underage, so alcohol wasn't an option, but tonight a stiff drink is definitely called for. I'd hidden all the alcohol in a spare refrigerator in the shop to keep Mia's friends from getting hold of anything, so I head outside. I think there's only beer, but I'll take what I can get.

Devlyn and my father are both in the yard, throwing things away, cleaning up, stewing over the events of the night. I walk right past them both, straight to the shop, saying nothing. I know my dad wants to strategize. I suspect Devlyn wants a big heart-to-heart, but I don't have the energy for any of that right now.

With one good push, I slide the door to the shop open, hearing it slam, not realizing how much force I released on the poor thing. I'm greeted by the shine of my motorcycle, a symbol of a life left behind. I walk right past her, too.

Opening the door to the old refrigerator, I lower my head, the cool air meeting my boiling skin. Then I feel her presence. Normally, it would soothe me, make me smile, but tonight there's only room for anger. I'm not angry with her and don't want to accidentally take my emotions out on her, so I grab a beer and turn around, taking a long drink.

Devlyn's blue eyes study me. "I can't talk right now," I say.

"Who said anything about talking?" she says with a stone-faced expression and reaches behind her, sliding the door closed.

I can hardly believe she's serious.

She steps closer to me and whispers, "I need you right now, and I think you need me."

I doubt it's the same for women. I doubt an angry woman wants to fuck, but an angry man wants to fuck—hard. Of course, we could use other means to get out our frustration, like exercise. But pounding a punching bag isn't nearly as satisfying as pounding a pussy.

Slowly, I place my beer down, our eyes locked. Normally, I might feel guilty about using a woman to feel better, but she wants this, too. All bets are off tonight. I don't care that my dad's outside, that Mia's asleep inside.

Stalking toward her, she doesn't move away, not in the mood for any cat and mouse games, either. Usually, she gets off on me teasing her. Usually, I get off on it, too, but tonight we both just want to get to the deed.

I run my eyes over her, still dressed for the party. Devlyn looks great in everything she wears, but I prefer her in dresses—easier access. "Take off your panties," I order.

"Remember?" she says with a flirty smile. "I'm not wearing any."

I must be really upset to forget that fun detail. Seductively, she walks to my motorcycle and hikes her leg across it, straddling it backwards, her dress pulled up to her upper thighs. The thought of her slick wetness on the leather of the seat makes my dick throb. Leaning past her, I push the start button and squeeze the clutch lever, revving it up. Her eyes go wide. I'd told her the bike didn't work. I never specified it was the brake system that's faulty.

Planting a sweet kiss on the nape of her neck, I give the lever another squeeze, causing the bike to vibrate. "Oh God," she moans, looking at me, wanting more.

I keep my hand on the lever, kissing her slowly, my tongue tangling with hers, the gentle hum of the bike between her legs. She reaches for my pants, but I give her another jolt. Her head tosses back, biting her lip, but I release the lever.

Her eyes dart to mine, and I flash her a wicked grin. "Reach under your dress and open the lips of that sweet pussy wider." Holding my gaze, she follows my orders, her eyes rolling back at the brief contact of her fingers.

This time when I rev the engine, her hips grind into the seat, her slick wetness helping glide her. Watching her get herself off, I match her rhythm with the engine until her whole body is shuddering.

Not giving her a second to recover, I turn the bike off and flip her around, bending her over. She gasps as I toss her dress up, exposing her perfect ass. "Hold on to the handlebars."

In one smooth motion, I free my cock and thrust into her hard. "You are mine," I groan, not wanting her to ever doubt that. "You hear me?"

"Yes," she breathes out.

Holding her hair, I thrust in and out. The only thing I want to think about is the feel of her as my cock slides deep inside. She uses the handlebars to force herself back on my dick hard, letting me know she can take all I can give. And I give it to her, banging the hell out of her, every moan from her sweet lips letting me know she's enjoying it as much as I am.

She whispers my name, her voice cracking with an undeniable vulnerability. It's my undoing. Through gritted teeth, I groan her name, hearing the same vulnerability in my voice, releasing inside her.

Lowering my head to her back, I hold her as tight as I can for as long as I can, until she wiggles slightly. When my dick slips out of her, there's a weird twisting in my gut. Ignoring it, I lower her dress, giving her ass a playful smack.

She gets off the motorcycle, reaching for my hand. We both just stare at each other for a few minutes, in shock over Sheena's abrupt appearance. I told her I didn't want to talk, but there's something she needs to know. I say, "This doesn't change anything between you and me."

She smiles, but shakes her head. "Garrett, you know it does."

Tightening my grip on her hand, I say, "No, it doesn't. I promise."

"Don't make promises you can't keep," she says softly. "Things are already different."

I start to argue with her, but her hand flies to her hip like a warning, and I know what she's referring to. "I will talk to Mia about us," I say. "But I can't do it like we planned. Not with Sheena here now. I can't give Mia anything more to deal with." She pulls that bottom lip between her teeth. Damn it, I know she's holding in tears. I pull her into my arms, kissing the top of her head.

"I should go," she whispers, stepping away.

"Devlyn," I say, but nothing else comes out.

"I understand, Garrett. I do," she says.

"When things have settled down," I say, "we'll tell Mia." She gives me a very unconvincing nod. Could things be anymore fucked up? "I just want to . . ." My fist clenches at my side. "That fucking bit . . ." I stop myself. My mother hated the word "bitch". Use of that word landed me and my dad in hot water. "Fucking Sheena."

"How's Mia?" Devlyn asks.

"Cried herself to sleep," I say. "How could Sheena do this? Just show up after eighteen years without a word? What the hell is she thinking?"

"What are you going to do?"

"No fucking clue."

"Mia's eighteen," Devlyn says. "You can't really stop her from seeing her mother if she wants to."

"Sheena doesn't deserve to see Mia," I spit out. "And I don't have to make it easy."

The saddest smile crosses her lips. "But you will," she says. "For Mia, you will."

Her hand gently lands on my cheek, then she walks away.

CHAPTER TWENTY-TWO

DEVLYN

NOTHING LIKE KNEADING dough to work out your frustrations. I pound into the gooey mixture, my hands red I've been at it so long. There was no sleeping after last night, so I came to the diner early. I'd be lying if I said I haven't eaten my weight in pastry this morning. I've got the food baby to prove it. Who am I kidding? I've got food triplets going on.

I've been hiding out in the back most of the morning because all anyone seems to want to talk about is Sheena. The only thing swirling in the air more than the aroma of my coffee are questions. What's she doing back? Why now? Will Garrett and her reunite? Will Mia forgive her mother?

Everyone has an opinion. Everyone wants to know mine since the general consensus is that I know Garrett and Mia the best. I'm keeping my mouth shut. I don't have any answers, anyway. It's all driving me crazy, so I decide to hide out and bake. Carbs never disappoint, so I'm making a few hundred. Biscuits don't judge me. Pastries don't gossip, and never has a scone made me cry, so I figure I'm safe.

Besides, the only thing I learned from listening to the town gossip is that Sheena is staying at a bed and breakfast in the next town, knowing that no one in Eden Valley would rent to her. Everything else is just hearsay and innuendo.

The oven timer dings, so I quickly rinse off my hands, grab a potholder and pull out a pan of freshly baked biscuits. Warm buttered biscuits are sex in carb form.

Sorry, Grandma! She'd roll over in her grave if she knew I was comparing her biscuit recipe to sex. I'm not sure how long this recipe has actually been in our family, but it's top secret. One little trick to making the perfect biscuit is frozen butter. Yep, frozen, not just cold. Frozen butter can be grated. That way, when it's mixed in, the butter spreads throughout. That's the only thing I can share without my mother disowning me.

Drake women like our biscuits big. These are around three to four inches tall. "There is no such thing as too big of a biscuit," my mother used to say. That could apply to men, as well. Not the three or four inches part, that would just be sad. Oops, sorry again, Grandma.

Plating them, I push the door open with my booty, my tutu crinkling up, and step out into the diner. I start placing them down on customers' plates. They may not have ordered them, but they are getting a little hot buttery treat, compliments of me. Hopefully, it makes them fill their mouths with something other than gossip.

"Devlyn, how are you dealing with . . ." Trudy, the mail carrier, starts to ask, but I shove a biscuit right in her mouth. That's the only acceptable way to tell someone to shut up.

She smiles through her bite then her eyes get huge. I knew my biscuits were good, but she looks like she's about to pass out. When I hear the door open behind me, I don't have to look to know why. The hairs on the back of my neck are telling me I'm about to come face-to-face with my nightmare.

Placing my tray down, I turn around. Sheena smiles at me. She's got some nerve waltzing into my shop, and of course, she looks perfect. Blonde, petite, brown eyes, and a stomach flatter than mine. Seriously, she's birthed a baby. Life isn't fair. I'm not even sure my socks match, and she's dressed to kill. Aside from her hair being slightly shorter, she looks exactly the same as eighteen years ago.

"Hi, Devlyn," she says, glancing around. "The place is just like I remember. The whole town is."

Everyone in the place is staring at me, wondering how I'm going to respond. "We aren't as welcoming as we were before," I say.

She glances at her feet. "I knew coming back here wasn't going to be easy, but you were always so sweet to Garrett and me. I was hoping . . ." I lean against the counter. This ought to be good. "I just thought maybe you and I could talk."

"I'm working."

"Over one cup of coffee. That's it."

"I'm not interested in anything you have to say," I say, turning away.

She grabs my elbow. "Then I'll listen. You can talk, and I'll just listen. Please, I'm desperate."

I yank my arm away. "Don't come in here again."

Like the stubborn, spoiled princess she is, she takes a seat at the counter, slamming her purse down. I have a mind to spill a whole pitcher of orange juice on top of her perfect blonde hair, but instead I smile at the man seated at the table in the corner.

He gets to his feet, his blue officer uniform a nice contrast to the shiny metal of his badge. "There a problem, Devlyn?"

"Loitering, trespassing, harassment," I say, smirking. "Whatever else you can charge her with."

"Fine," Sheena says, getting to her feet with a stomp. "You know, Garrett was always so blind when it came to you, but I saw right through you. Nothing more than a lovesick, awkward little . . ."

"Sheena!" Garrett barks from the front door of my diner. Mia stands behind him, mostly hidden by his frame.

I feel the heat on my cheeks, the tears welling in my eyes. Garrett's eyes run over me. He can't rush to me. He can't hug me. All I get is that look.

"Well, at least you're talking to me now," Sheena says, trying to look around him at Mia.

"Oh, holy hell," one customer whispers.

"This is getting good," another says.

"She was just leaving," I say, motioning to the town police officer to go ahead and throw her out.

Sheena pulls away. "I'm not leaving until I talk to my daughter." Everyone in the place knows that Garrett isn't going to let Mia see her mother get taken out by a police officer. "Please, Garrett," she says, taking a step to him. "I want a chance to get to know her. Maybe we could all have breakfast."

Mia peers up over his shoulder. "It's just breakfast, Dad."

I want to scream that breakfast is my thing with Garrett and Mia, not hers. Garrett doesn't like it, not one bit, but he nods his head to Mia, giving her the okay. I don't want to make this harder on him, so I give him a smile. A fake ass smile, but a smile still.

"Not here," he says, glancing at me.

"But we always come here," Mia says then looks at Sheena. "It's kind of our thing."

"Oh," she says, smiling at her daughter. "I don't want to mess up anything between you and your father."

Liar! Who does she think she's kidding with that line of bull crap?

"It's fine," Mia says. "We're all here. Right, Daddy?"

Another glance to me. Another smile from me, and they are taking a seat at their usual table, only this time Mia sits beside her dad instead of across from him. It looks like two against one.

Everyone else in the place is trying to pretend they aren't staring, but not me. I can't take my eyes off the three of them. Trudy pats my hand and whispers, "Have someone else serve them."

"I got it," I say. "I'm alright."

I fix Mia and Garrett's coffees just the way they like them then head over and place them down. Garrett's jaw is so tense it looks like his mouth is wired shut.

"I saw your graduation speech online," Sheena says.

"You watched it?" Mia asks, taking her coffee.

Sheena glances at Garrett. "Me and about a million other people it looked like."

"Oh, my gosh," Mia says. "I have to tell you about the women that showed up after to date Dad. It was so funny and . . ."

"Mia!" Garrett barks. "You wanted to talk to Sheena? Fine! But leave me out of it."

Mia looks down into her mug. I can count on one hand how many times I've heard Garrett scold Mia like that. He clenches his hands in a fist in front of his mouth. I can't decide if he looks like he's praying or trying to keep from wringing Sheena's neck.

I clear my throat. "Mia, honey, you want granola? Fruit?" She barely looks up at me. I step behind her, playing with her hair. Sheena's eyes study us, obviously jealous. Damn, it feels good to get under her skin. I probably shouldn't be doing this in my shop, it's not very professional. I probably should lay off since they have enough family drama, but my internal bitch is awake and she's pissed. Pissed about what Sheena did to Garrett and Mia, and ready to unleash years of hurt.

"How about those cookies and cream waffles that I only make for you?" I ask.

She looks up, giving me a smile. "That sounds good. Dad?"

I stare right at Sheena and say, "I know what he likes."

I see half a smile behind his clenched fists. Satisfied, I head toward the counter. Not to be beaten, Sheena calls out, "You didn't take my order."

Garrett's eyes fly to me. What the hell? His lover is supposed to serve his ex? This is all kinds of screwed up. What am I supposed to do? Mia's eyes are right on me, and Sheena knows it. I don't want to damage my relationship with Mia. Ah hell, I'll just spit in her food.

I step back to the table. "No," Garrett snaps, causing both Mia and Sheena to jump slightly. "Devlyn doesn't need to wait on you."

"It's fine, Garrett," I say.

One shake of his head, and Sheena nods to me to go. Good God almighty, this is more dramatic than a soap opera, and I don't know my part in it yet. Do I have a part? Or am I simply an observer, relegated to the kitchen?

I'm not Mia's stepmother. Garrett and I aren't even public knowledge. My mother would say I'm nothing more than a harlot.

Disappearing to the back, I gather the ingredients in my hands. I'm like an octopus in the kitchen. It seems like I can carry a whole shopping cart in my arms. I whisk the ingredients for the waffles.

Maybe I'm just the biscuit girl? The one he calls when he needs help. A friend. It's been that way most of our lives. Does sleeping with me a few times really change that? A tear rolls down my cheek. I don't want to think like that. Brushing it aside, I continue making their breakfast like I always have. My grandmother used to say that food picks up on the baker's feelings, so if you're sad, your bread will be, too. I hope that's not true, because Garrett's meat-lover's omelet is going to be one confused mess.

When I finish, I have two perfect plates of breakfast. Drawing a deep breath, I push the door open, finding Garrett stuck in the same position he was when I left him. Mia's smiling, Sheena's smiling, and everyone else in the diner looks like they want to vomit. I'm feeling a bit ill myself. My food baby has turned on me and is fighting back.

"You must have all kinds of questions," I hear Sheena say as I walk over with the plates.

"Are you leaving?" Mia asks. "I mean, do I have to ask you everything right now?"

I freeze. Sheena's eyes go to Garrett. "I don't have any firm plans yet."

Garrett is stone-faced. My jaw, however, is on the floor. No firm plans? She could be here for the foreseeable future. Until Mia goes off to school? Longer? Is she here for more than Mia? I see the plates falling to the ground before I even realize I'm shaking. The loud clatter and flying food only draw more attention.

"Devlyn!" Garrett says, getting to his feet. He takes both my hands in his, but only for a second.

My eyes fly around the room, everyone staring. Sheena has a stunned look on her face. Mia has the same expression, saying, "I don't think I've ever seen you drop a plate. Ever!"

"Your breakfast," I say softly, looking at the mess on the floor.

For years, it was breakfast in the diner with Garrett and Mia. Now it's a pile of crap on the floor. Sometimes life is poetic like that. I bend down, throwing chunks of food back on the plates, thankful they didn't break. Garrett kneels in front of me to help, his eyes glued on me, but I don't look at him, knowing I won't be able to smile this time.

"So you live in England?" Mia asks.

"Yes," Sheena says. "You'd think by now I'd have the cool accent, but no such luck."

"What do you do?" Mia asks.

"I work in finance," she says, smiling. "It's not very exciting."

Mia nods and clears her throat. "Are you married? Do I have any brothers or sisters?"

Garrett's body goes rigid, causing me to look at him, but his eyes are closed. "I've never been married," Sheena says. "And you're my only child."

Garrett's blue eyes open, catching me staring. "I've got this," I say, my voice soft but with an unmistakable chill.

Slowly, he gets up, taking his seat back at the table. I'm left on the floor with the mess. The irony is not lost on me—I've always been cleaning up the mess. Part of me wants to clean up slowly so I can continue to eavesdrop, but another part of me wants to get the hell out of Dodge.

"There's so much I want to know," Mia says.

Sheena reaches out, touching her hand. "We have time, Mia."

Garrett glances at her hand, but Sheena doesn't remove it. Mia asks, "You won't just leave again?"

"I won't," Sheena says. "I've taken a leave at work." Garrett's head shakes in obvious disgust. Sheena's eyes go to him. "Seems like you have some things you want to say to me, too."

"I'm only here to protect Mia," he says.

"Protect her from me?" Sheena asks, her voice rising.

"You forget I've heard all your lies before. I'm not going to have Mia fall for it like I did."

"I was a teenage girl. I was pregnant, confused, and alone. I . . ."

"You weren't alone. Alone is how you left me and Mia."

Mia bursts into tears. Releasing a deep breath, Garrett pulls her into his arms. I get up, placing the dirty dishes on the counter behind me and grab Mia a napkin. Garrett takes it from me. Mia seems to be using his shirt as a snot rag at the moment, and he doesn't care one bit. Got to love that!

"Can you not fight?" Mia sobs, pulling back to look at her dad. "This is my chance." Her voice gives. "My chance to know my mom."

Garrett lowers his head. Raising Mia alone was hard, but at least she never grew up with parents fighting all the time. He looks up at me. My heart starts to thunder. Please don't ask me. Dear God, please don't ask me what I think he's going to ask me.

"Devlyn, could you stay with Mia while Sheena and I talk?" he asks.

Yep, that's what I thought he was going to say. Wanna babysit my kid so I can go hang out with this other chick? My rational mind knows that's not what this is, but the heart isn't a rational organ.

Mia's upset. He doesn't want her alone. She's hungry. And only I know how to make cookies and cream waffles. So I hold out my arm. "Come on, honey, let's get you something to eat."

I know I'm going to regret this. Mia gets up, and I wrap my arm around her. Garrett gets to his feet, and Sheena follows. He walks toward the door as I walk toward the back of the diner with Mia. I turn around, watching him open the door for Sheena to walk through. Sometimes, I hate that he's a gentleman.

MIA HAS A stool pulled up to the counter in the back of the diner away from prying eyes. Her eyes are still red and puffy—no doubt a result of the combination of crying last night and this morning. She swirls the waffle around on her plate, lapping up the last morsels of syrup. It's been at least fifteen minutes since Garrett and Sheena stepped outside.

"Guess they're discussing a custody arrangement," Mia says snidely, tossing down her fork.

"This is a shock for your dad, too," I say. "Give them some time to . . ."

"I'm eighteen," she snaps. "I'll do what I want. That includes seeing my mother whenever I feel like it."

I grab a fork and lean over, stealing a piece of her waffle. If you want a teenage girl to open up, share some food with them. There's a reason why women share a pint of ice cream or a bottle of wine in almost every chick flick.

"She lives in England. I know she's here now, but who knows for how long," Mia says. "Dad has to understand this is my chance."

"I think he understands what you want," I say.

"Why'd she leave?" Mia asks, looking at me. "You have to know."

Because she's a selfish bitch isn't an appropriate response, so I bite my tongue, push back the vomit in my throat, and say, "I think she was just really young and overwhelmed."

"Then why have me in the first place?"

"I don't know, but I'm glad she did," I say, patting her hand.

"Why'd she never call me or write or anything?" Mia asks.

I don't have answers for her and don't want to say anything nasty about her birth mom in front of her. Sure, I was passive-aggressive and snarky before. I think Mia missed most of that, but I won't trash talk Sheena to Mia.

Garrett clears his throat behind me, startling us. He looks rough, like he's run his hands through his hair at least a dozen times.

"Did she leave?" Mia asks, jumping up from the stool.

"She's gone," Garrett says. "But you'll see her later."

"When?"

Garrett glances at me. "Dinner tonight."

"A family dinner?" Mia asks with a huge smile.

My heart breaks—for her and for myself. I hate the thought of Garrett sharing a dinner with Sheena. Maybe I'm a terrible person for feeling that way, but I do. Mia just wants a few normal memories—a dinner with both her parents.

"No," Garrett says. "You and Sheena."

Mia shakes her head. "Why don't you ever call her my mother?"

"I do."

"No, you don't," Mia snaps. "It's always Sheena."

Garrett exhales. "No, it's not."

"Why won't you have dinner with us?" Mia asks, her hand on her hip.

"I thought this is what you wanted," he says. "To have time with Sheena, to get to know her."

"I thought you were protecting me from her," Mia says, storming past him. "Guess you're not afraid she's going to abduct me to Europe."

He calls after her, but she just ignores him. Lightly, he bangs his head against a cabinet. "I can't win with her right now."

"She's angry," I say.

"I don't get why she's so pissed at me all of a sudden."

"Because you're safe," I say. He looks up at me. "It's easier for Mia to be mad at you because you stayed, you're safe. She can rage at you and know you won't leave her. She doesn't have that with Sheena." He reaches out for me, taking my hand. Placing the palm of my hand on his cheek, I say, "She's really mad at Sheena for leaving. She's just taking it out on you."

"Great," he says, his finger gently stroking mine. "I'm sorry about all that this morning. I told her not to come in here again, not to bother you."

"Garrett, be careful. You don't want her to figure out we're together. You don't want her to have anything to hold over your head with Mia."

"I don't want you upset. I saw you in there. You were hurt." He kisses my forehead. "I know this is a lot on you, too."

I'm happy he's worried about me, too, but I also feel guilty that he is. "So what did you and Sheena talk about?"

"There was a lot of silence," he says.

"Don't you think at some point you're going to have to have it out with her once and for all?" I ask.

"No," he says. "I have no intention of co-parenting with her, so . . ."

"You know that's not what I'm talking about," I say. His refusal to talk to her makes it blatantly obvious that he has a lot to say. "She didn't just hurt Mia. She hurt you, too. I would think you'd want to tell her to go to hell or yell at her or ask why or something."

"Men don't work that way."

"Bullshit!" I snap. "Being a man doesn't mean you can't hurt."

"Devlyn."

"I was there, remember?" I say.

He steps away from me. "I don't get you. I'd think the last thing you'd want would be for me to be around Sheena, but you seem to want me to . . ."

"No," I say. "I hate the idea of you with her."

He places his hands on my hips, pulling me close. "Then while Mia is having dinner with Sheena, will you have dinner with me?"

Running my fingers through his hair, I know he needs a distraction, but I'm not sure it's a great idea. I'd love nothing more, but if Mia or (worse) Sheena find out, it would only make things more complicated. No one needs that right now.

But Garrett is a hard man to say no to. I don't think he realizes that. I don't think he knows his smile makes me weak in the knees, his blue eyes render me speechless, and his body strikes me stupid. God help me if the man ever figures it out. He could probably get me to do just about anything, like one of those hypnotists that make you act like a chicken. I'd be walking around Eden Valley clucking like a hen, and he'd be the cock why.

A knock sounds at the kitchen door, and we step away from each other. Edward Hollis sticks his head in before stepping all the way in. "Sorry," he says. "I got at least a half-dozen phone calls about Sheena showing up here."

Garrett briefly fills his father in on what happened and the mother-daughter dinner plans. "I don't like it," Garrett says. "But I know Mia needs this."

His dad glances at me then back to his son. "We need to talk about Sheena," he says.

"Not now," Garrett says.

"When?" his dad asks.

Garrett shakes his head, squeezing my hand. "I kind of have my hands full right now. Plus, I'm behind on the Falls project."

"It's important," his dad says, and I get the feeling there's something I don't know.

"Dad," Garrett says, his voice sounding so tired and overwhelmed.

"Okay," his dad says, holding up his hands. "Can you at least tell me what you and Sheena talked about?"

"Nothing more than dinner tonight. Frankly, I didn't even want to agree to that," Garrett says. "I've got to go. I need to work on the pavilion today to make up some ground. Do you think you can find Mia and . . ."

"I've got it," his dad says.

Garrett turns to me and says, "I'll see you later."

I'm not sure if he's telling me or asking me. Either way, it doesn't really matter, my answer is the same—yes.

CHAPTER TWENTY-THREE

DEVLYN

I TRY NOT to be a judgmental person, but all bets are off in the checkout line of the grocery store. I can't help it. I place a bottle of wine, steaks, and bubble bath down on the conveyor belt by the cashier, noticing the kindergarten teacher from the elementary school in front of me with her forty-ounce beer, bag of salty off-brand chips, and bottle of sweet tea. I'm sorry, but this is the South—we don't buy our tea in a *bottle*. We brew it. That's just sacrilege. And what's up with the rest of her purchase? A forty-ounce and bag of chips? This woman is teaching the next generation. Don't they teach food groups in school anymore?

She turns to me, feeling my grocery store judgment no doubt, so I divert my eyes. The sun is out, but damn if I don't see some black clouds in the distance. I have to make it out of here before I get soaked again.

"Romantic dinner?" I hear a woman ask behind me. I know that voice.

Damn her for judging my groceries—that's my thing! Then again, Sheena is always intruding on what I consider mine. I look down on the belt, at my makings for a nice dinner with Garrett. The belt rolls forward, and I step that way. Good God, is there no escaping this woman? I guess if I'm going to be with Garrett, then I'll have to learn to deal with Sheena.

Before she returned, dating Garrett was a package deal: him and Mia. Looks like that package will now include one more.

I can't judge her purchase, either. Damn her, she's just buying breath mints. Seriously? Sheena doesn't wait for me to answer, saying snidely, "I was right before when I said things here are exactly the same. You're still following Garrett around like a schoolgirl."

The cashier picks up the wine, scanning and bagging it in an obvious hurry. I'm not sure if it's to save my ass or to avoid seeing a girl-on-girl beat down, but either way, I'm grateful. Reaching into my purse, I hand my credit card to the cashier.

"Sheena, it's been a long week. I'm going home to eat a nice dinner, have a glass of wine, and soak in the tub. Seems to me you're the one still obsessed with Garrett."

"I'm here for my daughter," she says.

"If you say so," I say, taking back my card and putting it away.

"Garrett is as handsome as ever, though," she says, flashing me a smile.

A quick debate starts in my head. Do I agree with her? There really is no denying that Garrett is a fine piece of male specimen. He's one of those universally handsome men, so to deny what she said seems like I'm protesting too much, but to agree with Sheena on anything makes bile rise to the back of my throat.

I gather my bags and start to leave as she quickly hands her breath mints to the cashier and whips out come cash. Unfortunately, the cashier is too quick with Sheena, who catches up with me before my foot hits the sidewalk.

"Devlyn," she says, touching my arm. "Look, I was . . . I'm sorry I was a bitch to you. I see how Garrett looks at you."

"Then you need to have your eyes checked."

"I understand you don't want me to know, but let's forget Garrett for a second." She takes a deep breath. "I see the way my daughter looks at you."

That one I don't deny.

"It hurts," she says softly. "A part of me is thankful you were around for her, but another part of me is so jealous I can't see straight."

Sheena, jealous of me? What universe are we in? Still, I get what she's saying. I've just never considered it before.

"Mia is very easy to love," I say.

Sheena smiles and gives me a little nod. "I'm about to have dinner with her. Just me and her. It's all I've thought about for years, and now I'm scared to death. What if she hates me? What if she never wants to see me again?" Her head shakes. "I'm sorry. This isn't your problem." Her hand goes over her mouth. "I can't believe I'm supposed to go walk into that house. That house!"

"Garrett's house?" I ask, my voice a little higher.

"His grandparent's old house," she says. "Or at least it was when he and I used to sneak inside it."

Thunder booms outside, causing us both to jump. "I need to go," I say, hurrying outside, needing to escape the storm that's coming, needing to escape what's brewing inside of me.

Walking quickly, I bite my bottom lip. In all these years, it never occurred to me to think about where Sheena and Garrett conceived Mia. It was too painful to think about him even sleeping with her, much less get into the logistics of it. The backseat of a car, a field in the woods, what did it matter?

His house? Where he still lives? That's where? The place where he and I? Every day of his adult life he's lived in the same place where he used to sneak away and . . . I can't. I just can't. I tell myself this is silly. I wouldn't expect a man I dated to buy a new mattress in between all his girlfriends. I shouldn't expect Garrett to buy a new house.

Yes, I'm going to be very logical about this. I'm not going to be hurt. This isn't about me. It's just a house—four walls, a ceiling, and floor. That's it. It doesn't have to have any more meaning than that. It only has meaning if I give it meaning.

I get into my car, starting it and blaring the air conditioner, but I don't drive off. I lean my head back, trying to stop the onslaught of negativity in my head. Staring into the sky, the dark clouds on the horizon threaten a picture-perfect, sunny summer day. At least I made it safely to my car before the storm unleashes itself this time.

I don't have a lot of experience between the sheets. We aren't talking double digits or anything, and none of the guys were virgins. None of them were man whores, either. I'm not one to be a notch on a bedpost, and I'm not delusional enough to think I can turn a man slut into a saint. I'm just crazy enough to hold a candle for the same boy since I was five!

Regardless, I knew my past boyfriends' histories. I never obsessed over it, but Garrett is different. Perhaps because I love him. Perhaps because I have to run into the girl who took his virginity in the grocery store checkout line.

We had sex for the first time in the same place he had sex with Sheena for the first time. Another blast of thunder hits as a tear rolls down my cheek. I close my eyes. I must look like a mental health crisis waiting to happen, sitting alone in my car, crying.

Did he think about her? Did she cross his mind? If even for a moment?

CHAPTER TWENTY-FOUR

GARRETT

I SEE HER sitting in her car in front of the grocery store all alone and pause on the sidewalk. In all the years I've known Devlyn, I've rarely seen her sad. She always offers a smile, always does for others, for me. Something about the way she's staring makes me wonder if she's running out of steam.

I walk over, knocking on the car window, tilting my head, concerned about her. She rolls it down, and I lean in slightly. "Hey," I say. "I was just walking over to your house. Sheena just picked up Mia."

She looks straight ahead out at the horizon, the sun doing its best to fight off the clouds. "I just ran into her in the grocery store."

Shit! I release a deep breath, knowing this isn't good. "Try to remember this is temporary. She won't be here forever." Devlyn just nods, unable to look at me. I reach in to take her hand, but she pulls back. "Did she say something else to you?"

"She said a lot of things," Devlyn says with sass. Normally, I like her sassy little attitude, finding it sexy, but not today. "How she's jealous of the way Mia looks at me. How she's nervous to see Mia. How handsome you are." Then she turns to me, and I see the anger in her blue eyes. "How you used to fuck her in your grandparents' house. Well, your house." Angry tears roll down her face. "The same place where you fucked me."

Don't let anyone ever tell you that words aren't a weapon, because she just pierced right through me.

Fucked her?

It's funny how when you are in bed having fun, being playful, a woman doesn't mind you talking dirty, using the word "fuck," but outside of the bedroom, if they say you fucked them, it's never good. Fucking a woman is bad, unless you are *actually* fucking them.

I want to yell that I've never fucked her, at least in the way she means it, but I'm not going to get into a semantics debate in a parking lot. The only thing that's important is that she *feels* fucked by me, and that's not alright.

I feel my jaw tense. This is the last thing I need, and so irrelevant. "I didn't think about that."

She cries. "It's where you conceived Mia. It represents your stolen moments with her, not me."

"It represents nothing," I argue. "It's just a house."

"It feels like more than that," she sobs softly. "It feels like a little box of memories."

I walk around her car and get inside. "Drive to my house."

Her eyes dart around, and she points to her backseat. "I've got groceries for dinner and . . ."

"My house," I say.

She puts the car in drive and heads that way. Memories are a funny thing. It's all about the ones you let in, the ones you focus on. If I let it, all of Eden Valley could be a bad memory. My mom used to ask me every day after school how my day was. Then she'd say, "Sounds like you had more good than bad today. I'd call that a blessing."

I didn't realize at the time how wise she was. Every day has good and bad. We should consider ourselves lucky for the days where the good outweighs the bad. Focus on that. Guess she instilled that in me without me even realizing it.

This town, my house aren't bad memories for me. I've had more good than bad happen here.

Devlyn pulls in front of my house, and I get out, walking around to open her door. I start up the steps then stop. "Mia got her first scraped knee right there," I say, pointing. "She pointed to the step and scolded it, 'Bad step'." Devlyn looks up at me with a small smile, and I open the front door. Closing it, I pin her to the wall, letting my lips hover close to hers. "Kissed you for the first time right here."

"But you also . . ."

"Nope," I say, placing my finger over her sweet lips. "These are *my* memories." I take her hand, leading her to the kitchen. "In that very oven, you helped Mia make her first gingerbread house when she was five."

Her eyes start to water. "I helped you make sugar cookies to leave out for Santa, too."

Smiling, I nod, pointing to the faucet. "Burned your finger, and Mia got her doctor's kit to heal you."

"Oh God, I forgot about that," she says. "She had the little lab coat and everything."

Leading her into the den, I point to the sofa. "The only time I've seen my father cry was right there. After mom died."

"He was so solemn at her funeral," Devlyn says.

"You brought him dinner every night for a whole month," I say.

"You know about that?" she asks.

"I know," I whisper, pulling her close. "When I look around this house, those are the memories I think about."

She peers up at me. "I want to believe you."

"Have I given you any reason not to believe me?" I ask.

"No," she says softly.

I get the feeling she wants to say more, but she doesn't. A woman who has something to say but won't is like a snake ready to strike. You know it's coming, but there's not a damn thing you can do to prepare. I've been down this road with women before, so I predict what's coming.

"Is this . . ." my voice cracks. Fuck, my voice hasn't cracked since I was thirteen. "Is this too much for you?"

She looks up at me, her eyes wide, thinking I'm giving her an out. Doesn't she know she's never getting rid of me? I'm in this for good.

"I'm doing my best to keep you from getting hurt," I say. "If there's something more you need, then I need you to tell me. I can't read your mind."

She nods and says, "I think I'll feel better after we tell Mia, and everyone knows. At first it was fun to sneak around, but it's not feeling very fun anymore."

"You know that can't happen right now," I say. She says she understands, but everything else about her—her eyes, her posture, her demeanor—tells me she's hurting. "Didn't you say you got stuff for dinner?"

She cocks a cute little smile. "A bottle of wine, steaks, and bubble bath."

"We should probably go to your place in case Mia and Sheena come back here," I say.

She nods, saying, "Just so you know, the wine and bubble bath are mine. You can have the steaks."

I grab her from behind, tickling her. "You aren't going to share?"

"Nope, I'm going to drink all the wine."

"Like the time you got so buzzed you thought cutting your own hair was a good idea?" I ask.

She cracks up laughing. "Took six months for my bangs to look normal."

I take hold of her, grabbing her ass. "No wine, no bath, no steaks. I'm taking you straight to bed."

She raises an eyebrow at me, like I'm in big trouble. Guess a man should never assume he's getting laid, but he can always hope. I place my hand at the small of her back, leading her out to the porch. What is it about that spot on a woman? The small of her back.

There are so many sexy spots on a woman. They are basically sexy by nature. Guess that's by design. Devlyn is no exception. In fact, she might be the blueprint for sexy—her ass, her tits, her legs, her lips, that perfect curve of her waist. There's so much to worship you might forget about the small of her back.

There is something so innately protective about a man placing his hand there. I can guide her where I want her to go, pull her closer to me. I know Devlyn has two dimples at the small of her back that are the sexiest things I've ever seen, framing the curve of her ass.

Maybe that's the thing about the small of a woman's back, your hand is dangerously close to their ass. Whatever it is, that simple touch shows the world she's mine. I know that's what she wants, what she needs.

Suddenly, she stops. I look up, finding Sheena staring right at us, and her eyes go to my hand. I don't want to stop touching Devlyn; instead, I want to curve my arm all the way around her and pull her closer, but I can't. I don't trust Sheena not to tell Mia.

"Is Mia here?" Sheena asks, her voice frantic.

I take a couple big steps closer to her. "Why would she be here? She's supposed to be at dinner with you."

"She got upset," Sheena says, starting to pace a little circle. "She ran off. I thought she might come back here."

"I knew this would happen," I snap. "What did you do?"

"I know you're mad at me," Sheena snaps back. "But I have every right to be mad at you, too!"

"I don't give a fuck if you're mad at me. I didn't do a damn thing to you. Now where the hell is my daughter?"

"Our daughter!" Sheena says quickly, glaring at Devlyn. "Everyone needs to remember whose daughter she actually is."

"Mine!" I say.

Sheena starts to laugh. "You think you can forbid me from seeing her for eighteen years, and that's going to change the fact that I'm her mother. Although I'm sure that was your asshole lawyer of a father's idea."

"What the hell are you talking about?" I ask. "You signed away your rights. I never . . ."

"Please," she says, throwing her hands up. "Thought you were being sneaky, burying that little clause in the legal paperwork that I could have no contact until Mia's eighteenth birthday."

"That's not true," I say. "You never made any attempts to contact her."

"Because I couldn't," she cries, pulling out a folded contract, flipping through and pointing to a paragraph. "Right here. A no-contact clause. I have to say that's really low. I was depressed and scared and making a difficult decision, and you had to put that in there. To say I could never call her or see her or get a picture or anything."

She breaks down in tears, clutching her hands over her heart. I stare down at the words on the paper, trying to read them, but it just looks like letters on the page, not making sense. I never actually read this before. I just signed it. Devlyn comes to my side, reading it. How did I not know this was in there? My father drafted this. Why would he do this? He saw how hurt I was after she left. What the fuck?

Still, Sheena is not going to play the victim in this. The only victim in this is Mia.

"You didn't have to sign it!" I say.

"I'd just had a baby and was leaving her and you. I wasn't thinking clearly. I thought that was what you wanted—to never see me again. I thought I should at least give you that. I thought I deserved your hatred. I thought that's what you wanted, and I couldn't hurt you again."

"I didn't know about this," I say, handing her back the papers.

"I find that really hard to believe."

"Believe what you want. I didn't know."

Sheena pauses a moment, considering my words, then begins to sob. "I couldn't come back."

"You wanted to?"

Sheena glances up at me, her lashes wet with tears, but she doesn't answer. "I know you want me to be the villain in this story, and that's fine, but I . . ."

I wave her off and try to refocus. "We need to find Mia."

"I'll try and call her," Devlyn says.

"I've been trying," Sheena says.

I give Devlyn a nod to go ahead then turn back to Sheena and ask, "What happened?"

Sheena's brown eyes cloud with a look I've seen before. Guilt. She stammers for words.

Devlyn steps closer. "Mia's not picking up."

Sheena shakes her head, straightening her posture. "She asked me why I never called or tried to see her, why I came back now. I told her I couldn't and showed her the no-contact clause."

"Mia thinks this is *your* fault, Garrett," Devlyn whispers, glaring at Sheena. "She thinks you did this. She thinks you kept her away from her mother."

"Fuck, we have to find her," I say. "Where are my keys?"

"I'll take my car and look for her, too," Devlyn says.

"I'll stay here in case she comes back," Sheena says.

Devlyn grabs my hand. "We'll find her."

CHAPTER TWENTY-FIVE

GARRETT

IT DOESN'T TAKE long to cover Eden Valley by car. I can cover the whole town a half-dozen times in less than an hour. I can call most of the town in that amount of time, too. No one's seen Mia. Everyone promises to call me if they spot her. Half the town is out looking, too. I stopped by Penny's house in person, knowing the bonds of teenage girls are strong and not trusting that Penny wouldn't lie to me, but Mia wasn't there.

Mia's still not answering her phone. She doesn't have her car, so she can't have gone far, but it's dark out now. It's not as though Mia's never been out this time of the night, but I always knew where she was, who she was with, when she was coming home. Now I know nothing.

I was prepared for this feeling when she went off to college, but not while she's under my roof, not while she's upset. People make stupid decisions when they're upset, do stupid things. I hop out of my truck, deciding that walking is best. It will help me burn off some stress and allow me to get to some places that I can't see from my truck. Walking, I make sure to look down every alley, between all the buildings. Hell, at this point I'm even checking out rooftops. I should have put that tracking app on her phone like every other parent in the universe.

I check the hardware store and Biscuit Girl. I text Devlyn every five minutes to see if she's had any luck. Sheena calls me at about the same interval. The words of the contract we signed swirl in my hand.

Absolutely no contact until the above-mentioned minor reaches eighteen years of age.

I need to find my copy of the paperwork and read over it. Maybe Sheena changed it? Maybe this is all some trick on her part?

She showed up on Mia's eighteenth birthday. That can't be a coincidence. Could she have really been waiting for that day all these years? Waiting for a chance to see Mia again? To hold her? To tell her she loves her?

My head is spinning so fast I feel like I've been on a bender for the past eighteen years. No amount of alcohol could ever fuck with my head more than tonight has.

Did Sheena change her mind and want Mia? Or did she simply want visitation? Did Sheena's change of heart have anything to do with me? Did she want me, too? Want us to be a family? When did she start having these thoughts? Days? Weeks? Months? Years after she left?

I stop walking. Everything is quiet. No insects are chirping. No cars. No sound except my heart against my chest, the memories invading my mind. Sheena's teenage voice ringing in my ears.

I love you, too, Garrett.

Rubbing my jaw, I lean against the lamppost, the memory of that summer swirling.

It was a night like this one—dark and quiet—a few days before the Fourth of July. I was holding Sheena's hand, walking her back to the house her parents rented for the summer. My dick was still hard from our dry humping session at my grandparents' old house. I was sure her panties were still soaked, too. The difference was, she'd gotten off, and I was in serious pain.

In the moonlight, I could still see the blush on her cheek. She swore that had never happened before. It certainly was the first time I'd ever given a girl an orgasm. I'd never done more than kiss a girl until Sheena. I wouldn't say Sheena was a "fast" girl, just that things between us moved that way. Neither one of us did much to stop it, but we didn't really talk about it, either. I knew I should be prepared, buy some condoms, but there was no way I could do that in Eden Valley. I'd have to borrow the car and drive to the next town if I wanted to make sure that my parents didn't find out.

I didn't know then Sheena had birth control covered. Still, if I'd only made that drive.

Sheena stopped by this lamppost, hugging me. I whispered in her ear that I loved her. It wasn't to get in her pants. It wasn't for any reason other than it was true. When she whispered it back, I believed her.

In the years that followed, I told myself that it wasn't true. That it was teenage hormones and not the real thing. The hurt I felt after she left was all the explanation I needed.

Love and hurt don't mix.

Only they do. As much as we try not to hurt the ones we love, they always end up being the ones we hurt the most.

Loving hard means hurting harder.

I see it with me and Sheena, and I see it when Devlyn looks at me these days. She's hurting. I'm doing my best to not cause her more pain, but it sure seems I'm failing.

"Garrett?"

My body tenses at his voice. That hasn't happened since I was a teenager, when I knew I was in trouble. Tonight, it's for a whole other reason.

"Any luck finding Mia?" my dad asks. "Devlyn called me looking for her."

I should've called him myself, but I had Devlyn do it, knowing what would happen if I talked to him right now.

"A no-contact clause!" I snap.

He stops dead in his tracks about four feet from me. "That's what I wanted to talk to you about this morning," he says.

"This morning?" I yell, pulling at my hair. "What about eighteen years ago? Or any time since then?"

"When Mia was born, you were in no position to make these kinds of decisions. Your mother and I . . ."

"Mom knew?"

He nods. "We wanted to protect you."

I can't believe this. "So it's true? You put that in."

"I did," he says, not sounding like he regrets it in the slightest.

"Anything else in there I don't know about?"

"It's all pretty standard," he says. "Sheena relinquished all rights. Was relieved of all financial responsibility."

"And she couldn't contact me or Mia for eighteen years?"

"We did it to protect you both." He steps a little closer. "Suppose she would've changed her mind a year down the road, or five? Then what? You'd have to share custody with her. No judge would deny her. She was young. She had no support. A judge would be sympathetic to her. We couldn't run that risk. I wouldn't let that happen to you."

"What about what I wanted? Or Mia?" I ask.

"What you want isn't often what you need," he says, turning my words on me. "I gave you what you needed."

"Dad, this wasn't your decision to make."

"Son . . ."

"She shows up on Mia's eighteenth birthday?" I say, shaking my head. "Jesus Christ, Dad!"

"You know I don't like it when you talk like that," he scolds.

Before I say something I'd regret, I start to walk off, unsure if I've ever been this angry with him before. He altered the course of my life, of Mia's life with those papers. He thinks it was for the best, but what if he's wrong? I'll never know. I'll never know what would've happened if Sheena came back sooner. How Mia would be? How I would be? This is a betrayal. A big one.

Still, I know he loves me. I know that. But that's the thing about love. Sometimes it leads us to do some stupid ass shit. Nothing renders a man more stupid than being in love. He hears what he wants, sees what he wants, and suddenly can't be rational to save his life. His dick rules the roost, his heart rules everything else, and his head is stuck far up his ass.

He calls after me. "I've got to find Mia," I call back without turning around.

Everything I've believed the past eighteen years is a lie. I thought Sheena just left and never looked back. I thought my parents were honest people. I never dreamed something like this.

My phone rings. Sheena again.

"Is she at home?" I ask.

"No," she says. "So you haven't found her?"

"No."

"Eden Valley is so small. Where could she be?"

My gut does a weird twisting motion. "Maybe she's not here?"

"You don't think she'd really run away?" Sheena asks.

"Before tonight, I would've said no, but now I don't know anything," I say, my eyes darting around.

"Is it always this much worry?" Sheena asks.

"Not usually," I say.

"I never worried about Mia much. I knew you'd make sure she was happy. Had a good life. I always trusted that." She takes a deep breath. "I worried about you a lot, though."

"Me?"

"It wasn't just Mia I gave up eighteen years ago," she says then clears her throat. "Find her, Garrett. Find our baby girl and bring her home."

"I will," I promise. "Stay there in case she comes back."

"I'm not going anywhere," she says, and I wonder if there's some hidden meaning in her words.

I hang up and continue my search. All the usual hangouts lead nowhere. There's only one more place I can think to look.

I head to the hardware store to grab a flashlight then make my way across town. Teenagers love to hang out at the Falls at night. They don't think we know it's the local make-out and drinking spot, but we do. Almost every day I work on the pavilion, there are empty beer cans and used rubbers laying about. The poor park service guy has to pick that shit up. There are trash bins, but they don't get used.

All the kids know they aren't to come out here alone at night. It's a waterfall in the middle of the damn woods. They could fall, get hurt, drown, or run into some unfriendly wildlife. There *are* such things as vicious squirrels. I made Mia read a whole article on a squirrel that terrorized a neighborhood out in California, hoping that would be burned in her brain, and she would never come out here on her own.

Of course, she joked and said only California squirrels are killers. God, I love that girl. Where is she? Flicking on the flashlight, I make my way over the wooden bridges that lead to the Falls. I don't call out her name, thinking if she knows I'm coming she might make a break for it or hide.

She needs to know the truth, that I never kept Sheena away from her, that this wasn't my doing. Everything will be okay if I can just explain. Well, things might not be okay between her and my dad, at least not for a while.

The light and the shadows play a game of tag as I make my way, the rush of the Falls calling me like a ghost. I've made this walk thousands of times, especially lately for work, but it's never felt like this. The legend of this place is built on a love story, but some of the greatest of those are tragedies.

Which brings me back to love and hurt. Why are they more often than not mingled together? Why is every high school student on the face of the planet made to read Shakespeare's *Romeo and Juliet*? It's touted as one of the greatest love stories ever written, yet everyone dies. Pain and love are so intertwined we can't separate it.

Just like the Falls. The legend here. A great love. A great loss.

Hurt and love.

Eden Valley is founded on it.

"Ouch, crap, stupid phone!"

"Devlyn," I call out, knowing her voice anywhere and scanning the tree line with my flashlight, searching for her.

"Ouch," she says again. "Over here."

Moving the light, I see her standing over by the pavilion and rush to her. "What are you doing out here?"

"Looking for Mia," she says, rubbing her shin.

I flash the light down, seeing the rip in her jeans, the huge scratch on her leg, blood soaking the fabric. Bending down to take a look, I say, "You shouldn't be out here alone."

"You're alone," she says.

"Well, at least I brought a flashlight," I say, examining her leg.

"I was using my phone," she says. "But then it died."

Getting to my feet, I say, "Doesn't look like it needs stitches."

"Whose bright idea was it to leave this big pile of wood out here?" she teases. "Maybe I should sue."

"Very funny," I say. "You could've really hurt yourself."

"It was the last place I thought to look for Mia," she says.

"Me, too," I say, the fear in my voice evident.

Handing her the flashlight, I scoop her up, carrying her out. "My hero," she says, shining the light in front of us and leaning her head on my shoulder.

"I need you to be smarter than this," I snap. "What if something happened to you?"

She responds by kissing me on the cheek. Devlyn is one of those people that just understands. She knows my voice is harsh because I'm worried. She doesn't take offense, knowing I don't mean it. It's just the worry and stress talking. She knows that. Devlyn is good at translating me. She might know me better than I know me.

"I can walk," she says sweetly.

"I can carry you," I say.

"Always so cocky," she says, wiggling a little bit. "Garrett, you're tired. Let me walk."

"No, you're hurt."

"Said yourself it doesn't need stitches," she says.

"Needs me," I say.

"Always," she says. With that, she wins, and I put her down, keeping my arm under her to help her hobble along. "What now?"

"I'm going to keep looking," I say.

"I'll come with you."

"You're going home and getting that cut taken care of." Before she can object, I plant a soft kiss on her lips. "I'll walk you home. We can look for Mia on the way."

"She's a tough girl," Devlyn says. "She knows you love her. She just needs some time to think."

"She thinks I kept her mother from her," I say.

"Does no one remember that Sheena's the one who left in the

first place?" Devlyn asks.

"I haven't forgotten that," I say. "But . . ."

"No buts!" she says, pulling away from me. "She left! End of story."

"She regrets that," I say without thinking.

"Now you are defending her," Devlyn bites.

"I'm not defending her."

"And when did this change of heart take place?" Devlyn asks. "A week ago? A year ago? Just how long has she been missing you and Mia?"

"We aren't talking about me," I say.

"Oh, yes we are," Devlyn says, putting her finger in my face. "Make no mistake about it. Sheena didn't just come back to see Mia. She came to see you, too."

"You're acting like a jealous girlfriend, Devlyn."

"I guess fucking me every chance you get doesn't earn me the right to be a little jealous."

Wrapping my arms around her from behind, I kiss the top of her head. "I'm telling you that you don't need to be."

"I'm sorry," she says. "I'm tired. I know that's no excuse. You don't need me acting all cray cray right now."

"I'm used to it," I tease then add, "We've got to find Mia."

I MIGHT BE the only person up at this hour. Well, the only person in Eden Valley, anyway. I know that's not true, either. I'm sure my dad isn't sleeping. I got Devlyn to go home, but I'm sure she's not sleeping.

A worried parent makes an insomniac look like a narcoleptic. Apparently, that's one trait of motherhood Sheena inherited. I see her through the window of my house, sitting at my kitchen table. I came home to check the workshop one more time. Of course, Mia's not there. A quick piss, and I'm going to make my loop through town again. As soon as the sun comes up, I'll start making another round of phone calls.

I open the front door, and Sheena leaps to her feet. I hold my hand up, indicating Mia's not with me, knowing she's got no news, either. She sinks back into the chair. "I shouldn't have come. It's my fault she's missing."

God help me! I have to be reaching my limit of emotional women. Guess I can hold my piss a minute longer. "Tell me again what you said to her."

She repeats what she told me earlier. "I just wanted her to know that I loved her. I wanted to be with her."

"What are you saying?" I ask, feeling my defenses shoot right up. "You wanted to be her mom? You wanted Mia?"

"I wanted both of you," she says, looking up into my eyes. "I always wanted both of you."

I shake my head in disbelief. "Sheena?" I say and step away from her slightly.

"I know," she says. "At first I thought it was just a normal reaction to have after giving up our baby. I went to birth mom support groups. Had a shrink for a while. I had this empty feeling inside me. It never went away."

"You regret leaving?" I ask.

"Yes," she says then shrugs. "No. At the time, it was probably for the best. I was in no condition to be a mother. I'm sure I would've fucked her up."

"I never thought that," I say. "I thought you'd be a great mother."

"I was," she says. "I did what I thought was best for my daughter. Just like I'm doing now. I came here because I thought it was for the best. I thought she'd want to see me. I never imagined this."

"We will find her," I say.

"Garrett," she says, reaching for my hand, "this is my fault. I need you to know that. Nothing you did or didn't do made me leave that day."

"We were so young," I say.

"And scared," she says, and I nod in agreement. "I was so grateful when the Eden Valley newspaper went online. I searched it every day for glimpses of you or Mia."

My face must show my shock. She was across the ocean searching for news about us?

"I didn't really have any friends in Eden Valley that I could call for news. Not that anyone here would help me, anyway. I've got to be the most hated woman in the history of the town."

"I don't remember being in the paper," I say.

"When you bought the store," she says, "there was an article about the change in ownership. And once there was a picture of Mia on your shoulders at some Christmas event. It was from behind. She had on this polka dot and striped romper-looking thing. The photo was black and white, so I couldn't tell the colors. Then there was the school honor roll listing every quarter. And . . ."

She keeps listing articles, like she has them filed in a card catalog or something. I can tell she hung on to those tidbits of information like her life depended on it.

"These are letters," she says, reaching into her purse and pulling out the box with the ribbon on it from Mia's party. "Every year on her birthday, I wrote her a letter, and I couldn't send it."

Hating her all these years was easier than this, witnessing her pain. I sit down beside her, having no idea how much pain she'd been in. I always assumed she was off living the high life while I was changing diapers and wiping up vomit. "I'm sure Mia would love to have those."

She nods, trying in vain to pull herself together. "I shouldn't be crying. It's just hard. I've missed so much, and now I've hurt her again. Maybe I should just go back home."

A few days ago, those words would have been music to my ears, but I know how badly that would hurt Mia. "You promised her you wouldn't just leave again."

Her eyes grow wide. "You want me to stay?"

Choosing my words carefully because I don't want them to come back and bite me in the ass, I say, "I think you need to keep your promise to Mia."

She nods. "This is why I stayed in Europe and never moved back to the states. I needed an ocean between us. That was the only thing that kept me from showing up on your doorstep again. Still, do you know how many times I went to the airport to fly here? Every birthday. Every Christmas. Hell, a few times I even bought the ticket."

"Why didn't you?" I ask. "Can't just be because of the contract."

"Fear," she says. "I'd get there and talk myself out of it. Telling myself to let you be happy. That I didn't deserve to see her. That it was selfish of me."

She looks at me with those brown eyes, the same ones Mia has, and I soften. It makes me uncomfortable. I've held onto my hate for her. That's what I'm comfortable with. I'm now conflicted, aggravated, tired. "I better get back out there and look for her," I say, getting to my feet then heading to my bathroom to take a long-awaited leak.

"Garrett," she says, causing me to turn back. "I think there's a lot we need to talk about, to say to each other."

Now is hardly the time.

"For Mia's sake," she says.

"For Mia," I say.

CHAPTER TWENTY-SIX

DEVLYN

SO I LIED to Garrett again. Geez, I'm making a habit of this, but he wanted me to go home and sit on my hands while Mia is missing. Not gonna happen. I did go home to clean up the cut on my leg and change my clothes, but now the search is back on.

Eden Valley is quaint and charming during the day, but there's something special about it at night. It's quiet and still, and you feel like you're the only soul here, but it's not scary or lonely. There's a peace to this town, to the people here. A peace that comes from knowing that your neighbor has your back. The people here look out for each other, which is how I know Mia will turn up. Someone here had to see something, has to know something.

I take a seat in the gazebo in the middle of town square. "Mia, where are you?" I whisper to the wind, hoping it carries a message to her. My feet hurt from walking, my leg hurts from banging it, my head hurts from stress, my heart hurts from worry. I'm now the very definition of the phrase "worried sick."

I've been a teenage girl. I've been a teenage girl pissed at her parents. I should be able to figure out where Mia is. I made pissing my mom off an art form when I was Mia's age. I was the freaking Leonardo da Vinci of teenage girl passive-aggressive behavior.

Once when I was mad at my mom, I rode on the back of a motorcycle with a boy without a helmet, making sure to cruise by the diner for extra drama. Another time, I showed up to church in a short red dress that left little to the imagination. But mostly, I hung out with the local teenage father—which left my mother in a perpetually bad mood. Garrett is good at lots of things and yanking my momma's chain is one of them.

"A boy," I cry out, feeling silly that I didn't realize it before. There is no easier way to get your parents' feathers in a ruffle than getting mixed up with the bad boy.

But Mia doesn't have a boyfriend. I know that doesn't matter. Boys are a dime a dozen, and there's always a bad boy around looking for some trouble.

I reach for my phone but find nothing, now realizing I left it plugged into the charger at home. I know Garrett's out searching for Mia, but I need to tell him my theory. I hate to do it, knowing Sheena could still be at his house, but I head back that way. She can't object to me using the phone to call him. If there is anything we can all agree on, it's that we need to find Mia.

I'm surprised when I see his truck in front of his house. I didn't think anything could tear him away from finding Mia. Maybe he found her? I quicken my pace. He could be calling my cell to tell me, and I wouldn't know. Please God, let Mia be safe and sound inside.

I start making promises to God in my head, vowing and swearing to do anything and everything I can think of. I'll stop gossiping. I won't swear anymore. I will no longer judge those unfortunate souls who are unlucky enough to end up in front of me in the grocery store line. I know God doesn't make deals, but I'm hoping he'll make an exception just this once.

A prayer on my lips, I walk through Garrett's front door. If God was listening, he just got a prayer full of expletives. Garrett's walking out from his bedroom, pulling up the zipper of his jeans. I see Sheena, too.

My eyes dart back and forth between her and his fly. My head yells at me not to react, searching for an explanation. He wouldn't do this—and certainly not now, with his daughter missing. A few hours ago, he swore I had nothing to be jealous of.

As usual, my heart wins, and tears rush down my face. Garrett looks down at his pants, holding his hands out. I turn and rush out the door, hearing him yell, "This isn't what it looks like!"

I don't have a car here. Crap! No way am I going to escape on foot. Garrett grabs me, turning me toward him. "I was taking a piss," he says, his voice sharp. "I heard the door open and ran out hoping it was Mia. That's it."

That's a logical explanation, and I know by his voice, his eyes, that it's true, but my heart doesn't recover as quickly as my head.

"I'm sorry you walked in when you did, but . . ."

"I don't want to hear you're sorry," I snap. "I can handle being second place to Mia, but not Sheena. Not again."

"You aren't."

"Then why were you even here with her? You sent me home. Didn't want me to search with you, but here you are with her."

"I came home for just a minute and . . ." he pauses. I hate it when people do that. It's like they are parsing their words, searching for the right ones. The truth is the truth. It should just roll off the tongue. "Something came up."

"I know what came up!"

His jaw tenses. "Sheena was crying and upset, okay? I came home to piss, and she wanted to talk. For Mia's sake."

Shaking my head in disbelief, I say, "She's using Mia to play you."

"Devlyn," he says, reaching out for me. "Do you believe me when I tell you nothing happened with her?"

"I believe you didn't sleep with her," I say. "But something did happen. You don't hate her like you did."

"Here's the thing," he says. "You either believe in us, or you don't." I want to yell that I believed in us before he even knew there was an us, but he lowers his head to mine and whispers, "I'm really hoping you do because I do. More than anything."

"I'm trying, Garrett," I whimper.

Pulling me to his side, he walks us back toward the house. When we reach the porch, I step away from him, but he takes my hand, leading me inside. Sheena's eyes are like a laser on our joined hands.

Garrett squeezes mine and says, "I'm sure you've pieced together by now that Devlyn and I are together." Sheena glances at me. No smile, no frown, no expression at all. It's kind of scary how in control she is. "Only a few people know. Mia isn't one of them."

"Why doesn't . . ."

Garrett shakes his head that she doesn't get to ask questions. "I expect you to keep this to yourself until Devlyn and I have had a chance to tell Mia ourselves."

"Of course," Sheena says.

I inch a little closer to Garrett, letting him know I appreciate this gesture. It should make me feel better, but it only makes me worry about how she could use this information against him. Against us. He looks down at me, giving me a small smile.

"Maybe I should call nearby hospitals," Sheena says.

"I did that earlier. Called some cab companies and the bus terminals from neighboring towns, too."

"Where the hell is she?" Garrett asks, growing more agitated by the second.

"I had a thought. It's why I came over," I say, looking up at him. "You aren't going to like it."

"What?"

"If I were mad at my parents and wanted to get even with them about something, I'd find some trouble. Maybe a boy?"

"I've called every boy in her class," Garrett says.

"Mia doesn't strike me as that way, anyway," Sheena says.

I try my best not to cut her a look that says "how the hell would you know?" I mean, she's known the girl for like two days.

"I think she's just hurting and needs some time alone," Sheena says. "That's how I am."

"I don't think runaway behavior is hereditary," I say. Unable to help myself, I add, "But on second thought, maybe it is."

Was that petty? Probably so, but it's just too damn soon for everyone to forget what she did.

Garrett glances at Sheena. "I'm going back out to look for her. Let me know if you hear from her." Then he places his hand on the small of my back, directing me outside. "Guess I need to take you home for the second time tonight," he says, raising an eyebrow and opening the door to his truck.

"I had to keep looking."

"I know, and I appreciate it," he says. "But you've got to open the diner in a few hours. Please go get some rest. I need to know that you're okay."

Garrett is my weak spot. We all have one. Some of us have more than one. Like coffee or chocolate or wine. For Garrett, it's Mia, and for me, it's him. I can't shake it. No matter how hard I try, he will always be my weakness. Maybe that's where the phrase "weak in the knees" comes from. Weak, so I can't run away. There is no escape. Who am I kidding? It's not as though I've tried very hard. Even if I could run away, I'm betting he would chase me. At least I hope he would. Let's hope I never have to find out.

PAJAMAS ARE ON. Teeth are brushed. Hair is combed. Lights are out.

Sleep is non-existent.

Every time I text Garrett for an update, he simply responds by ordering me to sleep, and that I'll be the first to know when he finds her.

I stare up at the ceiling fan in my room. When's the last time I dusted that? Throwing the covers off, I stand up in the middle of my bed, reaching up and barely grazing the blades of the fan with the tips of my fingers. Pretty good!

I tilt my head, trying to catch a glimpse at the top of the armoire. No telling what's living up there. Hopping off my bed, I walk to the kitchen to get a chair. Apparently, cleaning is a side effect of insomnia.

A small knock halts my progress. That's not Garrett's knock. He's more of a banger. Smiling at the pun, the knock comes again. I flick on the porch light, moving back the curtain to check who or what is making the sound. This is Eden Valley. There hasn't been a violent crime here that I can remember, but I'm not going to be the first victim.

Mia!

Flinging the door open, I pull her into my arms, crying like a fool and kissing the top of her head over and over again. She clings to me, sobbing into my pajamas. She's petite anyway, but right now she feels so young, so little. I'm so thankful to see her that I don't even think to scold her.

Pulling back, I hold her face in my hands, scanning her for signs of injury. Her blonde hair is tangled, her face tear-stained, and she's trembling. "I didn't know where else to go," she sobs.

I pull her inside. "I'm glad you're here. What happened?"

She shakes her head. "Dad lied to me about Mom. He's been lying to me my whole life."

"No," I say. "He didn't know about that part of the agreement. Your grandfather put that in without him knowing. Garrett loves you. He wouldn't keep something like that from you."

As soon as the words are out of my mouth, I realize Garrett actually *has* been keeping something big from her—*me.*

"Granddad?" she asks, and I nod. "But why? How could he do that to me?"

"I'm sure he was just trying to protect you and your dad."

"I never want to talk to him again!"

Patting her leg, I know that's a conversation for her to have with Garrett. "Let me call your dad," I say.

"No!" she cries. "Please, Devlyn, I've been so stupid."

I reach for her hand. "Stupid how?" I ask and then it hits me—the way she looks at me. I know before she says a word. Please let me be wrong.

"He's out of his mind with worry. I have to call him." She leaps off my sofa, rushing to the door. "Okay, okay," I say. "How about I call him, let him know you are safe, but tell him you aren't ready to see him?"

"He won't go for that," she says.

"Let me handle it."

"He'll go crazy."

"I know," I say. "But I'll take the heat for you."

"Thank you," she says.

I give her another squeeze, knowing I need to ask her some

tough questions. I'm not sure it's my place, but she might feel more comfortable being honest with me than her dad. "Did you take any drugs or were you drinking?"

"I had a few drinks," she says softly.

"Are you hurt?" I ask.

Her head shakes. I take one deep breath and close my eyes. "Did anyone force you to do anything?"

"No," she whispers. "I can make bad decisions all on my own."

"Hey," I say, looking into her eyes. "You're a good girl. No matter what happened tonight. That doesn't change that you are a good person. It doesn't change that I love you. Your dad loves you. Nothing changes that."

She gives me an unconvincing nod. "Would you mind if I shower? I walked like fifteen miles to get here."

That's really far, but I manage to hold my surprise. I know she's not telling me something, and I also know that I can't force it out of her. Teenage girls are very good at keeping their secrets. "Mia?"

She looks away from me. "There's this guy."

I knew it.

"He's older."

"How old?"

"Twenty," she says. "I knew he was interested, but I didn't want to get involved before I left for school. After I left Mom, I called him and had him come pick me up. He lives with like four other guys, and they were having a party. He turned out to be a jerk. I ended up having to walk back home."

There seems to be a big chunk of her story missing. Jerk to walking home—something in the middle. "A jerk how?" I ask.

"He was only interested in partying. When I wanted to leave, he wouldn't bring me home because he was having a good time. Dad always told me to have my own money, but I didn't tonight. The guy wouldn't even get me a cab, so I walked," she says. "I just feel stupid for going there. I was mad at Dad and just wanted to blow off some steam."

"Why didn't you call someone for a ride? Me? Penny?" I ask.

"I was embarrassed," she says. "I just needed to think. By the time I thought to call, my phone had died."

"I'm not going to give you some big lecture," I say. "I'll leave that to Garrett."

A small smile on her face, she nods and thanks me.

"Go shower, and I'll call your dad." I walk her to my bathroom, making sure she's got fresh towels and knows where everything is. I give her one of my oversized t-shirts to sleep in and promise to make her something to eat. When she's all set, I grab my phone.

Blowing out a breath, I dial. One ring, two rings, then I hear his voice, the worried tone, the exhaustion. I won't make him wait one second longer to know his daughter is alright. "Mia's here," I say. "She showed up at my house a few minutes ago. She's alright."

"Thank God," he says. "I'm on my way."

"She's upset and exhausted. Why don't you let her get some sleep and see her in the morning?"

"I'm seeing her right now."

"Garrett, she doesn't want to see you."

"Did you tell her that I didn't know about the no-contact clause?"

"Yes, I told her," I say. "She's had a rough night. She wants a few hours of peace and rest before facing you."

"Tough," he says. "I'll be there in five."

The phone goes dead. I give an exasperated grunt into my phone. I miss the days when you could slam a receiver down. That was always good for dramatic effect. Cell phones cost way too much money to do that, and I doubt slamming your phone because you're pissed off is covered under the protection plan.

Appealing to his rational side didn't work. I step out on my porch, knowing I've only got a couple minutes. I try to think of what to say to him, but I've got nothing. Nothing that's going to make him feel better.

I make one quick phone call to Trudy to let her know Mia is safe, knowing she'll make sure everyone else knows. Then I wait for Garrett. It's got to be almost two in the morning by now, but the air is still thick with humidity, making my skin feel sticky, like I need to shower again. The light of the full moon shines down on the street. The dark outline of his body comes into view, and even his silhouette looks tense.

"Where is she?" he calls out as soon as my property comes into sight.

"Inside taking a shower," I say.

He bounds up the front steps, reaching around me for the doorknob. "Garrett?"

"You don't want to get in the middle of me and my daughter," he threatens.

"She came to me. Of all the places she could go, she came here," I say. "Think about that. Do you want to get in the middle of that?"

His blue eyes glance at me. We both know he could go around me. I couldn't stop him. The only things I have on my side are words and his love for Mia. "Where was she?"

"I think she should tell you."

"I have to see her," he says.

"She didn't even want me to call you," I say. "When I told her I had to, she tried to bolt again. The past few days have been a lot on her. She needs a good night's sleep, a hot meal, a place where she doesn't feel torn between you and Sheena."

"I'm not leaving until I see her."

I'm not going to fight with him, even though he looks like he's gearing up for one, his muscles hard, his jaw set. I know Garrett. When he digs his heels in, he's as stubborn as they come. He makes a mule look like a laidback puppy dog.

"I'll sleep on your damn front porch if I have to."

There's not a doubt in my mind that's true.

"Garrett," I say tenderly, wrapping my arms around his neck. He squeezes me hard, his head buried in my hair. I feel all his worry and fear and know he won't feel better until he sees her. "She's okay," I whisper.

His head nods, his arms getting tighter around me. We stand there for what seems like forever, just holding each other on my porch under the watchful eye of the man on the moon. It must've been long enough that Mia changed her mind about seeing Garrett, or she wondered what the heck we were doing out here. I hear the click of the knob behind me, and Garrett releases me.

Mia cracks open the door, wearing my t-shirt, a towel wrapped around her head. She doesn't look either one of us in the eye. Garrett engulfs her in his arms and says, "You scared the shit out of me."

"I'm sorry," she says softly.

He pulls back, his hands on her tiny shoulders. "Where the hell have you been?"

Her eyes find mine, begging for help. "You both look exhausted," I say.

Garrett looks down at Mia. It doesn't take a rocket scientist to figure out she needs some rest, and Garrett is very predictable when it comes to Mia. He always does what's best for her. "Come on," he says. "Let's get you home."

Those begging brown eyes of hers find me again, tugging at my heart. She doesn't need the third degree from her father right now, and if they go home, there's a big chance of that happening, because he's been so frantic with worry. The past few days have been hard on him, too, even if he doesn't say it. I know.

"She's all ready for bed," I say. "Why don't you let her stay?" I can see the no forming in his mind, all the reasons they should go. "Why don't you stay, too?" The shock on his face is priceless. "I know you want to be close to her tonight. You should both stay."

Mia yawns a little, and that seals the deal. We all make our way inside. I get Mia something to eat and set her up in my spare bedroom under Garrett's watchful eye. To his credit, he doesn't push her for answers. The relief that she's alright is enough for the moment. He stays in the doorway until she falls asleep, which doesn't take more than a minute.

Grabbing a pillow and blanket, I make up the sofa for him. As much as I wish he could be in my bed, I know that's not going to happen. I feel him staring at me. "It's like we had our first fight, and you've been relegated to the sofa."

"Why do the guys always get kicked to the sofa?"

"You don't want to sleep with an angry woman," I say. "It's for your own safety. Remember Lorena Bobbitt?"

He walks past me, grazing my hand and taking a seat on the sofa. "Thanks for being there for her."

"I love her like she's mine."

He reaches out to me, wrapping his arms around my waist and burying his head in my stomach. "I wish she was yours," he says.

"But she's not," I say, pulling back. "She's Sheena's."

"You've been more of a mother to Mia than Sheena. Tonight proves that—again. The fact that Mia chose to come here."

"But I don't get credit," I say. "Sheena gave birth to her, so that trumps all the movie nights, hair braids, breakfasts."

"No, it doesn't," he says.

"Why do I feel a *but* coming?" I ask.

"The only butt I want is yours and the coming part better happen soon," he says with that smirk that I fall for every time.

"Go to sleep," I say, tossing a pillow at him.

CHAPTER TWENTY-SEVEN

DEVLYN

GARRETT, MIA, AND I are all asleep under the same roof. Go figure. Granted, Garrett is on the sofa, and Mia still has no idea her dad and I are an item. Still, it's surreal to have them both here, to hear both of them breathing softly, at peace.

I peek in to check on Mia before heading off to the diner. I didn't get more than a few hours of sleep. She's still out like a light.

Next, I check on Garrett. His feet are hanging over the edge of my sofa. One arm is hanging off the side, the other is thrown over his head. All the pillows and cushions have been flung about. The man is well over six feet tall. He wasn't made for my girly little sofa. Still, he's completely out. I blow a kiss at him, not about to risk waking him with a real one, then as quietly as I can, grab my stuff and head to the diner.

I'm used to being the first one up in Eden Valley. It's me and the birds. I usually don't see a soul, which is how I know that Sheena walking past my shop isn't a coincidence. No one gets up at this hour unless they have to.

I know Garrett talked to her after Mia showed up, but I don't know what he actually said to her. From the looks of things, she isn't happy that neither her daughter nor her ex came home last night.

"I was hoping you could give me an update," she says.

"Mia and Garrett are both still sleeping. I need to work. Consider yourself updated," I say, moving to unlock the door to my diner.

"Mia should be coming to me," she says. "You should be encouraging her to go to her mother when she's upset."

"Are you delusional?" I ask.

"Look, I'm here," she says. "I plan on being in Mia's life from here on out. You better get used to it."

"No," I say. "You better get used to feeling unwelcome by me and everyone else in this town."

"Not everyone," she says. "Garrett told me to stay."

She's not going to pull that one on me. "For Mia," I say.

"Last night was a wakeup call for us. Garrett and I talked. We have some things to work through. We are going to get along and make every effort for Mia. Don't interfere with that."

"I don't take my cues from you."

She steps closer. "Mia is my daughter. Stop trying to take what's not yours. What will never be yours."

"Are we just talking about Mia, or is Garrett included in that?"

"Garrett and I share a child. Nothing you have with him will ever match that."

"You have no idea what Garrett and I have."

"I know he doesn't want more kids," she says, a definite snark to her voice.

"He told you that?"

"Mia told me that," she says. "Which is pretty much like it coming from his own lips."

Garrett and I had the kid conversation when we first started seeing each other. We didn't agree on anything. He never shut the idea completely down, though.

"So you see," she says. "What I have with him, you never will."

She turns to walk away. My heart reeling, wanting to call her a bitch but not wanting to stoop to her level, I call out, "You're right," causing her to turn back. "I won't ever have what you have with him, but it's not because of Mia. It's because you left."

"You love to bring that up," she says. "You think you love him more because you stayed here pining after him all these years? Let me tell you something. Loving someone and leaving them is a lot harder than staying. I could've stayed. That was the easier decision, but I did the harder thing. I let them both go. I loved them enough to let them go."

"Do me a favor and do that again," I say with an evil smile.

She rolls her eyes at me. "Loving someone and staying versus loving someone and leaving. Which is harder? You better hope that you don't ever have to find out."

What the hell? She thinks what she did was love? That it was harder than what Garrett did? Harder than what I did? She needs to ride that crazy train right out of town.

I was raised in Small Town USA—we stick. We don't run when things get hard. We stay, we fight, we try harder. We don't fold up shop and call it quits. Loving someone means sticking with them through thick and thin.

She has some gall thinking that she loves Garrett more than I do, that she loves Mia more than me. She took the easy route—all the way to fucking Europe! I know that's not entirely true and judging her doesn't make me feel any better, but why does she insist on talking to me? Seeking me out?

"Devlyn, everything alright?" Edward Hollis says, hurrying down the sidewalk toward us.

"You sure do have the Hollis men wrapped around your finger," Sheena says.

"Just trying to get the day started," I say.

"Me, too," he says. "Already went to the cemetery this morning."

I smile at him. His love for his wife hasn't changed at all since she died. He's still as devoted as ever. Is it a trait that all Hollis men love like that? Does Garrett?

He turns his eyes on Sheena, who's giving him the same death stare. "I think it's best if you move along," he says to her.

"I told Garrett about the contract. He knows what you did."

Edward waves his hand at her dismissively. "Did you also tell him your parents knew about it? Agreed to it?" She looks around, searching for a response. "You want to act like we pulled a fast one over on you, but you were fully informed about what you were signing, what you were doing."

"I was a child."

"You were a mother," he says with a softness to his voice that I couldn't manage if I was him. "Garrett begged you to stay. My dear wife, bless her soul, begged you not to leave. Isn't that right?"

"I was . . ."

"I seem to remember the last conversation I had with you, too. Do you remember that? Because I do. I remember crying with you and promising to help you and Garrett. I tried to assure you that you weren't alone. I told you that I would forever be grateful to you for giving me Mia and that if you stayed, I'd love you like my own."

I'd bet she didn't tell Garrett *that* part of the story.

"I couldn't," she says, tears streaming down her face.

"So I protected Mia and Garrett," he says simply. "You can hate me for it. Blame me, but Garrett is my son. He might be upset with me now, but he won't stay that way. He'd do the same thing for Mia. That's what a parent does."

Wiping her face and without another word, Sheena does what she does best—leaves.

I watch her walk away, and the man places his hand on my shoulder. "Buy you a cup of coffee?"

Charm runs in the family. Laughing a little, I unlock the door to the diner. I flick on the lights and get a pot brewing while Garrett's dad takes a seat on a stool at the counter. "How you holding up?" he asks.

"Mia is overwhelmed," I say. "And Garrett is . . ."

"I asked about you," he says, reaching for a napkin.

"Right," I say, shaking my head. "I'm a little tired."

"I heard," he says. "My granddaughter came to you."

"It was nothing."

"It's everything," he says. "She thinks she hasn't had a mother all these years, but she has."

My eyes fill. I honestly didn't think anyone really noticed how much I did for Garrett and Mia. "I'm just the Biscuit Girl."

"The one and only," he says with that charming smirk that his son has, too. He pats the stool beside him. "Come sit and have a cup of coffee with an old man."

I REALLY SHOULDN'T have had that third cup of coffee with Garrett's dad. I've been behind all morning. Not even the caffeine high has been able to catch me up. Seems like everyone in town came into the diner this morning, chatting about Mia, asking me questions that I won't answer. I'm running on empty, so when Mia calls asking me if I can come back home, I'm pretty much dead on my feet.

I don't think I have it in me to negotiate a fight between her and Garrett or have some big conversation with him about Sheena. A blanket, pillow, and ten hours of uninterrupted sleep is what I need, and it's only eleven in the morning.

Opening my front door, I have no idea what to expect. Could be World War III? Could be tears and tissues?

So I'm completely surprised when Mia screams, "Surprise!"

She and Garrett pull me into my kitchen. Well, it used to be my kitchen. Now it's a littered mess of pots, pans, skillets, and dirty kitchen towels.

"We made you breakfast," Mia says, as Garrett urges me to the table to sit down. The kitchen might be a disaster, but the table is perfect.

Cloth napkins, wine glasses holding orange juice, the china my grandmother left me but I never have occasion to use. It looks like I'm having tea with the Queen, only this is better. The most important meal of the day with the most important people in my life.

"Dad, the flowers," Mia says, pointing to a grocery sack filled with bright yellow sunflowers. They remembered my favorite color is yellow? This grocery store purchase gets no judgment from me. Flowers are flowers, no matter where you get them.

Garrett places them in a vase filled with water. "This was all Mia's idea," he says. "She got up, went to the store, and got everything."

Part of me wonders if this is Mia's way of avoiding talking about last night, but I'll take it. She throws her arms around my neck and whispers, "Thank you."

Kissing her cheek, my eyes go to Garrett, grinning at us. "We made all your favorites."

Mia stands up with pride, listing off the menu. "Mango, banana, and orange smoothie and hot chocolate French toast."

My mouth falls open. "How did you . . ."

"We know what you like, too," Garrett says, giving me a wink.

I place my napkin in my lap as Mia places the food down in front of me. Surprised at how good it looks, I'm praying that Mia has better abilities in the kitchen than her father. Well, he is good in the kitchen, only it involves us on the floor naked, not him cooking.

Picking up the smoothie, I take a long drink. Mistake number one. I should have sipped it or smelled it first. It's a smoothie. It shouldn't be crunchy.

"I told you that you don't put the seeds in," Mia says, laughing and playfully swatting her dad. "She looks like she's about to choke." Garrett busts out laughing. "Try the French toast," Mia says.

This time I'm more careful, examining it with my fork before I take a bite, and I only take a little one. There's something really odd about it. I've made this recipe a couple ways—with unsweetened cocoa powder or with hot chocolate mix, but this is something else.

"What kind of chocolate did you use?" I ask.

"A candy bar," Mia says. "Dad used your blender to smash it. It's good?"

"It's the best breakfast I've ever had," I say, getting to my feet and hugging them both.

"Don't worry," Garrett says. "We're going to clean up, too."

Mia gets this look on her face, her big brown eyes working overtime. "Daddy, I really need to go see Penny . . ."

"You're grounded," he says.

I guess they did have a talk this morning. "I know, that's why I need to see her. Before my grounding goes into effect." She gives him the cheesiest smile. "She was worried about me last night, too. Please! I promise after this, just work and time with you and Mom until the Fourth of July like you said."

The fact that I'm not included in those plans slaps me in the face.

It shouldn't. Why would I be included? I'm not family. Mia doesn't know anything has changed between her father and me.

"Thirty minutes," he says. She kisses him on the cheek, hugs me, then is out the door. "She's like a different child this morning," Garrett says, leaning down to kiss my neck.

"Should've asked for more than thirty minutes," I say, giving Garrett a flirty smile.

He whisks me out of the chair, throwing me over his shoulder, and carries me to my bed. Laughing, he places me down, his body on top of mine. "This was a lovely surprise," I say.

"Wish I could take the credit," he says.

His fingers lightly comb through my hair. "Did you find out where she was last night? What happened?"

He nods. "I can't believe she didn't call me."

"Think she was pretty embarrassed."

"When I think about what could've happened," he says, his eyes closing.

"She's okay," I say, tenderly.

"Mostly she wanted to talk about Sheena," he says. "We had a long talk. She wants to spend time with her." He blows out a deep breath. "I need to give Mia some time. She's in a fragile place. Fighting with Sheena and putting up roadblocks will only hurt Mia. I need to know you understand."

"Don't I always?" I say, scooting up.

"Don't be that way," he says.

"What does this mean for me? For us? What are you saying? We can't see each other?"

"No, of course not."

Rubbing my eyes, I say, "I'm too tired to have this conversation."

"This might be a first," he says. "A woman who doesn't want to talk."

"I've already talked to Sheena and your dad this morning, so . . ."

"What?"

"Nothing," I say, not wanting to get into it all. It goes nowhere.

"I need to talk to my dad," he says. "I was planning on doing that when I leave here. What did Sheena say?"

"It's not important," I say. "I can't tell on her every time she runs her mouth."

"You can if she's upsetting you. I want to know."

I repeat what Sheena said, waiting to see if his head explodes when I mention the bit about him never wanting to have a baby with me.

"Oh."

Oh? That's what he says? Dude wanted to talk, and that's his big speech? "You want to have this conversation?" I ask.

Taking hold of my hand, he says, "Mia went through this phase where she really wanted a sibling. I told her I didn't think it was in the cards. God gave me perfect when he gave me her, so why mess with that? That's what I told her. It was years ago."

Our baby would be perfect, too, I think, but don't say it. Don't need to add more to his plate. There's a right time and place to have this conversation, and we will have it. Just not now. Not after last night. "Okay," I say.

He pulls me to him, his lips finding mine. "We're wasting our thirty minutes," he says.

"You know, grounding a kid is pretty much like grounding yourself," I say, unbuttoning his shirt.

"I might have to give her time off for good behavior," he says, removing my shirt.

"You'd unground her because you're horny?"

Off with my panties, he says, "Absolutely."

"I love that," I say, pulling him closer.

CHAPTER TWENTY-EIGHT

GARRETT

"MOM'S HERE," MIA calls out, rushing to the door.

Keeping some distance, I stand in the doorway of the den. Since their last visit ended up with Mia staying gone all night, we decided it was best for Sheena and Mia to visit at my house. That way I can keep an eye on things. Plus, I think Mia needs to see that Sheena and I can set aside our differences.

When they meet, they don't hug—although I can tell Sheena wants to. "Garrett," Sheena says, throwing me a smile, "thanks for this."

"Sure," I say.

She turns back to Mia. "I realized I never gave you your birthday gift." She reaches into her purse and pulls out the wooden box.

Mia's eyes light up. "Can I open it?"

"They're letters I've written you over the years, so maybe you should read them another time."

Mia hugs them to her chest. "Thank you."

"So I thought you might want to look at some photos, old home videos," Mia says.

"I'd love that."

They walk into the den, the table full of pictures, albums, keepsakes. It's a little documentary of Mia. Mia walks Sheena through every vacation, every Christmas. Mostly I listen. Listen to my daughter describe our life together.

And not just our life together.

How happy she's been.

I did that.

Could I do that all again? The diapers? The no sleep? The ear infections and sore throats? The homework? Everything in those pictures Mia's flipping through. Can I give another child all that?

As I glance through the pictures, I see my mom, my dad, people from town, and Devlyn. Usually, she's hidden in the background somewhere, but always there. I can catch a glimpse of her hair, her tutu, some part of her.

"Look at this one!" Mia laughs, holding it up to me. "You remember?"

I snatch it from her. "You said you tore that one up!"

She turns to Sheena. "I was completely obsessed with Harry Potter this one Halloween."

"Just one," I tease her.

"Anyway, I dressed up as Hermione, and Dad surprised me and dressed up as Professor Snape! He wore a wig and everything. It was awesome."

"This I have to see," Sheena says, reaching out for the photo.

"Wait," Mia screams, leaping up. "I think I still have the wig."

Laughing, she runs to her room. "Mia, don't you dare!" I playfully threaten.

Sheena picks up some more photos, a huge smile on her face. "I never thought I'd get to see all this." Then she looks right in my eyes. "Fatherhood agrees with you, Garrett."

"I heard you had a talk with Devlyn about that," I say. "If this is going to work, then I suggest you mind your own business and stay away from Devlyn."

"I don't remember you being so protective of her," Sheena says.

Wasn't I? If not, then I must've been a complete douchebag. Mia comes walking out, the ridiculous wig on her head, and starts giving one of Professor Snape's famous monologues from Harry Potter: "I can tell you how to bottle fame, brew glory, and even put a stopper in death."

She only stops because she starts laughing so hard, then takes the wig off and tries to force it on my head. Dodging her, Sheena grabs it, plopping it on her own head. Smiling, she looks at me then to Mia, quoting Snape again, "You have your mother's eyes."

Then it happens. I'm not sure who reached for who first, or if it was mutual, but either way, Sheena and Mia are wrapped in each other's arms. It's almost as if they're making their first memory together.

Mia looks so happy.

Sheena has the same look.

Wanting Mia to have this moment, I try to sneak out, wanting to make myself scarce the rest of the night. "Daddy," Mia says. "Where are you going?"

"Thought I'd give you two some time alone."

"I want you to stay," Mia says. "It's kind of like we're having our first Halloween."

Sheena squeezes her again. "And my letters are like I was with you for your birthdays."

"Maybe we could have dinner," Sheena says. "A family dinner."

"Yes!" Mia agrees.

"Wait," I say without thinking, then I look into my daughter's hopeful eyes, filled with so much need. God help me.

Mia wants a few normal family memories. I can't give her back all the Christmases, the awkward first days of school. I've spent my life trying to give Mia everything she needed. Now she needs this.

This isn't a want. This is a need, and as her father, it's my job to give her what she needs.

THEY SAY A woman's work is never done. The same holds true for us guys. Work, family, friends—we get pulled in a thousand different directions. Keeping your woman happy has to be at the top of that list. So when you've got more than one woman in your life, it's a balancing act. I've suddenly got three. I could care less about Sheena's happiness, except as it relates to Mia, but Mia and Devlyn are a different story.

The past few weeks have been delicate, to say the least. I have to make sure that Sheena doesn't do anything to upset Mia or Devlyn or both. I have to make sure that Mia is happy, adjusting okay, that I'm spending enough time with her alone, and with her and Sheena together so she has some semblance of happy parents, or at the very least, parents that don't hate each other.

Then there's Devlyn.

She's in a class all by herself. She's where I want to be focusing my attention, but I've been divided. I know that. She's a badass woman, though, handling things with her usual smile. Still, I know this is hard on her. Which is why I'm going to tell Mia about us before the dedication of the pavilion at the Falls. I want Devlyn by my side when they cut the ribbon. I want her standing with me and Mia.

Sheena's been here a few weeks now. She's planning on staying through the month of July, taking an extended leave from work. I don't want to keep pushing back telling Mia about Devlyn and me. It's not fair. I just hope it doesn't send her into Sheena's arms more than she already is.

That child has fallen hard for her mother. I guess I should've expected it. I fell just as hard eighteen years ago. Frankly, it scares the shit out of me. I know how bad it hurts when Sheena disappoints, and I still don't trust her entirely. Maybe what scares me even more is sharing my daughter for the first time. Sheena has already hinted at Mia visiting her in Europe, spending a holiday or summer there. Over my dead body!

I feel like I'm in a three-ring circus. In this ring, you've got the crazy ex. In the opposite ring, you've got my daughter. Center ring, you've got Devlyn. I'm the ringmaster, trying to juggle the wants and needs of all three. It's fucking exhausting.

It's about to end. It's time everyone knows how important Devlyn is to me. Most importantly, Devlyn.

Mia and I head out the door. Our mornings at Biscuit Girl haven't been as frequent as before, mostly because Mia wants to spend as much time as possible with Sheena. I'm also trying to keep Sheena and Devlyn apart as much as I can, so we don't make it to the diner every morning like we used to.

"Off to Biscuit Girl?" my father calls out like so many mornings before.

Mia simply looks the other way.

"Mia?" I say harshly.

She's still not forgiven him for the no-contact clause, refusing to even talk to him. Her disrespect has landed her in serious hot water with me in terms of her car—it's in a permanent time-out until she works things out with her grandfather.

"Yes, we're going to the diner," she says with attitude.

Dad gives me a little smile. The old man is nothing if not patient. He and I had our say, but we've moved on. Guys are like that. Unfortunately, teenage girls and grudges seem to go together. I have to wonder if Sheena has something to do with it, as well. She blames my dad, so Mia blames him, too.

As we walk, I proceed to give Mia the same lecture I've given her every day since she decided her grandparents set out to keep her from her mother—that her grandfather meant well, thought he was doing the right thing—but like every other day, it's falling on deaf ears.

"There's something else I want to talk to you about later," I say. "Something important."

"Mom?"

"No, not your . . ."

"No," Mia cries, pointing to the gazebo. "Mom's here."

Mia hurries over and gives her mother a big hug, and Sheena kisses her on top of the head. "I was hoping to catch you," Sheena tells me. "I brought breakfast. Thought we could all eat and then I was hoping to take Mia shopping. Maybe get a new outfit for the dedication."

"You're coming to that, right?" Mia asks.

Sheena looks over at me, and I give her a little headshake. "I think that's something you and your dad should go to together."

Sheena and I have gotten pretty good maneuvering this whole thing, which means she knows when to back down. Mia seems to be good with whatever Sheena says, seldom questioning her or her motives. It's a bit scary, to be honest.

"Should we go to the hardware store to eat?" Sheena asks, turning to me. "I brought you something healthy for breakfast. You have the worst eating habits."

"I'm always telling him that," Mia says, enjoying ganging up on me with her mother. "What did you bring?"

"Cottage cheese and . . ."

"Need my coffee," I say, pointing to the diner, and not mentioning I also need my morning smack of Devlyn's ass in her back room.

"I'll get it," Mia says, already rushing that way, too late for me to stop her.

CHAPTER TWENTY-NINE

DEVLYN

"COFFEE TO GO," Mia says, leaning up on the counter, looking way too chipper for a teenager in the morning. "For Dad."

"No breakfast?" I ask, trying to hide the disappointment in my voice that Garrett won't be sneaking in the back for a quick kiss good morning.

"Mom brought us breakfast," Mia says, pointing toward the gazebo.

Sheena and Garrett are standing there talking. It might as well be eighteen years ago. Me in the diner feeling jealous as all get out, and the two of them oblivious to anyone or anything around them.

"Mom's taking me shopping today."

"That's great," I say, grabbing a to-go cup.

"I know," she says wistfully. "I'm so happy she's here. We are doing all kinds of things together. We've gotten our nails done and . . ."

Does she not remember when I gave her her first mani-pedi?

She continues talking about all the wonderful things her and Sheena have done, most of which are things she and I used to do together. I've been replaced, or perhaps it was never my place to begin with. I want to be happy for her. I am happy for her, but I'm sad for me, not sure of my role in her life anymore.

"You know the best part?" Mia asks, as I place a lid on the piping hot cup, made just the way Garrett likes it. "It's that," she says, looking toward her parents. "Seeing them together. I used to have these fairytales in my head that Mom magically would come back, and her and Dad would get back together."

"You think they . . ."

She shrugs. "I have to wonder why Dad never really dated anyone serious. Maybe he still loves her. I mean, look at them," she says. "They're like, perfect together."

I know what she means. They look like the classic American couple—the delicate blonde woman with the tall, dark, and handsome man. Still, it's a pipe dream—the dream of a child. The dream of any child whose parents have split up. I know that. A part of me wonders if I wasn't in the picture, perhaps Garrett and Sheena would find their way back into each other's arms. That's certainly what Mia wants.

"It just means so much to me to have them both, you know?"

I nod, feeling my throat closing up.

"I want it to last forever."

This time I nod and fake a smile, having lost my voice.

She glances back out at them again. Garrett with his hands in his pockets, looking handsome as ever, and Sheena smiling up at him. "You think I'm being silly, don't you?"

This time I'm forced to answer. "I don't think it's silly to want your parents together."

"The Fourth of July is a special day for my parents. Mom wrote me these letters every year on my birthday. She probably forgot she wrote about that."

Special day? I really hope she's not referring to what I *think* she's referring to. I could've lived my whole life without that little piece of information.

"Anyway, I was thinking I'm going to suggest that after the dedication, Mom, Dad, and I all go to dinner, then I'm going to have Penny call me with some fake emergency. Mom and Dad will be left alone together. Maybe that will help them remember how they felt about each other. Do you think that might work?"

I consider that for a moment—if your Dad wasn't sleeping with me, then maybe so? Somehow my brain filters that into something socially acceptable. "Anything's possible."

"I really hope it happens," she says, almost bouncing toward the door. "I don't think anything could be better."

My heart heavy, I walk to the front window of the diner, watching Mia join Garrett and Sheena under the gazebo—smiling—the perfect little family. Mia hands him the coffee I made.

I watch.

And as always, I understand.

I understand what Sheena was ranting about the other day. Loving and leaving someone versus loving them and staying.

I've stayed. All these years, I've loved them and stayed.

My head realizes what I have to do before my heart. My head yells at my heart. You're a muscle, you should be stronger than this. I've been driven by my heart my whole life, but my heart has a weakness—Garrett and Mia. Still, even my heart knows this is the right thing to do. It's time to bow out gracefully.

I love them so much, I need to leave.

I need to walk away and give them a chance. A chance to be a family, the family Mia wants more than anything. I'm standing in the way of that.

Watching them, they look perfect together, like that's the way it should've always been. There isn't anything I wouldn't do for Mia, including giving up her father.

I wait for Garrett to look toward the diner, to look toward me. How many other times in my life have I waited for that same thing? Waited for him to finally look my way?

It finally happened. I thought we'd finally have a life together. Instead, we've had just a few stolen moments. I guess that's all there will be. That will have to be enough.

Waiting at the window, he doesn't look my way. This is the part where I have to walk away. A tear rolling down my cheek, I turn from the window.

Fuck you, Sheena, for being right—loving someone and leaving is the hardest thing I'll ever do.

I'VE NEVER HAD to fake an orgasm with Garrett. I've faked a lot with him over the years. Faked smiles. Faked not loving him. Faked only being his friend. So faking not wanting to be with him should be easy. I'm going to miss these times with him. With Mia spending time with Sheena, we've had more spare time together than I thought we would.

Naked in bed, his fingers lightly roam my body. It's time to go. I know that's what's coming. I know by the path his fingers draw on my body. Down my thigh, then back up my hips, my waist, my breast, all the way up my neck until he reaches my chin, turns my face up to him, and whispers, "We need to get up."

Another long, slow, deep kiss, and he's out of bed, reaching for his clothes. I do the same, knowing I need to be out of here before Mia gets home.

I hear his zipper go up. He'll be ready to walk me out in a few seconds.

Five

Four

Three

Two

One

Time to let him go.

"I need more than this, Garrett," I say, fastening the last of the buttons on my shirt. His blue eyes find mine. I'm not sure of the emotion behind them.

"I know," he says. "I'm going to talk to Mia tonight and tell . . ."

Crap, now he finally decides to tell her? "No," I state firmly.

"You don't want me to tell her?"

"I don't think there's anything to tell her," I say, motioning between us. "I need more than you can give."

"Where's this coming from?" he asks, his voice measured.

"I can't just keep waiting around for . . ."

"I'm telling Mia tonight."

"Then what?" I ask. "I'm thirty-three years old. I want a family, kids. My mom was right. I've been waiting on you my whole life, and if I don't get out now, I could spend the rest of my life waiting for you."

"This doesn't make sense," he says. "Ten minutes ago, I was balls deep inside you."

I don't tell him that I wanted one more time with him. One last time to memorize the way it feels to have him make love to me.

Cocking my chin, I say, "Then you hop up, ushering me out the door. As usual."

"You know you can't stay," he says, sounding so rational. Sometimes I hate it when men are so sensible. "This whole time, you said you understood I needed some time for Mia . . ."

"That's the problem. It's always Garrett and Mia, and screw everyone else. Well, I'm here. I've always been here. You take that for granted. It stops right now."

"Devlyn," he says, reaching out for me, but I move past him, walking to the front door of his house. "I'm going to tell her."

"It's too late," I say.

"No, it's not," he shouts. "Does this have something to do with Sheena?"

Irritated he'd even bring her into this, I snap, "No."

He draws a deep breath, like a fighter preparing to go twelve rounds. It's funny. Only when I'm ending things with him do I see how ready he is to fight for me.

"Let's talk," he says. "We can work this out." I move to open the door. "Wait!"

"That's the problem," I state calmly, though it takes everything in me. "I've been waiting. I waited too long. Not again. Not anymore."

He's just staring at me. He's never told me he loved me. Now I'll never hear those words from him.

"You want this over?" he asks. "Is that what you're saying?"

"I hope we can still be friends."

"Are you fucking kidding me with that?"

"I just thought once some time passed, we could go back . . ."

"Fuck that," he barks. "I'm not letting you do this. I have no idea where any of this is coming from!"

"There's nothing you can say to change my mind," I say, feeling my eyes well up. "This is what's best."

As I turn to walk away, he captures my hand. Our eyes meet, and before I know what's happening, I'm wrapped in his arms. I try to let go, but he only holds me tighter. Running my fingers through his hair, I say, "I'm sorry." Then I take a deep breath and whisper, "I love you."

He pulls back slightly to look in my eyes. I'm sure he hates that I said it first. He's macho that way. It's probably confusing the hell out of him to hear me say that right at this moment, when I'm leaving, but I had to tell him, at least once in my life.

Before he can respond, I take off, hurrying out of his yard. "Devlyn," he calls out. I forgot how fast he is, quickly capturing me by my waist. The only thing that saves me is the sound of a car pulling in front of his house. Sheena and Mia are home from shopping.

Garrett and I both glance at the car then back to each other. "I know," I say. "Now's not a good time. That's the thing with us, Garrett. It's *never* a good time, and I can't keep waiting. I won't anymore."

CHAPTER THIRTY

GARRETT

I NEED MORE.

Friends.

I'm sorry.

I've heard it all before from other women, but I really thought Devlyn was different, that she understood.

"What was Devlyn doing here before?" Mia asks, pulling out a new purse Sheena bought her.

"Um," I say, my brain spinning, unable to come up with a good lie. "The purse is nice."

Her forehead wrinkles up. "Daddy, you okay?"

"Fine," I say. "Just tired. Been working long hours to get the pavilion done."

"Okay," she says, placing the purse down. "What did you want to talk to me about?"

"What?"

"Earlier," she says. "You said there was something important you wanted to talk to me about."

"Oh, nothing," I say. "It was nothing."

If it was nothing, then why in the hell do I feel like this? She left me. Women have left before, and I never gave them another thought, but this feels different. It feels worse than when Sheena left.

"Oh good, because I wanted to ask you about something. I think Mom really wants to come to the dedication at the Falls. Is it okay with you?"

"Sure," I say, shrugging.

Who the fuck cares, really? There's only one person I want to be there, and I doubt she's going to show.

GUYS ARE IN a tough position when it comes to being dumped. On the one hand, you don't want to be a pussy and go crawling and begging for your woman to take you back. On the other hand, you want to fight for your lady. So you're caught between a pussy and a hard place.

How many phone calls does it take for you to go from a man who wants his woman to being whipped? How many visits does it take before you go from noble to stalker? How many flowers do you send before you go from sweet to lunatic? The answers aren't easy. It's tough terrain for us men.

Most importantly, I don't want to hurt Devlyn anymore. I really had no idea how bad she was hurting. I thought I was doing a good job at shielding her, but she fooled me. I shouldn't be surprised. She fooled me my whole life. I tell myself she needs some space, but giving her that feels like giving up, and I'm not about to do that. My heart won't let me.

She loves me.

She left.

She's not the first woman to say she loved me and walk out the door.

This is exactly what I didn't want to happen. This is why I never dated women in Eden Valley before. I should've known better than to get involved in the first place. Mia's little dating game is to blame. It opened the door, and I doubt it's going to be easy to lock it up again.

I peek in on Mia, who's still sound asleep. We aren't going to Biscuit Girl this morning or tomorrow morning or the one after that. Guess I better learn how to make myself a decent cup of coffee.

I'm not sure how I'm going to explain not going to Mia, although she's so consumed with Sheena that it's possible she won't even notice. Without breakfast, without coffee, I head toward the Falls.

Work calls. Work doesn't care if you just got your ass handed to you, you still have to show up. That's what I've always done. Show up. People are counting on me.

I'm out the door so early this morning my dad isn't even up. That's a first. On instinct, I start walking toward town square. Mia and I usually walk that way. I'm a few blocks from my house before I realize I've even done it, but I see I'm walking toward the diner, toward Devlyn. I've been walking to her my whole life without even realizing it.

The only saving grace in this whole mess is that not many people know about Devlyn and me, so there won't be questions from nosy neighbors, people taking sides. No billboards erected touting Team Devlyn. For sure, everyone would be on her side, although I don't have a damn clue what I did wrong.

That's not entirely true. I could've talked to Mia sooner. But you know what? Devlyn could've stayed a bit longer, and talked to me, too. She could've given me a chance to fix it. She obviously just wanted out. Mia was just the excuse.

I need to forget Devlyn Drake.

Common ways to forget about a woman. Number one: drink until you forget or just don't care anymore. Number two: screw another woman. Number three: do something for revenge, like bang their best friend, make sure she sees you with someone else, fuck a woman she hates, or the best yet—fuck her one more time, then treat her like shit afterwards.

My legs stop moving before my eyes even focus in on her. Devlyn's down the sidewalk from me, and like me, she's frozen still. How can I forget her when she's so close? Although I doubt distance would even work. I don't want to drink myself into oblivion to forget. I don't want to hate fuck her or anyone else. I don't want to seek revenge. I don't want her to hurt.

She said she loves me. I hate she said it first.

And I don't get it. Why bother to tell someone you love them if you are just going to leave? I never thought Devlyn and Sheena had anything in common, but I guess they do. They leave the people they claim to love.

If that's love, then I should be thanking my lucky stars that she broke it off. Seeing her standing there in her pink tutu and light blue *Butter my biscuit*s t-shirt, thankful is *not* what I'm feeling.

This isn't over.

She can say it is, but I know her. I know her better than anyone. I know her eyes, her lips, her sounds, the tremors of her body when she's coming. I know how she tastes, smells, and just where to kiss her to soak her panties.

Mostly importantly, I know her heart. She loves me, and Devlyn doesn't walk away from the people she loves. I know that firsthand. When she broke up with Scott, she cried, but she was fine. The look on her face right now is anything but fine. Devlyn usually glows. There's a spark about her, but even her tutu is droopy today.

As I walk toward her, she cocks her chin up like she wants a fight. I'm not going to give her what she wants. Any anger I felt melted away as soon as I saw her. Stopping in front of her, I ask, "Are you alright?"

Her lips pressed tightly together, she nods. You're going to have to lie better than that, baby, if you want me to believe you.

"You?" she asks.

"Not even close," I say.

"This is for the best," she whispers.

"Not for me," I say. "And from the looks of things, not for you, either. So who exactly is this the best for?"

"I have to go," she says, moving to unlock the door to the diner.

"You are forgetting something," I say, leaning over her shoulder and whispering in her ear. "You forget I love you, too." I hear her take a swift breath. She doesn't look at me. I tilt her chin up to me slightly to catch her eyes. "There will never be a moment I don't love you."

I hold her eyes for a minute, letting that sink in, letting her know she's not getting rid of me easily, that this isn't over. Some loves are never over. My mom and dad are the perfect example. Not even death could change the way my dad felt about my mom.

I don't know a lot about love, but one thing I do know for certain is that nothing will change my love for Devlyn.

My love is not conditional. It's not going to change with the winds. It's hers.

"I'm leaving town," she says quietly. "I thought you should hear it from me."

When you tell a woman you love her, you'd think she'd say it back, you'd fall into a kiss or bed, or at the very least a hug—not get sent a change of address form. Fuck!

"You can't leave town," I say. "You just broke up with me last night. You can't have plans to leave town already."

"My mom mentioned an opportunity to open Biscuit Girl Two at the beach last time she was in town, and I've decided to do it. This place here practically runs itself, but I'll be back periodically to check on things. I leave in two days."

"Two days . . ."

I stop myself. I know the reason for the quick exit. She knows if she hangs around, then I will win her back. She knows I won't give up. Better, she thinks, to put a couple hundred miles between us.

"Good luck with the dedication of the pavilion. I'm sure it's going to be beautiful," she says, reaching for the door to the diner. "Goodbye, Garrett."

CHAPTER THIRTY-ONE

DEVLYN

ALL I'VE DONE the past few days is go through the motions of life. Get up, get dressed, work, shower, then repeat. I smile when I'm supposed to. I laugh at all the right times, but it's all a lie. Every smile is hiding a tear, every laugh is masking a sob. Still, this is the right thing to do, to give them a chance to be a family like Mia wants. If Garrett told her about us now, she'd probably end up resenting me anyway, seeing me as the reason why her parents never rekindled their relationship.

The idea of opening a second location is a good distraction, just what I need at the moment. There are a lot of little details to consume my brain. My parents designed Biscuit Girl, and while I love most everything about it, it would be nice to build a place from the ground up. There are a few things I'd do differently. A perfect example is the bathrooms here. There's only one. I've always hated that, and there's not room to redesign.

Flooring, ceiling tins, wainscoting, paint colors—there's a thousand things to decide. Well, first I better make sure I like the bones of the new space. I've only seen pictures. The idea of designing my own kitchen from the ground up is appealing. Ovens, mixers, plates—I'm in my element. While everything will be new, I still want it to have a hometown, vintage feel. There will be no fancy soda machines like they have in places now, with the fancy touch screens where all the drinks come from the same nozzle. Who thought of that? Water comes out tasting like oranges, and orange soda comes out tasting like lime. It's disgusting. I'll have none of that in my new place.

I'm going to miss Eden Valley, the people, the small-town vibe.

There's something special about being surrounded by familiar, friendly faces. Like today, the Fourth of July. Everyone is wearing red, white, or blue, or a combination of the three. All the shop owners have some sort of patriotic theme going. For example, I've got our country's colors in my table flowers. Most every house is sporting an American flag, and later today, the whole town will gather together at the Falls for a potluck to dedicate the new pavilion. Things like that don't happen other places.

I look up from the counter, thinking about adding some ribbon to the flower vases, and find Mia sitting at her and Garrett's usual table. She's alone. They haven't been in the diner together since I broke things off with Garrett a few days ago. She looks up at me, giving me a small smile.

Some habits are just too hard to break, so I take a seat across from her. "Thought you'd be getting ready for the big dedication today?" She just shrugs. "Everything alright?"

"I don't know," she says. "Dad's . . ."

"What's wrong with Garrett?" I ask. "He's not sick or anything?"

"No," she says. "I've never seen him like this."

"How?"

"I think he's sad about something, but he just says he's tired or busy or makes up some other lame excuse."

My heart breaks.

"Do you still have your dinner plan scheme?"

A broad smile covers her face. "Penny and I have it all worked out. I just need Dad not to be in a perpetually bad mood."

"I'm sure he'll be happy soon. Maybe he's just stressed about the dedication."

"You're coming, right?" she asks.

I was planning on skipping it.

"I think Dad would like to have you there. Maybe that will cheer him up," she says. "You and him always goof around together."

Is that what we do?

"I'll try."

"It might be my last chance to see you before you leave to franchise Biscuit Girl."

"It's one little place on the beach. More like a hut, really. Hardly a franchise."

She giggles, holding her hands up like she's reading a marquee. "Devlyn Drake, biscuit queen."

I kiss her on top of the head. God, I'm going to miss her. The only person I'm going to miss more is her father. I'll miss him the rest of my life.

I SHOWED UP late on purpose, not wanting to chitchat with people beforehand, but of course, they are running late getting started with the dedication. Hopefully, my green palm print maxi dress will blend in with the trees.

Seems like all of Eden Valley is here. There's a lot of chatter, laughing, but I don't feel like talking to anyone, and I'm not staying for the Fourth of July festivities after, either. I'll watch the dedication then sneak away.

I make a circle around the pavilion. Garrett's design is fantastic. I knew it would be. It replicates the town's gazebo with its white latticework, but the roof is all glass, held together with beautiful old beams.

"I've heard people are already booking weddings here at the pavilion two years in advance," Trudy says, coming up beside me. I nod, and she pats my hand. "Garrett's been . . ."

"Not now, Trudy," I say.

She sees my eyes welling up and steps away, giving me some space. I make my way toward the back of the crowd as the mayor starts the ceremony. The sun is blazing in the sky, the Falls are roaring, and a bright red ribbon graces the entrance to the pavilion. The mayor, a few other city council people, Mia, and Garrett stand behind it. His father is standing in the front row, camera ready. It's the sweetest thing.

Mia looks beautiful in a blue dress that matches the color of

Garrett's eyes. I should know. He's staring right at me. The mayor is talking. People are clapping, but our eyes don't waver from each other. I'm not sure if he wants to rush through the crowd and kiss me or bite my head off. It's one of the two.

I can't help it, I smile. His eyes close, his head lowering slightly. I feel a few tears slip down my cheeks and quickly wipe them away.

"Garrett looks handsome, doesn't he?" Sheena asks softly, and my head darts up. Where the hell did she come from? "Mia and I bought that shirt on our shopping trip for him to wear today."

I try to ignore her, but she doesn't take the hint.

"He's always in black or white t-shirts. We tried to get him to wear a tie, but no luck."

"I like his t-shirts," I whisper, unsure whether she heard me. I look back toward the pavilion, finding Garrett's eyes back on me again. He looks even more intense than he did before. The mayor holds a pair of huge scissors out toward him.

Sheena starts up again. "You know, this is a special day for me and Garrett."

Tears rush from my eyes. Yes, I'm aware you screwed the man I love on this day. Garrett sees my tears, taking a step toward me, but Mia grabs his arm, her eyes following his gaze. She whispers something to him, and he takes the scissors from the mayor.

"Garrett and I broke up," I say to Sheena as the crowd bursts into applause.

"I didn't know," she says, the happiness evident in her voice.

Turning to leave, I say, "So you have no reason to ever speak to me again."

That is the only bright spot in all of this. I will never have to look at her, hear her voice, or be near her again. Thank you, God, for that at least.

CHAPTER THIRTY-TWO

GARRETT

WHY IS THE mayor so longwinded? Can the blowhard shut the hell up already? Devlyn's leaving and from the looks of things, Sheena said something to upset her again. It's hot as hell out here. This dress shirt isn't helping, but that's not the reason my blood is boiling.

The tears on Devlyn's cheeks—those mean something. I know her tears—the happy ones, the sad ones, the mad ones, the ones that come from laughing too hard. Those were sad tears.

I want to know why. I need to know.

So as soon as the mayor shuts up, I barge off the stage, making a beeline right toward Sheena. "What the hell did you say to her?" I bark through gritted teeth.

"Nothing," she says, looking around at the crowd, whose attention is now on us.

"I warned you to stay away from Devlyn."

"Calm down," she says, not wanting a scene. "I simply pointed out that Mia and I bought you that new shirt."

"She wouldn't cry over a shirt."

"Why was Devlyn crying?" Mia asks, walking up to us. "Why'd she leave like that?"

"Mia, I'll talk to you later. Please go find your grandfather and . . ."

"No," Mia says. "What's going on? You've been acting weird for days, and now Devlyn's crying. I want to know what's going on."

"Sheena said something to upset Devlyn," I say.

"Mom wouldn't do that."

"Yes, she would," I bark then zero back in on Sheena. "What the hell did you say to her?"

Sheena throws up her hands. "Fine, I might have said something about how the Fourth of July has important meaning for us."

"You *what*?"

"I don't get it," Mia says. "Why would that upset Devlyn?"

Sheena gives me a smug smile. Having had enough of this, I turn to my daughter and say to her what I should've said weeks ago. "Because Devlyn and I were seeing each other."

Mia's eyes grow wide and then cast down, like she's in shock yet trying to make sense of what I just said, like I suddenly started speaking in a foreign language.

"It started right around the time you went to the beach with your granddad, and she ended it a few days ago."

Her eyes dart up. "That's why you've been off?"

"Yes," I say, reaching toward her. "I should've told you sooner. I was going to, but then your mom came back into town, and you were dealing with a lot."

She looks over at Sheena, who holds open her arms, expecting Mia to fall into them. "You knew?" Mia asks her.

"Yes," Sheena says, glancing at me. "But your father asked me not to say anything."

Mia shakes her head. "Why did you say those things to Devlyn then?" she asks her mother. Sheena looks at me, panic setting in, having expected Mia to attack me for keeping a secret from her, but Mia has turned the tables. "Why would you hurt Devlyn like that?"

"I . . ." Sheena stammers, looking at me for help. I offer none.

"You hurt her on purpose," Mia says, her voice getting a little louder.

"It's not like that," Sheena says, reaching out for Mia, but Mia steps back like Satan himself is coming for her. "Devlyn and I have a history. She always had a huge crush on your father even when he was dating me."

Mia looks down at the grass, and I can see her brain searching for what to believe. "Your letters," she whispers. "I was so focused on what you wrote to me that I didn't . . . you dissed Devlyn's clothes, dismissed her feelings about Daddy. You thought you were so much better than her."

"You misunderstood," Sheena says.

"No," Mia whispers, but she might as well have been shouting for the way Sheena steps back. "Even in the diner that first morning after my birthday. I didn't hear what you said to Devlyn, but I remember Daddy barking at you, and Devlyn's eyes watering. You said something nasty to her then, too, didn't you?"

"Mia, baby, I . . ."

"I'm not your baby!" Mia cries.

Sheena's eyes flash to me. This is her nightmare, coming to life. "Your father and Devlyn kept this huge secret from you. I can understand that you're upset right now."

Mia glances at me. Yep, she's upset. Her brown eyes look like puddles of muddy water about to ripple over. She's realizing who her mother is for the first time. As a child, it's hard the first time you realize your parents aren't perfect, not superheroes. It's usually a gradual process. Poor Mia has had her mother go from someone who can do no wrong to the devil incarnate in five seconds flat. This isn't just about Devlyn. It's about what she did to us all those years ago, how she left. The truth of who her mother is just hit her. The woman who takes her shopping and writes her letters on her birthday is the same woman who left us, who hurts innocent people without a second thought.

Then there's me.

I lost my superhero status with Mia about the time she discovered boys, but she's still my little girl. I'm still the most important man in her life. We have a history to draw from—a well of love, fun, and happiness when times are tough. She doesn't have that with Sheena.

That's important. In bad times, we have to have good ones to remember. So when we fight, we fight fair. When we are mad, we remember the love. When we are filled with despair, we have hope. You can't fight the good fight with someone if you aren't sure if they'll stick around through the war.

If this were a war, Sheena would be a deserter.

Tears fall from my daughter's cheeks. "Mia," I say, placing my hands on her shoulders.

"I need some time, Daddy," she sobs in a little whisper. "I'm not running away like last time, but I need some time to think."

"Okay," I say. "But I need to know where you're going."

"I'll text you," she tells me, throwing a look at Sheena, making it obvious she doesn't want her to know her whereabouts.

Wiping her face, she heads through the crowd back toward town.

"You can't just let her go!" Sheena cries.

"Don't tell me how to parent my daughter."

"So we're back to her being *your* . . ."

"Is Mia alright?" my dad asks, coming up to us.

"What's wrong with Mia?" Trudy asks, walking up with a few other folks, all glaring at Sheena.

All of Eden Valley has Mia's back. Sheena has no goodwill stored up with them, either, so there is no reason to take her side. Their natural assumption is that Mia being upset is her doing. If I don't want them to attack like a bull in a ring, I better say something. "She'll be fine."

I place my hand on my father's shoulder, turning my back to Sheena. Everyone else follows my lead. Damn, it feels good.

I STUCK AROUND the pavilion for a little while, but my mind was stuck on Mia and Devlyn. While everyone else was busy with their sparklers and potluck, I snuck away, needing to check on my daughter. She asked for some time, but my dad genes prevent me from giving her more than a couple hours before I have to check on her. She texted me that she was at home, so I knew she was safe.

I didn't speak to Sheena again. She didn't hang around long after Mia left, either, probably afraid she'd be stoned by the townspeople. I tried a couple times to call Devlyn, but she wouldn't pick up. I suppose she's still leaving tomorrow. I have to see her before she goes, if for no other reason than to say goodbye. The very thought of her driving out of town makes my gut twist in knots, but first I have to deal with Mia.

I hop out of my truck in front of my house. It's dark out now. I look up at the sky. No fireworks here. Instead, flashes of heat lightning fill the sky. The silent hues of orange and yellow are more spectacular than anything man could ever make. If this were ancient Greece, you'd think the gods and goddesses were at war with each other.

Heading inside, I find Mia sitting on the floor in the den with a cardboard box open in front of her. She and Sheena have been going through old albums, baby books, and home videos for weeks. Tears staining her cheeks, Mia holds a letter in her hand.

"What do you have there?" I ask.

"A letter from my mother," she says.

"Do you want to tell me what it says?" I ask.

"It's actually for you," she says, handing it to me.

The paper is thin and brittle, the edges ripped slightly. Carefully, I unfold it, noticing the date isn't Mia's birthday like all the letters Sheena wrote.

This one is dated a few days after Mia was born.

Dear Garrett,

I heard about Sheena leaving.

You can do this. I wanted you to know that I know in my heart that you can do this. You will be the best father to Mia. I know that. I have no doubt that she will be an amazing child with you raising her. Please believe that because I do.

I will do whatever I can to help you both. Thank you for letting me hold her in the hospital the other day. It was the first time I'd ever held a baby. I'm glad it was yours. I'm glad I got to do that with you.

I know you must feel so alone right now, but you're not.

I'm here.

I'll always be here for you and for Mia.

Whatever you need.

Always here,

Devlyn

I'd totally forgotten about this letter. In the aftermath of Mia's birth and then Sheena's departure, I'd forgotten all about it. Devlyn never forgot. She *lived* those words all these years. She believed in me when no one else did. How did we end up in this shit storm?

"Where'd you get this?" I ask.

"It was folded up in my baby book," she says. "The one Grandma made for me."

I know the one. My mom started it when Mia was born. She kept records of Mia's first word, her first tooth, first step. I'm not sure how Devlyn's letter ended up in there.

I read through it quickly once more. My eyes dart to Mia. "You said this letter was from your mother?"

"It is," she says. "I realized something today. I know who my mother is." Mia looks up at me with those big brown eyes. "Sheena gave birth to me, but Devlyn is my mom. She always has been."

I was right earlier when I thought Mia was realizing who her mother was, only I didn't realize it was this.

"I didn't understand it at first," Mia says. "I was so mad at Sheena for what she did to Devlyn. Like crazy mad."

"You love Devlyn a lot," I say.

She nods and asks, "Do you?"

"Very much," I say through the lump in my throat.

"I always thought I wanted Sheena, you, and me to be a family. But what I really needed was you, me, and Devlyn. I had that all along."

"You are one smart young lady," I say, squeezing her.

"Then why don't I know what to do about Sheena?" she says, her heart heavy. "Why'd she have to come back here?"

I lean her head down on my shoulder. "I've asked myself that more times than I can count," I say.

"She's a terrible, awful bitch," Mia cries.

Normally, I would correct her, but I'll let that one slide. "I think you know it's more complicated than that. You don't have to figure it out now."

"What about you and Devlyn?" she asks. "You gonna figure that out?"

"I'm not sure I can," I say.

She angles herself toward me. "Well, what did you do?" she asks. "Why'd she break up with you?"

"Wish I knew. One minute things were fine, and the next she was ending things."

"And you didn't do anything? Or say anything stupid?"

"Have some faith in your old man," I say.

"Dad, I've seen you on dates. You have no game!"

"I've got all kinds of game," I laugh out.

Shaking her head, she says, "Tell me what happened exactly."

Mia and I are close, but there is no way I'm telling her that. Tilting my head, I ask, "So you really would be okay with Devlyn and I dating?"

"No," she says, giggling. "I want you to marry her."

I hold my hands up. "One step at a time there, baby girl."

She pushes on me to get up. "Brothers and sisters, too, please."

"You've obviously been talking to Devlyn," I tease, but she doesn't laugh and her face goes stark white. "Mia?"

"I *did* talk to her. We didn't talk about babies, but . . ." Mia looks up at me, her eyes wide. "It's my fault Devlyn broke up with you," Mia whispers.

"No, it's not your fault."

"When did she break it off?"

"A few days ago," I say. "Why does it matter?"

"Did she break up with you the day Sheena met us at the gazebo with breakfast? The day I went in to get you coffee?"

It's been a long few days. I have to think for a second. "Yeah, why?"

She gets this look on her face, like *don't be mad at me*. "That day when I went to get you coffee, I told her about this plan I had to get you and Sheena back together."

"What plan?"

"It doesn't matter," Mia says. "I went on and on about it. How I wanted you, Sheena, and me to be a family, how nothing would make me happier. How I thought the two of you could rekindle something. What a great couple you'd make."

"Mia, you know that's never gonna happen."

"I know that *now*," she says, "but that day . . . Daddy, I must've really hurt Devlyn. I swear I didn't mean to."

"I know that," I say, hugging her. "Devlyn knows that, too."

She shoves Devlyn's letter at me. "Don't you see? It's right here in this letter. *Whatever you need.* I told her I wanted you and Sheena to be together. That I *really* wanted that to happen. She broke up with you for me, to give me a chance to have us be a family—you, me, and Sheena. Devlyn did that for me."

Devlyn would do anything for Mia. I know that, but this? Sacrifice her relationship with me? She loves Mia that much? That's putting your money where your mouth is. Mia comes first in my life. God knows I've sacrificed relationships for Mia before, but I never expected to have a woman love my daughter enough to do that. Fuck, if Mia's right and Devlyn dumped me for her . . .

"I have to stop Devlyn from leaving," I say.

Mia nods at me, a huge smile on her face. Grabbing her cheeks, I plant a big kiss on top of her head before heading toward the door, not caring how late it is.

"Dad," Mia calls out, causing me to turn back around. "Better change your shirt first."

She's right. Why'd I agree to wear this damn thing, anyway? A quick change, and I'm heading to find Devlyn. A woman breaking things off with you is never easy, but she did it for my daughter. It makes sense. It changes everything.

Mia meets me by the door. "Think I need to go talk to Granddad," she says, giving me a little smile.

It's time for both of us to mend some fences. Kissing her on top of the head, I pull out my phone, trying to call Devlyn again. No answer.

"She's not answering?" Mia asks.

I shake my head. "Not for days."

"What are you going to do?"

"I guess I'll just go over to her place or the diner and . . ."

"Wait," Mia says, pulling out her phone. "Let me try something."

I watch as she types out a message to Devlyn, asking her to meet so they can say goodbye, laying it on thick about a gift she'd picked out especially for Devlyn. Then we wait, both our eyes burning a hole in Mia's phone, praying for the little circles to pop up that indicate Devlyn is responding.

Mia looks up at me. I can see how much she wants this to happen, not just for me, but for her, too. I give her a hug, wishing I'd known that weeks ago. The phone dings.

I'm getting an early start. Meet me at the Falls at sunrise.

I kiss the top of Mia's head. "I'm a genius, I know," she teases.

Now I just have to wait until morning.

CHAPTER THIRTY-THREE

GARRETT

IF YOU ASKED me two months ago what life in Eden Valley was like, I'd have said slow and uneventful, the perfect place to raise a child. The last few months had been anything but slow. Last night was the exception. It seemed to drag on and on, waiting for the sun to peek through the clouds, waiting for my chance to see Devlyn and win her back.

To think this all started with a high school graduation speech—the dating hunt Mia had me on, Sheena showing up, the no-contact clause, building the pavilion, and falling for Devlyn. I'm ready for things to settle back down, to settle down with Devlyn.

Mia didn't get any sleep last night, either. After she and my dad hugged it out, she stayed up honing her matchmaking skills and developing a plan. She had this whole romantic scenario in her head, where she shows up at the Falls, talks to Devlyn, then I step out from the woods—the gift Mia promised.

No fucking way am I letting Mia win Devlyn back for me. She's done enough. This is between Devlyn and me. Mia's been between us too much. I let that happen when I shouldn't have. This morning is about me and Devlyn, and no one else. I had to practically threaten Mia to get her to keep her butt at home.

Pulling my truck up to the Falls, I see Devlyn's car there. She showed up. As I walk past it, I see the back filled with suitcases and boxes, and my gut twists. She's really packed and ready to go. This is my one shot. I can't blow it.

I'm not one of those people that rehearse what I'm going to say in big moments. I prefer things to just come to me, to speak from the heart, but right now I'm wishing I had a little something worked out in my mind—at least a place to start. In all my tossing and turning last night, I didn't come up with anything.

It's as if the world is just waking up, the birds are singing, the sunlight is peeking through the trees. It's warm out even for the early hour, and the pressure of the moment is sitting squarely on my shoulders.

When I come through the clearing to the Falls, I see her. Her fingers are lightly stroking the woodwork of the pavilion, her hair is loose and down, catching the rays from the sun, and she's wearing a white tank top with a long pink skirt with pineapples on it.

For a second, I just watch her, the way she moves, the morning breeze in her hair. This can't be the last time I see her. I won't allow it.

People spend their whole lives searching for the meaning of life—money, fame, success, wisdom. All that's great, but what we should be asking is, "What's the meaning of love?"

Love in its purest form is unselfish, unconditional, fearless, passionate, compassionate.

It's not about what you want in this life—or even what you need. It's about who you love and who loves you. The meaning of love can be summed up in one word—Devlyn.

Her blue eyes look right at me, a moment of shock in them. Then her head shakes, and she's heading toward me, or more accurately, trying to head around me.

"Mia!" she scolds no one.

"Devlyn, just listen."

"It's too hard," she says.

"There's nothing hard about loving you."

She pauses, wiping a few tears from her cheeks. "I have to go."

Capturing her waist, I say, "I told Mia about us." She looks up at me, a mix of sadness and surprise in her eyes.

"It doesn't change things," Devlyn said.

"I know why you broke it off with me," I say. "You did it for Mia. Because of what she told you about wanting Sheena and I to be together." She looks down. "That's why, isn't it?"

"Please, Garrett, it's what's best for Mia."

"Did it ever occur to you that I don't want Sheena?"

"I figured if I wasn't in the picture, then you'd . . ."

I can only shake my head.

"Don't shake your head at me," she says, pulling in her tears. "I see the way she looks at you. It's not a stretch to think she could get you back into her bed."

"If you really believe that, then you don't know me at all," I say. "There's not a chance in hell of that happening. Or of she and I getting back together."

"Not even for Mia?" she asks like she's testing me.

"Not even for Mia," I say.

She's quiet for a second. I'm hoping she's letting that sink in, but if I know Devlyn, the more likely scenario is that she's contemplating her next move.

"What about Mia?" she asks. "She can't have done a one-eighty and all of a sudden given up on her dream to have her parents together."

"She saw how Sheena treated you," I say. "That made her realize a few things about who her mother really is." I reach for her hand, and just when I think I'm about to get to her, she pulls away. "You know what? Let's say that I'm lying, and Mia still wants Sheena and I together."

"Okay," Devlyn says.

"The thing is, Mia doesn't get to make that decision for me." Her perfect, full lips open to argue with me, but I beat her to it. "Besides, love is not a decision. I didn't just *decide* to love you, so now I do. I'm sure if it was that easy, you would've decided *not* to love me a long time ago."

She smiles just a tad. "I decided to stay all these years. Like I decided to leave now."

"You think if you leave that you won't love me anymore?"

I see her start to crumble and I reach out, taking her cheek in my hand. "I know I'll still love you," she says softly. "And Mia."

"Mia is the one who sent me," I say, pulling out the letter Devlyn sent me all those years ago. "She found this."

She opens it up, seeing her handwriting. I can see the recognition in her eyes. "I can't believe you still have this," she says, her voice soft. "After all these years."

Watching her read her own words, I'm hopeful. Her blue eyes are wide. Tears are running down her cheeks. I think I may be winning her over. At least she isn't running away from me anymore.

"This is all still true," she whispers.

"And I'm not sure I ever thanked you," I say.

"Garrett, you were always grateful," she says, trying to let me off the hook.

Shaking my head, I say, "Maybe for the hair braiding lessons, the breakfasts, the movie nights, but I don't think I ever told you what that meant to me, to have you there, to know you had my back. The way you took on your parents when you were just a kid. Hell, you changed the way this whole town looked at me."

She futilely wipes her cheeks. "It was nothing."

"It was everything to me and to Mia." I take her hand. "This is what Mia needs. She knows that now. More importantly, you are who I need. Who I want."

Her eyes close, a rush of tears falling from her cheeks.

Without another word, my lips crash into hers. No speech I rehearsed could say everything that this one kiss can. I love you. I forgive you. I'm in awe of how much you love my daughter. I want you. I need you. None of it holds a candle to the feel of her body pressed against mine, her tongue wrestling with mine, her hands on my back, and mine in her hair.

Slowly, we pull apart, and I nod my head toward the Falls. The first rainbow of the day brightly arches over the water.

The legend is right.

She will be mine forever.

EPILOGUE

TWO MONTHS LATER

DEVLYN

BISCUIT GIRL TWO didn't die when Garrett and I got back together. It got fast-tracked. He loved the idea and supported me wholeheartedly, as long as it didn't mean me relocating. We've spent a few weekends at the beach fixing up the place together. Well, Garrett fixed and I admired how good he looked doing it. Mia came with us until she went off to college. She loves being so close to the ocean, so it worked out well all around. Bonus, it gave my parents a chance to get to know Garrett and me as a couple.

My parents watch out for the place when I'm not there, and Garrett and I have matched our schedules so that we can be there together. Truthfully, I think it's been a good distraction for Garrett with Mia now at college.

The day he moved her into her dorm was bittersweet. He asked me to make the trip with them, but I stayed back in Eden Valley, figuring that should be between father and daughter. I'll never forget the look in his eyes when he walked through my door after having left her hundreds of miles away. I expected him to say he didn't want to ever do that again, but instead he took me in his arms and joked, "Next time I do that, I'll be in my fifties!"

That's the way he told me he wants more kids. I loved that. It wasn't a big, sit-down discussion. It wasn't a fight. It was easy.

That's the way our love has been lately. Easy.

Sheena leaving helped that situation. She went back home not long after the Fourth of July. Mia refused to see her, so there was no reason for her to stay. I wish things were easier for Mia in that department. Mia has her guard up when it comes to Sheena these days. I hate that has anything to do with me. Mia hasn't cut off all contact, and to Sheena's credit, she calls Mia a couple times a week. Mia just has to decide what role Sheena will play in her life, and unfortunately, she's struggling with that.

Garrett and I are planning to go see Mia for parents' weekend next month, and I was beyond excited when Mia specifically asked that I come, too. We don't have plans to see her until then, which is why I almost pass out when I see her leaning up against the door of my diner on a random Friday afternoon wearing a pale-yellow sundress.

"What are you doing here?" I cry, rushing to her and giving her a huge hug.

"Skipped my Friday classes and came home," she says.

"What's your father going to say about that?"

"Figure it's easier to ask forgiveness than permission," she says.

"I've taught you well," I say as she laughs. "Is everything alright? Are you okay?"

She nods towards the closed sign on the diner, a sign that *should* be turned to open. "Daddy knows I'm here."

"Why is the place closed? Where is everyone?"

"Come with me," she says, taking my hand.

"MIA, WHAT'S GOING on?" I ask for the twentieth time since leaving the diner. She stops at the entrance to the Falls. "Are you in some kind of trouble?"

"No, *you* are," she says with a smile, nodding toward the bridge that leads to the waterfall.

Out of nowhere, Garrett steps through the tree line, wearing a gray suit with a white dress shirt, the top few buttons undone. I look back at Mia, who nudges me toward her dad but doesn't follow.

"Garrett, what's going on?" I ask, shaking my head and smiling.

Without warning, he drops to one knee. Some girls imagine this moment their whole lives, planning out their weddings, picking out venues. I'm not one of those girls. I always knew the man. The rest just didn't seem important.

Because I'm so unprepared, I blurt out, "Holy crap."

If there's a videographer hiding in the bushes filming this, I'll need a retake when my heart starts beating again.

"Devlyn," he says, his voice so sure, "I was wrong when I said all love is hard. Falling in love with you was so easy that I didn't realize it even happened. I love you. You've been my past, my present, and I'm hoping you'll agree to be my future. Will you marry me?"

I fly into his arms, knocking him to his butt and kiss him. We're laughing and kissing, and I hear Mia yell behind us, "The ring! Dad, you forgot the ring!"

Smiling, he rolls his eyes then reaches into his pocket. I see him blow out a deep breath. Silly man, doesn't he know I don't care about the ring? I'm going to love whatever he picked out for me *because* he picked it for me. When he pulls out the delicate band holding the center diamond, tears run down my cheeks. How on earth did he afford that? With Mia in college?

He reads my mind. "Turns out that old bike was worth more than I thought."

"Garrett!" I cry out. "It's so beautiful."

He slips it on my finger, helping me to my feet. Wrapping my arms around him, I hug him with all my might, then he kisses the top of my head, loosening his hold and nodding toward Mia. I look back at her, and she's holding her arm up, tapping her watch. "Do you need to be somewhere?" I ask.

"Yeah, your wedding!" she laughs out.

"What?" I say, turning back to Garrett.

He flashes me that drop dead sexy smile of his. "See you in fifteen at the altar."

"What?" I say again, as Mia appears by my side, holding a garment bag.

"Daddy, you've already broken like a hundred wedding rules,"

Mia says, shooing her hand at him. "I've got this."

"Wait?" I say, grabbing Garrett's hand.

"It's all planned," he says. "Everyone is here. Your dad is waiting to walk you down the aisle to the pavilion at the Falls."

"The wedding is here? Today?" I ask, needing more clarification. My brain is not working.

He flashes me a sexy grin. "Right now, DD."

He's busting out the nickname. He knows I hate that, but he also knows I can't resist his charms.

Cocking his head to the side, he says, "Won't be able to call you DD anymore if you marry me today. You'll be Mrs. Devlyn Hollis."

The name I secretly used to scribble over and over again as a schoolgirl. It's coming true.

"Look at me," I say. "I'm completely undone. No makeup, my hair is all crazy, I don't have a dress."

"I've got the dress," Mia says.

Garrett directs my eyes to him. "This is the way I love to see you. Beautifully undone."

"You really want to marry me right now?" I ask.

Nodding and smiling, he says, "Figure I've kept you waiting long enough." I give him a playful smack. He cups my cheek in his hand. "Please don't make me wait one more second to make you my wife."

MIA HOLLIS
Wedding Toast

LET ME START off by saying if anyone is filming this, please don't post it on social media. The last one got me in a lot of hot water.

I talked a lot about my dad in my last speech, so this time I want to talk about my mom—Devlyn.

From one unexpected blessing to the next—that's what you are to me. And to my dad.

It's silly that we didn't expect you, because you've been the constant in our lives. My very first memory is being in the gazebo. I had to be only three or four, and the three of us were eating strawberries. I don't remember anything else but the three of us.

While preparing this speech, I asked my dad how he fell in love with you. If he knew it while we shared the strawberries? Or was it when I lost my two front teeth, and you dressed up like the tooth fairy to make me smile because I thought I looked ugly? Or a thousand other moments after that?

He told me he fell in love with you a little bit every day. That it happened slow and easy.

Don't tell anyone, but I saw him blush.

"Love is hard to explain, Mia," he said.

Well, I didn't like his answer. I felt like I was asking whether he loved you back then, and his response was, "Love-ish."

Of course, Garrett Hollis would never add "ish" to anything.

"Love isn't hard," I told him. "You tell me that the things we want are often not the things we need."

Love is what we need. What we all need more than anything. To know that we are loved, but more importantly, to love someone else.

Love is the thing we both want and need.

I'm glad you both found it in each other. Whether it happened slow or fast? Was hard or easy?

Daddy, Devlyn—I mean Mom. That's going to take some getting used to.

It's funny how you can miss what's right in front of you. The thing I wanted. The thing I needed. I already had it—because I had you.

Both of you.

ALSO BY PRESCOTT LANE

To the Fall

Toying with Her

The Sex Bucket List

The Reason for Me

Stripped Raw

Layers of Her (a novella)

Wrapped in Lace

Quiet Angel

Perfectly Broken

First Position

ACKNOWLEDGEMENTS

MY DAUGHTER'S VOICE echoes in my head as I write this. She whispers, "Dad bod!" Throughout writing this book, she insisted I give Garrett a "dad bod." Her suggestion for the cover was the same. I didn't follow her advice, but she kept me in stitches the whole time I was writing this book, so I thought that deserved a shout out.

There's an army of people to thank for bringing Garrett's story to the page.

My editor, Nikki Rushbrook, for smoothing out the rough edges while honoring the voices of my characters.

To Michelle Rodriguez, beta reader extraordinaire, for support and her ability to pimp a book like no other.

To Michele Catalano, for her artistry, bringing my book to life in cover design.

To Nina Grinstead and the team at Social Butterfly, for being there—when things go right, and when things go crazy.

To readers, thank you for every laugh, every smile, every tear, every heartbreak that books bring you. You make it all possible.

Hugs and Happily Ever Afters,
Prescott Lane

ABOUT THE AUTHOR

PRESCOTT LANE IS originally from Little Rock, Arkansas, and graduated from Centenary College in 1997 with a degree in sociology. She went on to Tulane University to receive her MSW in 1998, after which she worked with developmentally delayed and disabled children. She currently lives in New Orleans with her husband, two children, and two dogs.

Contact her at any of the following:

www.authorprescottlane.com

facebook.com/PrescottLane1

twitter.com/prescottlane1

instagram.com/prescottlane1

pinterest.com/PrescottLane1